*Marrying Simone*

*By Anna Jacobs*

**THE PENNY LAKE SERIES**

Changing Lara • Finding Cassie
Marrying Simone

**THE PEPPERCORN SERIES**

Peppercorn Street • Cinnamon Gardens
Saffron Lane • Bay Tree Cottage
Christmas in Peppercorn Street

**THE HONEYFIELD SERIES**

The Honeyfield Bequest • A Stranger in Honeyfield
Peace Comes to Honeyfield

**THE HOPE TRILOGY**

A Place of Hope • In Search of Hope
A Time for Hope

**THE GREYLADIES SERIES**

Heir to Greyladies • Mistress of Greyladies
Legacy of Greyladies

**THE WILTSHIRE GIRLS SERIES**

Cherry Tree Lane • Elm Tree Road
Yew Tree Gardens

⁓

Winds of Change
Moving On
The Cotton Lass and Other Stories
Change of Season
Tomorrow's Path

*Marrying Simone*

ANNA JACOBS

Allison & Busby Limited
11 Wardour Mews
London W1F 8AN
*allisonandbusby.com*

First published in Great Britain by Allison & Busby in 2020.

A CIP catalogue record for this book is available from
the British Library.

First Edition

ISBN 978-0-7490-2395-9

Typeset in 11.5/16.5 pt Sabon LT Pro by
Allison & Busby Ltd

The paper used for this Allison & Busby publication
has been produced from trees that have been legally sourced
from well-managed and credibly certified forests.

Printed and bound by
CPI Group (UK) Ltd, Croydon, CR0 4YY

# Chapter One

## Perth, Western Australia

When Simone Ramsey arrived at the school, her grandson met her in the playground as arranged and walked with her to the hall.

A young teacher standing at the door said brightly, 'You must be Mrs Ramsey. I'm sorry but the junior hall's too small to fit all the children, so I'll have to send Tommy off to play games with the other non-performers.'

Simone watched open-mouthed as her grandson shouted a goodbye and ran away. It didn't surprise her that he wasn't performing. It was already evident to anyone who heard him sing that he wasn't musical. Very evident! It did surprise her, however, that Clo had wanted her to attend today. Surely her daughter had known Tommy wasn't going to sing in the concert? Or had he pretended he was in it?

The hall was stuffy even though this wasn't a really hot day, because March was often more humid. Why hadn't they switched on the air conditioning, for heaven's sake?

As she waited for the concert to begin, it occurred to Simone how often this torture was going to be inflicted on her during the next decade or so. Tommy was the eldest grandchild. She shuddered. She'd already gone through this sort of thing with her two daughters when they were young and not enjoyed it at all.

They'd now produced four children between them – and might produce more, for all she knew – and would probably expect her to keep attending in their place year after year while they carried on with their working lives. The arithmetic of that number of concerts made her gulp.

She should have refused to come today as the grandparents on the other side of the family had done. She had seen them refuse to attend nursery or school functions several times now. They simply smiled and said, 'No, sorry, can't make it this time.'

Why couldn't she follow their example? Because she was a softie, that was why, and a pitiful liar, always had been. Her daughters knew her well enough to see through any attempts to say no.

There was another reason she should have refused. Experience had already taught her how variable these school concerts could be: occasionally excellent, mostly rather tedious and sometimes downright appalling, especially if the teacher hadn't had any previous experience at organising musical events for young participants. Why was she so weak about saying no?

The trouble was, Clo had asked her to go to the concert in front of Tommy and he'd looked at Simone with such happy expectation on his face that she hadn't been able to refuse.

She was an idiot! Perhaps there was still time to leave.

Unfortunately, just as she was about to stand up and only fifteen minutes past the advertised starting time, an older teacher came out on the stage, smiled brightly at the captive audience and spoke into a faintly fizzing microphone. 'Welcome to our school concert, everyone. I'm sure you're going to enjoy it. Our Year 2 choir will start our show with a lovely song about the sea.'

Simone sank back on her chair with a sigh as a group of children filed on stage, shuffling and pushing one another. The teacher at the piano played the same note twice and sang it herself. This was clearly the signal to begin because the children began to yowl loudly, sounding more like a chorus of midnight cats than a group of human singers.

She winced. Half these children were too young to hold a complex tune like this. Whoever had chosen it had made a bad mistake.

She wriggled in another vain attempt to get comfortable. You'd think the school would provide bigger chairs for an adult audience. These were highly unsuitable for a woman in her fifties and she'd pinned up her hair too tightly. It was irritating her. She'd thought of having it cut but her daughters had both protested that she wouldn't seem herself with short hair, and it hadn't mattered enough to her.

The choir got tangled and faltered to a halt, so had to be restarted. She glanced along the row of fellow sufferers but could see no way of sneaking out without drawing attention to herself. She should just leave anyway but she didn't quite like to do that. She was a coward.

The next item was a Year 1 class playing a variety of percussion 'instruments' allegedly in time with a recording. They didn't have much sense of rhythm, but they were overflowing with enthusiasm for making a lot of noise.

Simone let her thoughts wander. Her husband had died suddenly four years ago and though she was used to living on her own now, it could be hard to do things like this alone.

She'd met a guy of her own age a couple of years ago and had enjoyed Phil's company greatly until he moved in with her. He was definitely not domesticated, and she'd soon realised exactly why his ex-wife had left him.

Their cohabitation hadn't even lasted three months. She wasn't stupid enough to let anyone treat her like a servant and when he'd told her two weeks running that he was a bit short of money and couldn't pay his share of the household bills 'just yet', that had been the final straw. She'd dumped his belongings on the front lawn while he was at work and had all the locks to the house changed.

'Never mind,' she'd said carelessly to her daughters when she told them, 'I'll be able to babysit for you more often.'

Big mistake. Since then she'd found herself in great demand. She loved her grandchildren dearly – how could you not? – but she wanted to do something more interesting with her life than sit watching TV while her grandchildren slept and their parents went out enjoying themselves.

To make matters worse, for the past year many of her friends and acquaintances had started introducing her to eligible men. Ha! There hadn't been one she really fancied. But some of the men had taken a while to stop pestering her. With one or two, she suspected that was because she was financially independent rather than due to an overwhelming attraction.

People began applauding and she realised the concert had ended. Well, that was a relief anyway.

'Weren't they cute?' the woman next to her said.

'No. Dreadful.' That got her several dirty looks from people nearby. Too bad. It was the worst school concert she'd ever attended.

When she went outside, she looked for Tommy, but he seemed to have vanished. Clo had said he'd catch the school bus at the usual time, so that Simone wouldn't need to go out of her way to take him home afterwards.

The buses were all lined up with children bobbing about inside. The ones who'd been performing in the concert were running across the oval to join them, shrieking and yelling.

What a total waste of an afternoon!

She was wasting her life, too. She sat in the car, feeling depressed, wondering how to change that. There had to be a more meaningful way of spending her time.

When she got home, Simone stared at the row of family photos on her mantelpiece and the dreadful thought returned. Years of school concerts lay ahead of her.

Both her daughters and their partners worked full-time and didn't go to many daytime school functions. And even the evening ones were usually too tiring after a day's work. She frowned as it occurred to her yet again that they didn't find it too tiring to go out in the evenings to cafés or friends' houses, or even too expensive for all their claims of tight budgets. Partly thanks to her free babysitting, no doubt!

Did anyone run classes in how to tell white lies to family members whom you loved dearly but who were driving you mad? If so, she'd be the first to enrol.

The phone rang just as she was getting ready for bed, but she didn't pick it up straight away. She listened to Deb leaving a message on the answerphone – another request for babysitting because a sudden wonderful opportunity had arisen for Deb and Logan the following evening.

'You won't believe it, Ma, but we've been given theatre tickets to a gala opening night, and there's a reception afterwards, so you may as well sleep over because we'll be late back.'

It was rare that Deb's outings ended before midnight anyway, so what did 'late' mean this time? Simone was an early-to-bed person and staying up till the small hours disrupted the following day for her, because she woke around her normal time of 6 a.m. and struggled for lack of sleep.

She hesitated, hand hovering near the phone, then shook her head and made no attempt to pick it up as her daughter ended the call with a request to get back to her and confirm the arrangement.

'No, thank you, Deb. I can't face it,' she said aloud.

Easy to say that now, but how was she going to say it to her daughter?

The following day the phone rang early in the morning. Simone checked who was calling before picking up and was delighted to accept a spur-of-the-moment invitation from her best friend, Libby, to go round for an Indian takeaway and drinks that evening.

She danced round the living room after she'd put down the phone. A genuine excuse for not babysitting this time. She could cope with refusing now. And Libby never tried to find her a new husband. Yeah!

Later, she left a message on Deb's phone at a time she knew her daughter would be unable to pick it up because staff weren't allowed to receive personal calls during working hours.

'Hi, darling. Only just got your message as I had an early night. Sorry, but I can't babysit for you tonight because I'm going out myself. Got to dash.' She put the phone down hastily and backed away from it.

There was another phone call from Deb in the late afternoon. Once again Simone listened to the message being recorded and her heart sank.

'Hi, Ma. Are you sure there's absolutely no chance of you changing what you're doing tonight? All my other babysitters are busy, and this is such a golden opportunity to see that play in style. Please take pity on us.'

Simone didn't return the call in case she let herself

be persuaded to change her plans. In fact, she left home a little early in case Deb called round in person to plead with her. That had happened before.

Her friend Libby opened the front door, beaming at her. 'Oh, I'm glad you came early. I'm famished after running up and down those playing fields all day.'

'You love running.'

Libby grinned. 'Of course I do. I wouldn't be a sports teacher otherwise, and it keeps me fit, but I do get tired sometimes by the end of the day. And hungry. We'll order as soon as Greg gets home from work.'

She stopped talking to study Simone's face. 'Hey, what's the matter?'

'Nothing.'

'Come on. I've known you since we were kids. I can recognise when you're upset.'

Greg came in just then, but Libby wasn't letting go. 'Simone was about to tell me what's upset her. Pour her a glass of wine and she can sleep over tonight so she doesn't drink and drive. If anyone ever needed cheering up, it's her.'

Simone leant back in her chair, relaxing as she always did with these two. 'I'd love a glass of wine.'

When the food order had been phoned through, Libby said, 'Right. Tell all.'

So Simone explained her dilemma, ending, 'Am I being selfish?'

'Not at all. It's about time you made a stand. I know they love you and you love them, but your family are running you ragged, taking advantage of your kindness since you got rid of rat man. I've been wanting to give you a nudge about it for a few months now, but Greg kept saying it was none of my business.'

Simone felt tears come into her eyes. 'You don't think I'm being selfish, then?'

Libby came across to give her a hug. 'No way.'

As they were settling down again, Greg snapped his fingers and exclaimed, 'I've got it! I know exactly what you can do to change things, Simone.'

The two women looked at him expectantly. Greg was a man of few words but rarely claimed what he couldn't deliver.

'A colleague of mine at work, Michael Westing, was asking only yesterday whether anyone knew a family who'd like to do a house swap for a few months. His in-laws in the UK want to come and stay in Australia for a while because his wife, who is their only child, is having her first baby. They have friends who do house swaps regularly and thought this might be a good, low-cost way to stay here, while still leaving their daughter and Michael their privacy.' He beamed at her. 'That might be just the thing for you.'

Simone gaped at him. 'Swap my house with strangers? I don't think so.'

'Not complete strangers, friends of a friend. They'd swap both their house *and* car, and expect the same from you in return, so you'd get an overseas holiday at the cost of an air fare.' He waited expectantly and when she didn't say anything, added, 'It'd be a perfect way for you to loosen the shackles of your loving family for a while.'

'And for you to do something *exciting*,' Libby put in. 'After all, you're from England originally so you can catch up with your relatives there.'

Simone stared from one to the other, still having trouble dealing with this idea. 'I don't know these relatives. We left the UK when I was six. That's a crazy idea.'

Greg reached across to pat her hand. 'Don't be so hasty. You don't have to decide this minute.'

But she wasn't off the hook yet because Libby took over. 'It'd do you good to get away, Simone. You gave up your job when Harvey died, so you've nothing to tie you down here.'

'Well, the business was dependent on Harvey's skills. I only used to run the office. I couldn't keep things going on my own without him and when I had a brilliant offer to buy it, I bit their hand off. My accountant agreed it was the right thing to do. And then there was all that insurance money. I'd not expected that much.'

'I didn't expect you to stay at home, though, Simone. I thought you'd get a part-time job, or do some charity work or something. Since you split up with rat man, you've almost turned into a hermit.'

'I looked at Jobs Vacant sections when I'd got over things a bit. Part-time jobs aren't usually very interesting. I don't *need* to work so I don't have to put up with doing something tedious. If I don't go mad and spend all my money on extravagances, I need never go out to work again.'

'That's what rat man wanted you to do, wasn't it? Stay home and wait on him hand and foot, as well as providing a house for him at zero cost.'

'I thought we'd agreed that the least said about him the better. You were right about him and I was wrong. I'm well over that mistake.' But she'd have trouble trusting anyone again.

'Yes, I know, but I still get mad every time I think about him trying to take you for a ride. Admit it, though. You're bored out of your mind half the time.' Libby's voice grew softer. 'Don't you think it's time to spread your wings a little?'

Greg took over again. 'Michael told me about the place where his in-laws live. It's in a leisure village in Wiltshire and I'm sure you'd find it easier to make friends in a set-up like that.'

'What's a leisure village?'

'A small housing development on a campus of its own with a whole range of activities provided, rather like a miniature village. The other owners are mostly older people, apparently.'

'Oh, retirement homes. I've looked at them here and the houses are tiny. It'd be like living in a cupboard.'

'This isn't like the Aussie retirement places. I've seen the photos and the houses at Penny Lake are quite big, and you'd have all sorts of activities available right on site. Owners pay an annual membership fee and take their pick from golf, a gym, a swimming pool, a hotel with restaurant and bar. Oh, and apparently there are lovely country walks near this one, as well as the lake it's named after. You can just walk out of your front door and join in.'

'That does sound rather nice.' She enjoyed swimming, though not in the sea, which was too bumpy for her. And she'd been doing a lot of walking lately. It helped fill the time.

They waited and she couldn't think what else to say.

Libby took over in a coaxing voice, 'It sounds like a safe place for a woman on her own to live.'

Greg added, 'The Dittons have only been living there for a few months. They love it and wouldn't be leaving it and going overseas so soon after moving in if it weren't for their first grandchild being on the way. Their daughter has been trying in vain to get pregnant for several years. They're thrilled to pieces but she's not been well, so has to rest a lot. Her parents want to help out without interfering too much.'

Simone had talked vaguely to Libby about finding something new to do with her life, but going away to England for a few months would be more than a bit OTT for a first step. The England she vaguely remembered from her childhood before her parents emigrated would have changed beyond recognition and she wouldn't recognise a single one of her relatives now. Her parents hadn't even taken photographs of them when they went back for a visit.

No, she couldn't do it! Definitely not. She opened her mouth to say so but Greg got in first.

'I know what, I'll ask Michael and his wife to call round to your place tomorrow evening and show you the photos of her parents' house. I've seen them and it looks lovely. They can suss out your house while they're at it and send photos of it back to her parents. I'll phone him now, shall I?'

As she hesitated, Libby nodded energetically at her, with *that look* on her face. No one could be as stubborn as her friend when she thought something was right, so Simone gave in. 'It won't hurt to see what's involved, I suppose.'

'And we'll come round tomorrow too. I haven't seen their photos, only heard about the place,' Libby said. 'Ah, there's the doorbell. Our food must have arrived.'

They chatted about other things over the meal and Simone enjoyed her friends' company as always. It was lovely to go somewhere and be sure no stray men would be joining them. If the samples of colourless, ageing manhood who had been trotted out to meet her so far were typical, she'd never want to remarry. However pleasant they'd been, none had attracted her in the slightest during the past couple of years.

Perhaps rat man had put her off men for good. She smiled. Funny how the nickname Libby had given him had stuck and defused some of her embarrassment. All Simone's family and friends called him that now.

She wasn't looking to remarry. Definitely not.

Only what was she going to do with her life? She didn't know, only that she couldn't go on like this, had to find something more.

When she went to bed, she looked in the mirror and told herself firmly that she wasn't going so far away for several months. Definitely not. She'd make a show of considering it then refuse graciously.

Whatever Libby said or did.

## Chapter Two

The following morning Simone went home as soon as she woke, not even staying for breakfast because Thursday was a working day for her friends.

As the day passed, she was even more certain that she wasn't going to agree to a house swap, even if these people were pleasant and their relatives' home looked like a beautiful advert. But she didn't have their phone number and her friends were both at work. Anyway, she didn't like to cancel at such short notice.

She felt increasingly nervous as the afternoon passed and was relieved when Libby turned up before the others to support her.

'Greg's coming with his friends, then he'll drive me home.' Libby brandished a bottle of Prosecco. 'I brought this to celebrate the deal.'

'What deal?'

Libby stared at Simone. 'Uh-oh! I know that expression

of yours. You've already decided to refuse, haven't you? Before you've even met them or seen photos of the house. Well, don't you dare tell them no until you've seen what they have to offer and talked it over with me afterwards.'

'But if I don't—'

Libby held up one finger and waggled it at her. 'No buts! You weren't such a coward before, Simone. Harvey would be ashamed of you. And you couldn't get a better time to go. It'll be spring and summer there. You might not even see a winter this year.'

She froze. Only Libby would have dared say that to her. The trouble was, her friend was right. Simone was starting to worry herself at how timid she was getting these days about meeting new people or going to new places on her own. And yet she longed to change things – only how to do it? She seemed to be stuck in a rut, with a reasonably pleasant life and it wasn't enough.

The doorbell rang just then and she went to open it. Greg introduced his friends, a pregnant woman and a man who kept shooting proud, fond glances at his wife.

'Michael and Harriet, meet Simone, who's known Libby since primary school, heaven help her.'

Harriet beamed at her. 'I'm so glad to meet you, Simone. I do hope you'll like the look of Mum and Dad's house. It's brand new and looks gorgeous. It would mean so much to me to have them here for the last few months and the birth.'

Simone mumbled something, not wanting to dent their happiness yet.

Libby gave her a little shove. 'You and I will show

them round this house while Greg opens the bubbly.'

'I have a bottle in the fridge, if we run out.' She had a feeling she'd be drinking more than one glass.'

Simone led the way round the house and if she said so herself, it was looking good. Harvey would be proud of the way she'd looked after it.

Her visitors took dozens of photos with their phones as they went, oohing and aahing at how well it would suit Harriet's parents, and what a nice feel it had.

After that Greg took Michael out to see the car, which would be included in the swap – if it took place.

Simone didn't go out with them. What did she know about the technicalities of cars? They were tin boxes on wheels as far as she was concerned and what mattered most to her was the comfort of the seats and the effectiveness of the safety features.

Libby winked at her. She'd obviously guessed already that Simone was going to find it hard to spoil their delight. 'How about us ladies make a start on the bubbly?'

'Not for me.' Harriet patted her slightly bulging stomach.

Simone got out some ginger beer for her visitor then accepted the glass of Prosecco her friend thrust into her hand and took a big gulp. It tasted lovely but it didn't help her nervousness about refusing.

The men came back to join them and once they'd all got glasses they toasted the coming child and nibbled a few nuts, while the visitors began to show Simone photos of the house in England on an iPad. They started with an overview of Penny Lake Leisure Village, then panned slowly along Bob and Linda's street to their brand-new house. Room by room they went through it then asked for Simone's email address so they could send her a copy of the tour to review later.

As she, Libby and Michael accepted a second glass of bubbly, she had to admit to herself that it was a lovely house, not at all like the small retirement homes she'd seen in Western Australia. And the nearby countryside looked really pretty too, as did the small lake to one side of the leisure village.

When Simone had finished looking through the photos, Libby took charge. 'Simone will get back to you within twenty-four hours. It's a big decision to make . . . in her circumstances.'

Their faces fell and Simone felt guilty as she saw tears of disappointment tremble in Harriet's eyes. The two of them left soon afterwards.

Once they'd gone, Greg exchanged glances with his wife and went out to their car, saying, 'I'll listen to the car radio while I wait for you girls to have a little chat.'

Libby held up one hand to stop Simone speaking. 'All I ask is that you think about it. Right? I'll come round tomorrow after work and we'll have a chat before you contact them.'

'But I already know that I don't want to—'

'Shh. Do not decide now, think about it really carefully. You're surely not going to waste a golden opportunity because of being *nervous*? They don't have fire-breathing dragons roaming wild in Wiltshire, you know. It's a beautiful rural county with some lovely places to visit – including Stonehenge. And remember, you have family in that part of England as well. Ask your parents what it's like.'

She shrugged. Her parents were off touring in their caravan and would be mostly out of touch for a few weeks, roughing it. She knew they'd visited some of their British relatives but they hadn't said much about them. Anyway, she wasn't going to England, so she wouldn't need to contact her parents about that, would she?

Libby gave her a hug. 'See you after work tomorrow. And don't you dare break your promise to me.'

As her friends drove off Simone said aloud, 'You should have stuck to your guns, you fool, and said no straight away.'

She was going to be very firm with Libby tomorrow. Definitely. She'd rehearse what to say until she was word perfect and stick to it. She could manage that, surely? Libby was her best friend, after all. She'd understand.

But it wouldn't hurt to look at the leisure village and the house again. It'd be something to do. This house could feel so empty after guests had left.

The following day Simone couldn't settle to anything. Libby was right about one thing. It would be foolish to dismiss the idea of a house exchange out of hand.

She made a cup of coffee and sat stirring it, trying to look at the situation objectively. It was certainly a cheaper way to take an overseas holiday. Could she do it, though? Swap houses and go to stay in England for a few months? It seemed a strange idea to live in someone else's home among all their possessions – not to mention letting them into your home in return. She'd never considered doing anything remotely like that before.

Well, she had nothing to be ashamed of. She looked after her home and anyway, she could put away her most precious objects.

She'd been too young when her family left England to remember that country clearly and had only seen it since in photos or on television, not noticing a lot because she wasn't really interested. Picking up the cup, she took it across to her computer and sipped as she searched for images of Wiltshire.

Wow! It did look to be a beautiful county. She studied the green, lush fields of ripe crops, the picturesque houses and villages, and wondered why she'd never gone on holiday to England. Her parents had done it a couple of times, combining it with a round-the-world trip each time. They'd been full of themselves when they got back and had urged her and Harvey to do it too.

But they hadn't said much about the relatives there.

She knew why she hadn't gone: because Harvey hated flying. And because it hadn't mattered much to her. After all, her parents and daughters were here in Australia. Harvey didn't have any close relatives left, but he was very close to their girls and to her parents.

If she went, she'd be so far away, on the other side of the world. How could she bear not to see her family for months? Especially the grandchildren, who were shooting up fast.

And look how lonely she got even here sometimes. Evenings were the worst part of the day when you lived alone. They'd be far worse in a place where she didn't know anyone at all, she was sure.

She shivered suddenly as she thought of the practicalities of what an exchange would involve: not only learning to use equipment and manage a stranger's house, but driving around in a strange country. No, she couldn't do that on her own.

But how did she say a convincing no to Libby when her friend was right about one thing: it was the sort of offer most people would have grabbed with both hands?

She went into the kitchen to get herself another cup of coffee before watching the early evening news, something she always did. Then she remembered there had been some Prosecco left last night. Libby had capped the second bottle and put it in the fridge. Oh, what the hell? It was a bit early to start drinking but if she'd ever deserved a comforting glass of wine it was now.

She poured some, pleased that it was still fizzy. She checked the label. She'd remember it because this one was particularly nice, not too dry and acidic.

As she reached for the remote to switch on the television, the doorbell rang and her daughters came in without waiting to be asked. They knew she kept the front door locked so always came with keys at the ready. She wished they'd not barge in like that, but hadn't liked to make a point of it. They wouldn't have done it when their father was alive, though.

'We've been doing the week's grocery shopping and thought we'd stop off on the way back and have a cup of coffee with you, Ma. The guys can look after the kids for a bit longer today.' Clo walked across the kitchen and put the kettle on.

Deb kissed the air near Simone's left ear. 'I was a bit worried when you weren't available to babysit the other night. Are you all right, Ma?'

'Of course I am. I went round to Libby's on Wednesday and stayed over, that's all. We had a great time.'

'Well! You really should check your phone more often. I'd been trying to get in touch with you. You could easily have gone to Libby's another night and babysat for us instead. We missed out on a very special evening.'

That assumption annoyed her. 'I'd been looking forward to going out that night. It wouldn't have suited me to have missed out. Why do you always think my wishes are less important than yours?'

They both gaped at that.

'As for checking my phone, Libby and I always switch them off when we want a good old natter. Anyway, it's rude to answer a call from someone else when you're visiting people so I wouldn't have checked for messages anyway. We're not all glued to our phones twenty-four seven, you know.'

Clo gave her a scornful glance as if she thought her mother was being stupid. 'Talking of Libby, she rang me at work at lunchtime and asked me to help her persuade you to accept an invitation to stay in the UK,'

'*What?*'

'You weren't really considering it, were you, Ma?'

'Well, I—'

'Because you aren't the travelling type and you're so

naïve about the world outside Australia. I hate to think how people would take advantage of you.'

They both stared at her, waiting for the expected agreement with that and frowning at one another when she didn't say anything. She picked up her glass and took a defiant gulp.

'You don't usually sit drinking on your own at this time of day, either,' Clo added disapprovingly, 'so you must be upset. Libby should know you better than to try to push you into it, shouldn't even have suggested *you* do something like that.'

Simone opened her mouth to explain but just then Deb's phone warbled its annoyingly loud jangle and of course she immediately took it out of her bag to answer it. She was as programmed as one of Pavlov's dogs.

*Quod erat demonstrandum*, she thought angrily. One of Harvey's favourite Latin quotes and Deb had just demonstrated the truth of that programming. Her younger daughter had picked up the call automatically, not even thinking about how rude that might be, and then walked out into the hall to answer it. Clo would have done exactly the same.

They did it all the time, interrupting conversations with their mother to chat to distant friends.

Why had she put up with it for so long?

She took another mouthful of wine and got more disapproving glances from both of them as Deb came back into the kitchen. She'd thought they'd got over their latest health kick about not drinking alcohol at all during the week. Apparently not.

'Don't let Libby push you into anything, Ma,' Clo said soothingly. You know it wouldn't suit you and you have trouble saying no to her. That's probably why you're drinking so early.'

'I'm drinking because I enjoy an occasional glass of wine in the evening. *I* am not the one who gave up drinking during the week. That's your choice. I don't drink enough to need rules, thank you very much.'

They rolled their eyes at one another, then Deb said in the tone of one clinching an argument, 'Anyway, I'm sure Dad wouldn't have wanted you to travel so far on your own.'

'Your father's been gone for four years now and much as I miss him, I'm well past running my life by what he would have wanted. Besides, I'm more than due a holiday, don't you think? You all go somewhere each year. Why shouldn't I?'

'We'll take you to Bali next year and have a nice family holiday together. We were only talking about it the other day.'

And they'd expect her to babysit the kids every evening while they were there, Simone thought bitterly. Like that family weekend in Busselton they'd all had last year. She'd been left to sit around quietly in a hotel room in the evenings with a book to read, keeping an eye on the children. She'd been gobsmacked that the weekend away she'd looked forward to and bought new clothes for was just more babysitting.

But she hadn't complained or refused to do it, had she? She had to learn to assert herself or she'd turn into a cabbage.

The words were out before she thought the consequences through. 'A holiday in England sounds somewhat more exciting than one in Bali, don't you think?'

They both gaped at her as if she'd suddenly spoken a foreign language.

'Ma, have you gone mad? You'd hate it, you know you would.'

That was the final straw. 'Why would I hate it? Wiltshire is where Nana and Pops come from. We still have relatives there. It's a lovely part of England.'

'You always said you didn't remember much about it.'

'I've been looking it up online. I need to get out of my rut and this is a really great offer.' She saw Clo look at her scornfully and start to open her mouth, so said slowly and clearly, 'I'm definitely going.'

They immediately started trying to talk her out of it, and the more they said the more they persuaded her to do the opposite.

So she was useless at finding her way round new places, was she? Wrong. Why did they think that?

And she liked a quiet life, did she? It hadn't always been this quiet, though. It was damned near silent half the time these days and she was fed up with it.

She was a bit old for adventures. She glanced at her image in a mirror. Not exactly elderly at fifty-six. A bit plump, maybe, for this scraggy generation's taste, but that filled the wrinkles nicely, she and Libby always joked.

She'd miss the grandchildren more than she realised, surely? Well, of course she would, but not as much as her daughters would miss the free babysitting. Oh, no!

And finally, she'd be terrified of driving in England.

That was the final straw. She raised her voice, cutting off Deb's next remark. 'Why do you say that? I have an unblemished driving record and I used to drive Harvey all over the place, in other parts of Australia as well as here in Perth. I wasn't afraid in Sydney's traffic snarls, but he was. Even rat man said I was a good driver.'

They rolled their eyes at one another yet again, and Clo used her soothing tone as if speaking to a child. 'Calm down, Ma. See how it's upsetting you already.'

'See how you two are upsetting me, you mean. You'll be buying me a shawl and a rocking chair next, and chaining me in a corner in case I lose my way round the house.'

'Look, we—'

The front doorbell rang and she bounced to her feet to answer it. 'Ah, Libby. Do come in. I was just telling Clo and Deb how much I'm looking forward to my trip to England.'

Libby hugged her and danced her round the kitchen–diner area. 'So they persuaded you to go, did they? Well done, girls.' She beamed at the two younger women.

Simone kept hold of her friend's arm and gave it a hard squeeze. 'On the contrary. They don't think I could *cope* with it, me being such a timid, elderly moron.'

'We *know* she'd be out of her depth going on her own,' Clo said firmly. 'Come on, Ma. I know it's tempting but you really aren't the sort to go gallivanting around a foreign country alone.'

'Not all that foreign. I still have dual nationality.'

Libby gave Simone an understanding squeeze of the arm in return. 'Good for you.'

'I'll be fine tottering round but maybe it'll make you two happy if I buy a Zimmer frame to take with me.'

Though Simone had meant it as a sort of joke, she heard the sharp edge to her voice. 'As soon as you girls have left I'm going to ring up Michael and Harriet and tell them I'd love to do the swap as soon as possible. I promised them I'd call with my answer this evening.'

'Phone them now.' Libby held out her mobile and gave Simone a challenging look. 'This is Michael's number.' She tapped something on her phone and handed it over as it began ringing.

'Ma, at least sleep on it. You don't want to do something you'll regret,' Clo said urgently, reaching out as if to take the phone away.

Simone moved further away. 'I've slept on it once. Do I keep sleeping on it till someone else takes up the offer? Ah, Michael. Simone here. I'd like to take up your in-laws' offer of a house and car swap.'

She heard him call out to his wife, 'Harriet, she's going to do it!'

Excited distant squealing made her smile. It was good to make someone happy.

'Look, Michael, I've got my daughters here. Can I ring you later to discuss the timing and the details?'

As she ended the call, her daughters picked up their shoulder bags, radiating outrage.

'Well, it's your own decision, Ma, and I just hope

you don't regret it,' Clo said loudly and slowly.

'We'd better get going.' Deb did a kissy-kissy in mid-air as usual. Heaven forbid she should actually touch anyone and smudge her make-up. Even her children knew better than to do that to their mother, young as they were. You'd think she was going into battle and needed war paint the way she got ready for work each day.

Clo sniffed disapprovingly. 'I still think you're rushing into this without thinking it through properly, Ma. But on your own head be it.'

'Of course it's on my own head what I do with my life. Did you think *you* were in charge of it?'

She waited till she'd waved them goodbye to come back and collapse into her favourite armchair. Looking across at Libby, she asked faintly, 'What have I done?'

'Stood up for yourself. Go get 'em, girlfriend!'

'I need another glass of wine. Join me?' She wasn't going to change her decision or she'd never hear the last of it, but oh, she was suddenly quite terrified.

'Just give me half a glass. I'm driving.' Libby grinned. 'Bossy, aren't they, your girls?'

'Yes. And so are you.' Then she giggled suddenly. 'Did you see their faces?'

They both howled with laughter then raised their glasses in a toast.

'To England!'

'To a wonderful holiday!'

# Chapter Three

Harriet came to see Simone the following morning to go through the basic arrangements, and they agreed to start the swap towards the end of May. This would be well into spring in Wiltshire and the countryside would be lovely by then.

Simone went to have a preliminary chat with a travel agent but decided not to make a booking until she got a firm date from the Dittons.

Harriet phoned three days later very early in the morning. 'Are you free? Something interesting has come up that I'd like to discuss.'

'Sure. Why don't you come round now?'

After the call ended, Simone hastily put the tins of food back into the kitchen cupboard she'd been cleaning out and tidied everything up. If she was going to let someone else live in her home for several months, she was determined that every corner of it would be immaculate.

When she heard a car pull up in the drive, she peeped out of the window, then went to open the front door before Harriet could get there. 'Come in and sit down. Can I get you a cup of coffee or something?'

'No, thanks. But I will sit down.' She gestured towards the laptop she was carrying. 'Could we sit at a table? I want to show you something.'

Puzzled, Simone did as her visitor had asked and waited while Harriet got online.

'I'll get straight to the point. My parents have found a super-special price for a business class flight and want to come sooner than we'd arranged. Any chance of you agreeing to that?'

'How much sooner?'

'This week.'

The silence was deafening. She couldn't think what to say and managed only a feeble, 'When this week?'

'Saturday.'

'That's only four days from now and I still have to book a flight.'

'That's why I wanted to come round. I have the details of the website they found where there are super-specials on international flights, some of them due to last-minute cancellations. How about we look at it now and see if we can find you a cheaper flight too? If not, there's no problem. They can still come early and stay with us till you're ready to leave.'

Since she'd found out the prices, Simone had been hesitating as to whether to book business class or not, because she was tall enough to find economy class seats very uncomfortable. But the super-specials for flights available in the short term on this site made her gasp. Wow! They'd save her a big chunk of money and make business class seem far less eye-watering in cost.

Then she noticed a cancellation offer blink abruptly into place. It was for tonight at quarter to seven from Perth airport, arriving in London just after five the next morning. If she could leave then, she'd save $3,000 on her return fare and get a non-stop flight. 'Look at that!' She pointed to the screen.

Harriet whistled and looked at her.

Simone took a deep breath and clicked on the icon to say she was interested before anyone else could do it. 'You're right about bargains.' Then she thought about the practicalities. 'But how can I go so quickly when I haven't done what's needed to get the house ready?'

'It looks immaculate to me. Leave the food in the fridge as is and they'll do the same for you. You can both eat up whatever's left. And if you don't mind, Michael and I can move things out of your wardrobe and drawers and take notes about what we put where.'

'I can do that part of it in an hour or so if I just dump my things in the empty drawers and wardrobes in the other bedrooms. I had a pretty good clear-out of my own things after my husband died a few years ago, you see. I don't want anyone to have to clear out my years of rubbish, as I had to do for Harvey.' She took a deep breath. 'I'll do it. Let me get my credit card.'

She grabbed her bag from the kitchen and was back in a minute, taking out her purse on the way. She completed the cancellation offer there and then, because she doubted she'd find another special as good as this one. The travel agent had already told her the non-stop flights were booked up months in advance and the Dittons would have to change planes midway. Her flight would arrive in the UK two days before they were due to leave, given the time differences.

'Perfect!' Harriet said. 'My parents can pick you up from the airport and take you to their house, and you can drop them at my aunt's house the day before their flight. She lives near Heathrow. If you don't mind, I'm sure she'd like to come and stay with them here.'

'I don't mind at all.'

Harriet hesitated, then gave Simone a quick hug, looking suddenly tearful. 'I can't tell you how much this means to me, how grateful I am to you.'

Simone returned the younger woman's hug. 'I'm glad. And I do hope it'll help your pregnancy go more smoothly to have your parents with you.'

'Thanks. Look, if we go round the house now, you can explain how everything works and I'll take notes.'

'Good idea. Though it's all very straightforward. I don't go in for fancy gadgets.'

'We can take you to the airport this afternoon. What time do you want to leave home?'

'I'd like to get there about three hours before the flight leaves. And can Michael deal with my car, show them about driving it, I mean? My insurance covers any driver I nominate, but there will be road tax due in a couple of months.'

'He'll be on to that. And I'll get Dad to cover your car insurance in England.'

They went round the reverse cycle air conditioning and other appliances, with Harriet taking notes but, as Simone had said, there was nothing fancy or difficult.

'We'll be able to get in touch easily if anything else crops up. And my parents will look after your house, I promise.'

'Yes, of course. As I'll look after theirs.'

'I can see that. Yours is immaculate.'

Simone didn't let herself smile. She could make her house look immaculate in a few minutes. Had perfected that when the kids were little.

Once Harriet had driven away Simone went along to her bedroom and proceeded to give her pillow a good pummelling, which was one of the best ways she knew to relieve severe stress.

She felt as if fate had grabbed her firmly by the scruff of the neck and was sending her to England '*will-she, nill-she*' to paraphrase Shakespeare.

Then she pulled herself together and started on the practicalities, removing her sheets and putting them on to wash before returning to the bedroom to pack two suitcases and her backpack. Fortunately she'd already mentally sorted out the clothes she was taking. She'd need some of her winter stuff from here in Australia as well, because it could be cool in England, even in spring. And if she needed anything else she could buy it there.

Thank goodness there was an increased baggage weight allowance in business class, so she could fit quite a lot in. After she'd packed she'd clear out her wardrobe.

On a sudden thought, she sent a text to her daughters and Libby, saying it was very urgent she see them as she was leaving for the UK TONIGHT!!! (in capital letters and bold). Could they get off work a bit early?

By the time they were due, she'd dried the sheets and remade the bed, packed all her bits and pieces into the hand luggage, got her laptop and phone ready and was going round the house checking every room.

Clo was the first to arrive. 'What's up, Ma?'

'I'll tell you all at once.'

Clo looked at her watch and gave one of her aggrieved sighs. Fortunately Deb and Libby arrived soon afterwards.

'Good thing I didn't have a class,' Libby said cheerfully. 'I claimed a family emergency and left early.'

When Simone told them how quickly she was leaving, her daughters looked at one another in horror and Libby beamed at her.

'I didn't think you'd go through with it, Ma,' Deb muttered.

*Join the club. Neither did I*, Simone thought, hoping her smile was convincingly confident.

Clo stared at her mother as if she'd never seen her before. 'Aren't you scared?'

She shrugged. 'Somewhat nervous, I must admit, but the Dittons will be picking me up at Heathrow, so it's just a matter of getting on the plane in Perth and getting off it again in England. Did I tell you I scored a non-stop flight in business class at an absolutely knock-down price because of a cancellation? That's why it's happening so quickly.'

Libby let out a low whistle. 'Well done you.'

Her daughters left soon afterwards but her friend stayed.

'Want me to take you to the airport?'

'The Westings have offered.'

'Let me do it, then I can hold your hand, so to speak, till it's time to board. I don't want you panicking and backing out.'

'I won't. I daren't, now I've told the girls. But I'd like to have you there.'

'We'll see if we can get you a sim card at the airport so that you can still use the same mobile phone in the UK.'

'I hadn't thought of that. Um, I'm going to miss you, Libby.'

'We'll stay in touch and if you're still there in the next school holidays, I may even come over to visit you.'

'Oh, do! Now, just let me phone the Westings and tell them they're off the hook for taking me to the airport. I've already given Harriet some house keys.'

As Libby gave her a farewell hug at the airport, she said, 'I'm so excited for you, Simone.'

'I'm excited too.'

It was clear from her grin that Libby was well aware that this was a lie, so Simone plonked a kiss on her cheek, took a deep breath and walked away from her. After going through customs she waited in the comfortable business class lounge for half an hour, then was called to board. Nervousness made her stomach lurch as she walked slowly down the narrow passage that led on to the plane.

When the flight took off, she let out a huge sigh and sagged back in her seat, glad this part was over and done with, and that she didn't have to pretend to anyone. Talk about riding the whirlwind for the past few hours.

She was delighted with the amount of seating space she had and the little side table. The service provided by the cabin staff was excellent and she felt herself calm down still further. She didn't expect to sleep a wink, but since she had a proper bed, when the cabin lights dimmed, she decided to lie down anyway.

Several hours had passed by the time she woke, but there were still eight more to go and they seemed to tick by very slowly. She watched a popular movie half-heartedly, read some of a book she'd been in the middle of, but couldn't have given any details of what had happened next, and tried to tell herself that this really would be an exciting and life-changing experience.

But she still couldn't convince herself that she'd really wanted an adventure of this magnitude.

Her biggest consolation was that for once she'd stood up for herself against her daughters' smothering love – and increasing selfishness. The time she'd spend away might make them appreciate her more once she got back. But oh, she'd miss them and her grandchildren so much.

She'd miss her parents too, hadn't even been able to phone them to say goodbye because they were out of touch electronically at the moment. They were enjoying being 'grey nomads' driving round Australia towing a small but luxurious caravan, though her father always insisted 'bald nomad' would be more appropriate for him these days. That had become a family joke. They were cheerful, enjoyed life and were lucky to still be in good health in their late seventies.

She'd only been able to send them an explanatory email telling them what she was doing. They'd approve when they read it, she was sure. They'd be surprised, too. Her father in particular teased her regularly about being a timid homebody. No one could accuse her of that now!

The flight seemed to go on for ever and she kept checking her watch. It just showed that time was relative. An hour passed quickly when you were enjoying yourself and very slowly indeed during this flight.

# Chapter Four

Russ Carden walked slowly round with Molly Santiago as he did a final inspection of the interior of his newly finished home. She and her husband were the creators and owners of the Penny Lake Leisure Village but he had other businesses so she was the one who handled all the sales of land and organised the building work. A capable and charming woman.

Everything seemed fine to him but she pointed out one area of wall that had missed its final coat of paint in the second bathroom and an insect screen that hadn't been properly fitted into the window in one of the spare bedrooms.

'I'll send someone to fix them as soon as I can, Russ. Most builders here don't install insect screens in the windows and doors of their houses so some of our tradesmen are still developing their skills in that area.'

He nodded. 'Thanks. Once you've lived in countries where they're standard, you appreciate the difference they can make. I don't enjoy sharing my home with insects that bite or sting.'

'Will you please try using the lift on your own now, Russ? I want you to be happy with it.'

He wasn't happy to need a lift but the accident had left him with various slowly improving physical weaknesses that still had to be allowed for when carrying heavy things or going up and down stairs. That galled him.

As a tourist, the last thing you expected when travelling in Australia was to be caught up in a major bushfire crisis, but this fire had hit suddenly and spread rapidly. The authorities had handled it well and Russ would have been all right if it hadn't been for a drunken idiot who hadn't followed police instructions about how to drive out of danger.

Russ had been driving along sedately in the patient convoy of slow-moving motorists who were being escorted to safety when someone had tried to overtake them on a blind corner. The driver had killed himself and his passenger by this careless act but unfortunately he'd taken the nearest two cars with him as well as he spun out of control. They'd all crashed into a huge fallen, half-burnt tree that had been bulldozed to the side of the road.

Russ still had nightmares about the feeling of sickening helplessness and the way everything seemed to go into slow motion as his car spun towards that tree, which was still smouldering at one end.

The other driver who had been caught up in the accident had survived with less damage to his body, but Russ was lucky to have survived at all. He knew that.

But he didn't *feel* lucky when he found himself facing months of rehab, in order to be able to do everyday things that had been so easy before.

*Oh, stop dwelling on that and look to the future, you moron*, he told himself and pressed the lift button to go down again. It worked smoothly with very little noise. When he joined Molly again downstairs, he said, 'It's fine. Where do I sign?'

She gave him one of her lovely, understanding smiles. 'Eager to move in?'

'Very eager.'

'Here you are.'

She held out the clipboard and he signed on the dotted line at the bottom with a flourish. He wasn't worried about the two minor defects not being remedied because he reckoned she was as honest as she'd seemed. That was one of the reasons he'd contracted her and her husband to build him a house here in the leisure village they'd created from previously bare meadows. That and the smiling, friendly faces of the other residents.

He didn't watch her walk back to the sales office. As soon as she'd left he rang the removal company he'd booked provisionally and his day immediately went another step brighter. Yes, they'd be happy to move his small collection of furniture the very next day, as long as they could turn up at eight o'clock to load it.

He was so eager to move something in today, he drove the hour back to his grotty rented flat in Swindon and collected together a load of oddments of various sizes and shapes, like his great-grandmother's old copper kettle, his wok, a few ornaments he treasured, wrapped in bubble plastic, and some boxes of books and CDs.

After grabbing a quick lunch, he drove them across from his flat to the new house. Smiling ruefully, he admitted to himself that the removal men could easily have brought these as well as the other stuff and this was mainly an excuse to wander round his new home again and gloat at its spaciousness.

By the time he'd transferred everything from his car into the house, his shoulder and knee were aching. With a growl of annoyance, he dumped things in the appropriate rooms and rode the lift back down to what Molly called the kitchen–family area.

Only he didn't have a family, did he, just fond memories of the wife who'd died.

That had been years ago now, but though he'd met some very pleasant women since, he'd never been tempted to go as far as marriage again. So he would be living here on his own and that was fine. He was used to it, was looking forward to resuming his busy working life.

He sneezed suddenly and became aware that the whole house smelled of some sickly air freshener that was making his nose tickle and his eyes water. He found a couple of gadgets spraying the stuff automatically every now and then, and turned them off with a grimace, putting them outside the back door. Pity it wouldn't be safe to leave the windows and doors open overnight. It'd be the first thing he did tomorrow, open up every window he could so that the house could be filled with clean, fresh air.

Back at the flat he made tea – cheese on toast followed

by an elderly piece of fruit cake from the nearly empty freezer – then he finished the last bit of packing.

Not that he had a lot to pack. He hadn't taken out of storage more than the absolute minimum needed when he moved here, knowing it would only be for a few months. He'd rented this place because he'd needed somewhere to live that was away from his aunt's well-meaning fussing. Vera had been wonderful to him, but she did talk a lot and he'd never been fond of chatting for the sake of it. In his professional career as a nature photographer he'd relished silence except for the sounds of life outdoors.

Anyway, she lived in a flat near the centre in Leicester. Not a convenient place for him, either for work or his new home.

As for his half-sister, he hadn't heard from her for ages. The last time he heard Justine had been living in Strasbourg with some rich French guy. But she'd rarely bothered to keep in touch, so who knew where she was now?

Well, he hadn't been brilliant at communicating with her, either. She was twenty years younger than him and he'd already left home when she was born, so he had never really got to know her properly.

Justine called herself an artist, but she was into modern, incomprehensible stuff that looked like a child's crayon drawing to him. No wonder she found it difficult to make a living. She'd made up for that with a series of wealthy men.

He left the clothes he would need for the morning on a bedside chair and stuffed his dirty clothes in the linen basket. He'd put the sheets in with them in the morning.

*My last night in this cupboard of a bedroom*, he thought happily as he lay down. He'd be so glad to close the door of this cramped little flat behind him for a final time.

In the morning Russ was awake by five and then had to fill the time until the removal people came by fiddling around online. Once they arrived, he kept an eye on them but it was soon obvious that he was doing more harm than good by trying to help, so he left them to it and sat on a hard chair in one corner of the bedroom. He pretended to look out of the window, but actually he was simply existing, longing to leave.

When the men had cleared the place out, they told him they'd be having a half-hour coffee break before taking his things to his new house, because they'd already spent time loading stuff from their warehouse. Good. This gave him time for a quick check that everything had gone and the flat was clean before he left.

As he drove past the leisure-village hotel and across to his new home he caught a glimpse of Penny Lake sparkling in the morning sunshine. How nice it would be to live within walking distance of a body of water. He should get some good photos from that. Most people wouldn't know half the species that lived there.

If he'd been the singing type he'd have burst into song as he opened his front door, but that might have scared the neighbours. He grinned. He definitely wasn't famous for his musical ability!

It felt wonderful to stroll inside, absolutely wonderful,

even without any furniture there to make it look like a home. He had left the new electric kettle standing ready in the kitchen for a ceremonial first brew and while he waited for it to boil, he walked round the ground floor opening the windows. Once he'd made himself a pot of tea, he raised his mug in a silent toast to his new home.

The smell of the so-called air fresheners was still lingering and he sneezed twice, so took the lift up to open all the bedroom windows as well. He didn't intend to use the lift all the time but the physio said he should take it easy at first when he moved back into a two-storey house, and he would. Well, he would try to rein back his eagerness to sort everything out.

As he stood sipping the last of the tea, a small florist's van drew up outside and a young fellow came towards his house carrying a bouquet. Must have got the wrong number. He opened the door.

'Mr Carden?'

'Yes.'

'Compliments of Molly and Euan Santiago.' He held out the bouquet.

Russ was so surprised it took him a minute to accept the bouquet, then he stood watching the van drive away amazed by this gesture. He couldn't remember anyone ever buying him flowers, though he'd bought them for other people at various times, usually for women.

He looked down at them and murmured, 'Beautiful!', loving their delicate perfume. Unlike harsh, artificial scents, these didn't make him sneeze and they gladdened the eye with their delicate colours.

He walked back into the kitchen, cradling them carefully in his arms. Did he even have a suitable vase? He wasn't sure, but the flowers would stay alive just as well in a bucket till his furniture arrived.

The bouquet made him feel truly welcome. Special. At home. All the things he hadn't felt for a good long while.

Molly's kind gesture also brought some of those stupid, weak tears to his eyes. Oh, hell! Since the accident his emotions had been rather fragile. But he hadn't had a home of his own for over a year, what with his time in rehab and then staying with his aunt. And he'd never owned a house himself, only half of a huge mortgage when he was married. He'd been careful with his money since then and owned this house outright.

Vera had been wonderful to him after he came out of hospital. He'd needed help in the early days of his convalescence with the many small tasks of daily life, like shopping, cooking or merely carrying a mug of tea across the room without slopping it on the floor. It had been embarrassing to be helped by an almost eighty-year-old.

Still, that was typical of his aunt. She was in excellent health for her age and had helped a lot of people over the years. She admitted she tired more easily these days than she had in her energetic middle years, which probably meant she was now behaving like a fifty-year-old. He smiled at the thought of her. And of his brother.

He just wished they would stop matchmaking, though. Once he started getting better, Vera had kept introducing him to women of his own age and she'd egged his brother on to do it too. Steve hadn't been hard to persuade. Just because he'd been happily married for years, he thought everyone else ought to be as well. Well, he'd fallen lucky. There weren't many people as delightful as his sister-in-law, Katie, and even their kids had grown into nice young adults.

However, Russ did *not* want to get married again. One ride on that wonky roundabout had been more than enough for him, thank you very much. His career had been taking off before the accident because he'd sold a television series of nature programmes about the almost invisible world around humans' dwellings. He was hoping to pick up on that again and Sally, his agent, was behind him one hundred per cent.

By eight o'clock that evening he had sorted out his furniture, his clothes and other smaller possessions, and he was utterly exhausted. He locked up and went to bed at nine o'clock, hoping not to be woken by nightmares, not only of the car crash but of the roaring noise the flames had made when rushing towards the small town where he'd been staying.

He hadn't realised bushfires could be so loud or travel so quickly. If he hadn't been driving, he could have got some fantastic photos.

To his amazement, Russ slept right through the night. Now there was a good omen. He got up smiling, eager to start his first full day here, grimacing when he used the lift because he was a bit stiff and had found some more bits and pieces to carry downstairs. He'd forgotten how many boxes he'd put in storage and had mixed upstairs and downstairs items in his hurry.

Soon after breakfast there was a knock on the door and he opened it to find the neighbours, whom he'd seen and waved to a couple of times, standing there holding out a small flowering plant.

'We're the Dittons from next door, Bob and Linda. This is to welcome you.'

'How kind. Pleased to meet you. I'm Russ Carden. Do come in and have a cuppa.'

'No, we won't at the moment. We know what it's like when you've just moved into a house. There's so much to do.'

'Well, you must come round for a drink sometime then.'

'That'll be great one day but probably not until later in the year, thanks,' Bob said. 'This is hail and farewell, I'm afraid. We're swapping houses and cars with an Aussie woman who lives near Perth so that we can be there for the birth of our daughter's first child. We're picking our swappee up at the airport this evening.'

His wife smiled at Russ. 'We wanted to ask you to keep an eye on Simone at first. She hasn't been to England since she was six, so she might not know how to do some of the everyday things.'

'Oh. Well, I'll do my best, but I don't know this area very well, myself. I've been living in Leicester and Swindon and before that I was overseas.'

Bob chuckled. 'We're not expecting you to babysit her – she's in her fifties after all – just to be aware of her situation and lend a hand if necessary. We've asked our other neighbours to do the same. Most of them are very friendly, you'll find, but not over-friendly, thank goodness.'

'Yes. Right. I'll, um, keep my eyes open and do my best to help if needed. Thanks again for this.' He nodded towards the little plant.

'Good. Got to get back now. Lots to do. We're leaving in a couple of days.'

And they were gone.

Russ went back inside and dumped the plant on the side of the sink, feeling somewhat aggrieved about the reason they'd called round. He didn't feel like keeping an eye on anyone, didn't even want to chat to the neighbours, however nice they were. Not until he'd settled in.

All he damn well wanted was some peace and quiet to make a new home for himself and start rebuilding the career that had been interrupted by the accident.

Russ went back to unpacking and arranging his bits and pieces of furniture, using the stairs a few times, enjoying getting organised.

He did his midday exercises carefully, never missed the various activities prescribed by the physio because he was determined to finish rehabilitating his leg and arm as quickly as he could.

It all went well but he had to take a rest in the early afternoon. He wasn't stupid enough to press on through pain. He'd probably done too much in the past couple of days.

He took things more easily for the rest of the day. There was no hurry to sort every single thing out, after all. It was a pleasure simply to be here.

# Chapter Five

It was a huge relief when the pilot announced they'd be landing at London Heathrow in twenty minutes, just after five in the morning. The cabin staff began a rapid clear-up and passengers got in their way as they gathered their personal possessions together.

Simone felt nervous but told herself not to be stupid. She muttered what had rapidly become her mantra: *I can do this.*

After the plane had landed, the disembarkation went smoothly and as her British passport got her through customs quickly, her anxiety began to ease. Neither this passport nor its predecessors had ever been used until this trip. She'd only kept a current one at her parents' insistence that it could be very useful to have when you were travelling outside Australia, which she might want to do one day.

She never had until now, though, still wasn't sure she was doing the right thing.

Thank goodness someone was meeting her – and thank goodness for the large signs telling you where to go in airports.

As she walked out into the terminal pushing her luggage trolley she breathed a sigh of relief that she had got through it all smoothly and looked round for Bob and Linda Ditton. She'd seen what they looked like, easy to remember with long, curly grey hair for Linda, a bald head and spectacles for Bob.

Only they were definitely not there, either singly or as a couple.

She went past the people waiting to meet visitors and hung about nearby, watching others enjoy their reunions. She envied them. Being met by strangers wouldn't be the same as being greeted by loved ones. Still, at least she was being met.

Only, the minutes ticked past and there was still no sign of the Dittons. She kept glancing at the clock or her watch – or trying not to when she found only two or three minutes had passed. They must have been caught up in traffic.

When more than half an hour had passed and a whole new set of people had arrived to wait for the next group of arrivals, she began to wonder if the Dittons had got the date or time wrong, or even had an accident on the way here.

Harriet had given her their mobile number, so after fiddling around for a little longer, she pulled out her phone with its new sim card – *Thank you, Libby!* – and dialled it.

'Hello!' a woman's voice said.

'Is that Linda?'

'Yes.'

'Simone here. I'm at Heathrow. Um, I was told you'd be meeting me.'

'*Oh, no!* We thought it was this evening not this morning. Oh dear, I'm so sorry! Just a minute.'

Simone heard her yell for her husband then explain the situation to him.

'Are you still there, Simone? Look, it'll take us just under two hours to get to Heathrow. We'll set off straight away. I can't apologise enough for the mix-up.'

'No, no! Wait. I'll catch a taxi.' Whatever it cost, she couldn't bear the thought of hanging around the terminal for hours longer.

'You don't need to do that. We're happy to come and get you.'

'I'd rather find a taxi. I'm not fond of airports.' Especially after seventeen hours on a plane.

'Neither am I. Oh dear, I feel so guilty. What a dreadful welcome for you!'

'Look, I have your address. I'll be there as soon as I can. I'll go and find a taxi straight away.'

When she'd disconnected, Simone stood for a few moments coming to terms with the situation, telling herself not to panic. *I can do it! I can!*

She took a few deep breaths and kept repeating those words in her mind for the sheer comfort of them and gradually calmed down. Of course she could do it. Catching taxis wasn't rocket science, even in a foreign country.

Should she have waited for the Dittons? No, she didn't want to stay in this crowded airport for one second longer than she had to. She was desperate for fresh air and daylight, instead of hurrying people and what seemed like miles of garish artificial lighting.

As a loudspeaker made an echoing and utterly incomprehensible announcement, she looked round at the various signs informing travellers of their choices and found one saying simply 'Taxis' so set off with her trolley in the direction it indicated.

There. She'd found the taxi rank.

The driver of the first car in the line said he was too near the end of his shift to take her on a long trip into the country. He studied her, eyes narrowed, and added, 'Get a fixed price for your journey, love. It'll be cheaper.' He even told her roughly how much she should pay.

'Thank you. That's very kind of you.'

'Well, you look like a tired, lost soul to me, and surely that's an Aussie accent?'

'Yes, it is.'

'I like Aussies.'

She didn't like his description of her, though. Did she really look like a lost soul in need of pity? Squaring her shoulders, she moved to the next taxi, trying to look more confident. 'I need to go to Wiltshire. Can you take me, and how much would it cost? I'd like a fixed price.'

He named an amount and it was close to what the first driver had suggested, so she accepted and let him load her luggage into the boot.

A guy in a uniform came and grabbed the trolley,

whisking it away. A mother snatched a small child out of his way and gave it a warning shake. A young woman stopped dead and began arguing with a guy in some incomprehensible foreign language.

All Simone wanted to do was get away from this noisy chaos. Hopefully she'd be able to go for a walk this evening. She loved being out in the open air, hadn't enjoyed being shut up in a plane.

'Want to sit in the front?' the driver asked as he closed the boot on her luggage. 'You'll see more of the scenery that way.'

'Thank you. That'd be nice.' She fastened her seat belt, relief running through her as she leant back. He closed his door on the noisy world and the car slid away from the kerb and began to thread its way through traffic.

After they'd exchanged a few remarks, he too asked, 'Is that an Aussie accent?'

'Yes.'

'First time here?'

'Not exactly. I was born here but my parents emigrated when I was six so I don't remember much.'

'It'll all have changed way beyond recognition since then.'

How the hell old did she look? she wondered, feeling a bit miffed.

'I hope you have a good holiday. Mind if I put some music on? It'll take just over an hour and a half to get there, depending on traffic.'

'Go ahead. I don't mind at all.' She'd prefer not to talk, wanted to study her temporary country of residence. She didn't know why, but she didn't feel like someone starting a holiday. She felt numb more than anything, slightly disoriented and nervous. Definitely nervous.

*What have I done? Why ever have I come here?*

There were several lanes of traffic meeting and separating as they left the airport, with vehicles changing from one lane to another like demented ants everywhere she looked. It reminded her of her visit to Sydney. But the lane discipline of these drivers seemed better, well, mostly better, and the signage was excellent.

She could cope with driving here, too, she told herself firmly. But not today. Today she was too tired.

Soon they were away from the worst of the traffic, though the M4 freeway they were driving along was still busy. No, they were called motorways here, weren't they, not freeways, she reminded herself.

Gradually the traffic thinned and they began driving intermittently through pretty countryside alternating with industrial areas. Some of the trees on the motorway verges had delicate young foliage though none seemed fully in leaf. It still looked lush and green after the dryness of a West Australian autumn following a hot summer. Well, it was spring here, wasn't it?

What did Blake's poem call it? 'England's green and pleasant land'. That definitely fitted the countryside round here.

They passed turn-off roads every few miles and she watched the names of towns she'd only heard mentioned before flash by. Then at last she saw the sign for Swindon, which she knew was the nearest big town to the smaller one where she'd be living. But the driver didn't take that turn-off as she'd expected and her heart did an anxious skip.

'Um, wasn't that the way to Swindon?'

'That first turn-off leads to the east side of the city. We take the second one, because your destination is at the western side.'

And there the sign was soon afterwards with the name of her new town on it: *Royal Wootton Bassett*. She relaxed again.

'Not far now,' he told her cheerfully.

They went quickly through the small town, which didn't seem to have woken up properly yet. Well, it wasn't quite eight o'clock in the morning. She'd set her watch to the right time on the plane.

They turned off after the town, passing through another small place called Marlbury then twisting along some narrow country roads, before coming to a sign saying 'Penny Lake Leisure Village'. They were here. Oh, thank goodness!

Following his satnav's instructions, he drove slowly through an entrance with gorgeous hanging baskets of flowers on either side, past a car park and hotel, then across to a group of houses and a few more being built. People in yellow high-vis jackets were just starting their morning's work on the new houses at the far end of the street as he came to a stop in a drive partway along.

'Here you are, love. Nice place, isn't it? Is this where you're staying, or are you just starting off here?'

'I'm staying here for a few months. I did a house swap.'

'Lucky you. There's a golf course right on site.'

'I don't play, I'm afraid.'

'I'd be out on it every day I could if I lived here.'

As Simone fumbled for her credit card, the front door of the house opened and a man hurried out. 'Simone? Oh, good. I'm Bob and I'll get this.' He pushed away the card she was holding out and handed the driver his own. 'It was our mistake entirely, so you shouldn't have to pay. You go inside and I'll bring your luggage.'

She told him how much had been agreed for the fare and got out, thanking the driver, before pausing to take a quick look at the house. It was a detached residence built of wood which was painted the same colour as the other houses on the street, even though they were all of different styles. The whole place looked very attractive.

Her temporary home was a two-storey house with large windows on either side of the front door. It had a nicely balanced appearance with a traditional roof shape and that pleased her. She didn't like ultra-modern houses with bits of roof sticking out at odd angles as if they'd been put on wrongly.

She realised there was a woman standing patiently at the door and she was keeping her waiting, so moved across to join her. It suddenly occurred to her that she'd coped with a small crisis perfectly well today. She smiled at the thought, feeling as if she'd grown taller, somehow.

'I'm Linda.'

'Simone.'

'You must be exhausted.'

'Not too bad. I managed to get some sleep on the plane.'

'Come in. Welcome to your new home.'

Taking a deep breath Simone walked steadily forward into her new life.

*I can do it.*


Russ heard a car draw up outside and went to look out and check that it wasn't for him. No, it was a taxi and had stopped in front of the house next door. Bob rushed out to it, waving what looked like a credit card.

The woman who got out was taller than Bob, probably nearer to Russ's height, and she had a tan she couldn't have got in an English winter, so she must be the Australian they were swapping houses with.

*Duh! Obvious. Well done, Sherlock Holmes!* he thought mockingly.

He couldn't help thinking what a lovely figure she had. Curvaceous. He wasn't into scraggy women like his half-sister.

The stranger went inside with Linda while Bob unloaded her luggage from the taxi and carted it into the house.

Russ smiled as he went back to sorting things out and making lists of stuff to buy. He was turning into a peeping Tom. Well, he enjoyed watching people even if he didn't always want to chat to them. He'd had a surfeit of people in the hospital, always poking and prodding at him.

He carried on, saving the best task until later in the afternoon. He'd dumped his photography equipment in the so-called formal living room, which he intended to set up as a studio, a proper, dedicated studio for the first time in his life. Well, he'd make a start on setting it up. He'd have to buy some new furniture, supplies, stationery, all sorts of things to equip it properly.

He was really looking forward to doing that because there hadn't been room to set up his equipment at his aunt's house or at the cupboard-sized flat. He went to stand by the rear window and stare happily at the lake, which he could see one part of from here.

He'd promised himself that this studio was going to be the best he could make it. Buying and selling houses was a pain, so this one was to be permanent. What did older people call their final houses? Death nests. He grinned at the thought. He'd cheated death for the time being, thank you very much. And the physio said another couple of months should see him back to normal.

He looked round the studio with a proprietary eye. Perfect. He'd had an extra window built into the blank side wall and light was streaming in. He was going to use the garage for a darkroom, so that the studio would stay spacious and tranquil. His car wouldn't notice whether it was raining or even snowing.

He picked up his notebook and began to go through his provisional list: two desks, new desktop computer, easel, big cupboard for his cameras and supplies, filing cabinet. He intended to get back into all aspects of his work from now on. He'd missed the photography itself most of all and soon he'd be going on real trips out into the countryside.

He didn't have any firm contracts at the moment, due to the accident, though he had a few ideas to broach to his agent. He had just finished the television series when he had the accident and she'd said it was selling well. She'd be happy to pitch any ideas to them again once he'd recovered. He'd contact her tomorrow to say he'd moved in.

He took his grandfather's old camera out of its bubble wrap and cradled it against his chest. He didn't rely only on modern digital equipment, though that was wonderfully versatile. Sometimes an old-fashioned camera like this one could produce subtleties for stills which, in his opinion, digital's sharper focus could erase or miss.

He had a lot of photos of Australia to download from the time before the accident. He had only vague memories of the days after it. Most of his work had been stored online and had survived.

He put his camcorders into the cupboard. He'd be needing them again soon with all the wildlife round the lake tempting him to go out and invade their privacy – just a little.

He loved what he did for a living, was lucky to earn a decent amount from his various artistic passions – and even luckier that years ago his brother had persuaded him to take out income guarantee insurance as well as house insurance after his marriage broke up. He'd hate to have had to break into his retirement savings to get through the past year.

A robin landed outside on the back patio and began singing, making an amazing amount of noise for such a tiny creature, and flittering about in delicate little hops.

He grabbed a camera and moved cautiously closer to the French window, managing to ease it quietly open to capture the robin's joyful movements before it flew away.

That seemed a brilliant omen.

Abruptly he became aware that his body was aching and a sense of weariness was making him long to sit down. His stomach rumbled and he glanced at his watch. Past six in the evening. Where had the day gone? No wonder he was feeling ravenous.

He walked across to the kitchen area, stopping on the way to admire the flowers, now properly arranged in a vase he'd forgotten he owned until he unpacked it.

He'd overdone it today – and had enjoyed every blessed minute of it, aches and all.

Should he go up to the hotel for a meal? No, he couldn't be bothered. A bowl of cereal would have to do. Or baked beans on toast? With a banana for dessert.

Yes, he could just about summon up the energy to make that.

# Chapter Six

'Welcome to England, Simone. We've put you in the main bedroom and we're camping out in one of the others tonight. Easier to clear up after ourselves without disturbing you all over again.'

'Thank you, Linda. That's very thoughtful.'

'If you don't mind, Bob and I will move to my sister's tomorrow morning. She's offered to come and pick us up to save you a journey. It takes time to get over jet lag.'

Bob brought one of Simone's suitcases in and dumped it near the foot of the stairs then nipped outside for the other as the taxi drove away. Still holding the second case he said, 'I'll show you your bedroom.'

Simone picked up the other suitcase and followed him upstairs to a light, airy room with its own en suite. 'This is lovely! I'm going to enjoy sleeping here.' Except for the ornaments, of which there were rather a lot: fussy, old-fashioned ladies in long skirts and frills, cute animals whose eyes were too big like those of cartoon characters.

'I'll leave you to settle in. I'll have a cuppa waiting for you downstairs when you're ready.'

She closed the bedroom door with relief. She'd been dying to use the bathroom, hadn't dared leave her trolley unattended at the airport.

Afterwards she went downstairs, leaving her unpacking until later because she was hungry and thirsty.

They shared a simple midday meal, all exquisitely polite to one another. She found it hard to maintain a conversation with complete strangers with whom she didn't seem to have much in common, however nice they were. Or maybe she was just overtired.

'If you'd like some gentle exercise,' Bob said, 'we could take you for a stroll round Penny Lake. It's about a mile in all and easy going.'

'I'd love that. I've heard that it's better to try to stay awake and fit into the new time zone after a long flight but I'm finding it hard to keep my eyes open. A walk will keep me going for longer, I'm sure.'

There seemed to be less need to chat while walking and Simone loved the idea that such a pretty little lake was right next to where she was going to live.

After that she went upstairs and unpacked, resisting the temptation to lie down on the bed, still fighting sleepiness.

By the time they went up to the hotel for an early evening meal, the time difference was winning the battle over sleep and she could only manage a light meal. She couldn't stop herself yawning several times as they walked the short distance back. 'I think I'll go to bed now if you don't mind.'

Linda made a sweeping gesture towards the stairs with one hand. 'Go for it. You've done really well to stay awake for so long. I hope you sleep soundly.'

Tired as she was, Simone realised she hadn't texted her daughters and Libby to say she'd arrived safely. By the time she'd done that she'd woken up again, so it took her longer than she'd expected to fall sleep.

She woke in the middle of the night and couldn't get back to sleep for a couple of hours. At home she'd have made herself a milky drink but she didn't like to do that here, afraid of disturbing her kind hosts.

The next thing she knew someone was shaking her shoulder gently. She opened her eyes, not knowing where she was for a few seconds, then saw Linda standing beside the bed looking down at her a little anxiously.

'Are you all right?'

'What? Oh. Yes. Is it morning already?'

'More than. It's nearly eight o'clock and we have a lot to do before my sister arrives. I'd like you to meet her before we leave.'

'Oh, my goodness! I *never* normally sleep in past six.'

'Well, no one would blame you for doing it this time. And eight o'clock isn't exactly sleeping in. You must have been exhausted. I wouldn't have woken you yet but I wanted to suggest something.'

'Oh?'

'Look, don't take this wrongly but I was a rather

successful hairdresser before I retired and I'd like to give you a re-style before we leave, as an extra apology for yesterday.'

'It's very kind of you, but I usually just pull my hair back. It's easy.'

'I know, but it's the wrong style for your face. You need it shorter and fluffier. At the moment you're pulling all the waves out. You're lucky to have bouncy hair. You should be taking advantage of it.'

'Oh. Well. All right. If you don't mind.'

Linda beamed at her. 'Mind? I shall enjoy it! I like to keep my hand in. Anyway, if you could get up now, we'll finish it before my sister arrives. I'll introduce her in case you need to get in touch with her, then we'll check whether there's anything else you still want to know before we leave you in peace. There's plenty of food, so you don't even need to go out shopping if you want a lazy day or two to get over the jet lag. And we have lots of books and DVDs. Just help yourself.'

Linda was still trailing words as she left the bedroom. 'Leave your hair wet after your shower.'

Simone got up, had a hurried shower, then went down, desperate for a cup of very strong coffee to finish the job of waking herself up.

Linda got her to sit down in the utility room and set to work on her hair, snipping and muttering and turning Simone's head, first one way, then the other.

There wasn't a mirror in here so there was no way of seeing what she was doing, but from the way she worked, Linda seemed to know what she was doing.

When she'd finished, she stepped back and beamed.

'Marvellous. I was so right. I just *know* you're going to be pleased. Come into the living room. There's a big mirror there.'

Simone followed her meekly, more interested in getting something to eat than fussing with hair – until she saw herself.

'Oh, my goodness!'

'Suits you, doesn't it?'

'I don't think I've ever had a style that suits me more.'

'Well, get your hair trimmed at Celeste's salon in Marlbury. It's on the High Street, you can't miss it. And tell her I sent you.'

'Yes. I will.' She couldn't help hugging Linda. 'This is marvellous. Thank you so much.'

'My pleasure. Now, let's get you fed. You must be so hungry.'

As Simone was finishing breakfast, Linda's sister, Jodie, arrived. The resemblance was strong, especially when they smiled. She fixed the best smile she could manage on her own face in return and chatted to them as she ate another piece of toast.

Bob left them to it and loaded the last of their things in Jodie's car then came in for a final goodbye.

Suddenly they were gone and all was quiet.

Simone let out a long sigh of relief. It felt wonderful to have the house to herself. She did a slow tour of it and that made her even more determined to put away some of the myriad ornaments.

Every mirror that she passed reflected back a stranger's face, the short, jaw-length hair made so much difference.

She kept stopping to beam at her reflection. She'd take a selfie and send it to her daughters. She stopped moving and frowned at herself on that thought. It was they who'd pestered her to keep her hair long.

Why had she let them dictate to her in so many ways? That was going to stop from now on. Definitely! She sauntered round the rooms carrying out a detailed exploration this time.

The freezer didn't have much in it and what there was verged on junk food in her opinion. There were a couple of frozen ready meals with so many ingredients listed on the back panel she grimaced. A cocktail of chemicals and artificial flavourings rather than nourishing food.

Since Harvey's death she'd eaten very healthily and had discovered that she felt better when she ate fewer carbohydrates. She'd always loved fresh vegetables and salads but he'd liked 'proper' cooked meals.

'I might have to go shopping today,' she said aloud then got annoyed when she realised she was talking to herself again. That had to stop.

Only, where were the shops? She got out the folder that Linda had given her and found to her relief that this had been covered. Oh dear, she hadn't even thought of doing that for them in her mad scramble to get ready. Still, they'd have their daughter to show them round.

She wished she had someone of her own here. 'Oh, don't be such a wimp,' she muttered and went out to the car, a smallish vehicle, fairly new-looking. She grimaced at the garish yellow colour but remembered reading a few years ago that this was one of the safest colours for cars. After clicking the key tab to unlock it she got into the driver's seat and adjusted it to suit her longer legs.

Might be worth driving round the hotel car park a few times to get used to it. She closed the door and something immediately started donging loudly at her. Ah, the seatbelt sign was blinking at her. When she fastened the belt, the annoying noise stopped and she was allowed to start the car.

She drove across to the hotel, round the nearby car park twice and then back to the house again. Piece of cake. Not a bad little car, actually, except for the colour.

When she got back she saw a man staring at her from the window of the house next door. He raised one hand in a greeting so she did the same. The Dittons said they'd told him about her but she couldn't remember his name. He didn't come out, so she didn't go and introduce herself properly. If he didn't want to get too friendly with the neighbours, that was all right by her.

She might as well get on with her first proper outing in the car. She wasn't worried about driving it now that she'd tried it out, but she was more than a little concerned about finding her way around the countryside on her own because the Dittons didn't have a satnav. She might have to buy one if she was going to do some exploring. Yes, why not?

She checked the boot for shopping bags and found a stash of them, just as she had in her own car in Australia.

When she went to get her handbag, she stopped in the kitchen to check the cupboards and fridge again, making a preliminary shopping list.

She felt distinctly nervous about driving about in a strange country and her heart began beating a little faster than usual. She was able to use her Aussie driving licence here, but it would be prudent to see if there was a set of road rules online, in case there were any significant differences.

Then she realised these cogitations were all delaying tactics and she was still standing there like an idiot at a fair. After checking that the house was locked, she got into the car again, took a deep breath and set off.

Linda's directions were excellent and took her straight to a large shopping centre on the outskirts of town. *There you are, you fool!* she told herself. *What were you so worried about?*

Everything, she admitted. She was worried about every single new thing she was going to face here, because she would be facing them alone.

For the first time she was truly glad she'd taken on this house swap, worries or not. She'd *needed* pushing out of her comfort zone.

Inside the huge complex she strolled round to see what shops there were, watching people, getting her bearings. It wasn't all that different from the shopping centre she used in Australia.

'Idiot!' she told herself.

She hadn't realised she'd spoken aloud until a woman next to her scowled, clearly thinking this was aimed at her. 'Oh, sorry. I was talking to myself.'

The woman didn't reply, merely rolled her eyes and walked away.

Simone found somewhere to buy a satnav, which made her feel better. After that she went back to the food hall and had a good old spend-up in the fresh food section of the supermarket. Frozen ready meals, indeed! She was going to make a luscious plate of salad for tea, with a chunk of the ready-roasted chicken she'd bought for protein and fresh raspberries with ice cream for afters. She'd bought some bottles of white wine too. She'd sip a glass as she watched television afterwards and hopefully would manage to stay awake a little longer tonight.

As she arrived back at the leisure village, the words echoing in her mind were: *I did it!*

But her elation faded because the evening was very quiet and seemed to go on for a long time. It got dark a lot later here, too. Like many of the evenings since she lost Harvey the hours had dragged, but that felt worse here.

She'd have phoned her daughters for a chat only they'd be in bed asleep now, since Western Australia was seven hours ahead timewise.

The following morning Simone phoned her daughters. It was teatime in Australia and she assured them that she was coping just fine. She also had a quick word with her grandchildren. That brought tears to her eyes as she ended the call and it took her a minute or two to calm down afterwards. She was going to miss them dreadfully. They'd have grown so much by the time she got back.

To distract herself she looked through the pile of tourist leaflets the Dittons had left for her. Now that she'd bought a satnav, she could go for outings, first of all to nearby villages to get to know the area, then maybe longer outings staying overnight.

That would keep her busy during the day, but she would need other ways of filling her time during the next few months. She had never been one to merely sit around idling.

She went up to the snack bar at the hotel in the late afternoon, just for a change of scene, and got chatting to the young waitress, who was thinking of working her way round the world with her boyfriend. When she found out that Simone was from Australia, she eagerly asked questions until called across to serve another customer.

The lass didn't seem to have any idea of how big Australia was. Very few Europeans did. Simone had found that before when chatting to tourists in Perth who planned to drive up to the north of the state 'for a couple of days', not realising it was a full day or more's gruelling drive just to get there on roads which were not smooth motorways.

Simone had a very clear idea of how small Britain was in comparison to Australia, but even so it had already offered her a few surprises.

It was going to take time to get used to driving along narrow country roads between high hedges, and she had been surprised at how many huge thundering trucks there were on both major and minor roads. No, they called them lorries here, at least she thought they did.

She would take her time and get used to things gradually. No worries.

And maybe she could join the local library.

\* \* \*

The next day Simone got up at six o'clock as usual, in spite of having had another wakeful patch during the night. It was an effort but it made her feel as if she was getting closer to a normal daily schedule.

She went out for a drive round the district at just after eight and was surprised at how crowded the roads leading to the M4 were. The rush hour seemed still to be full on. She'd remember that in future.

When she got back, she didn't let herself phone her daughters again but did have a quick chat with Libby. Ending it brought tears to her eyes.

She cried again when she saw a news item about some really bad bushfires in Australia. To her relief, they were in the eastern states, over two thousand miles away from her home and family, but her heart went out to the people who were losing not only their homes but personal treasures like family photographs. Some of them, who'd been taken by surprise, had lost every single possession except for the clothes they stood up in.

Every year some communities were affected but these fires were more widespread than usual. She'd have to contribute to the funds for helping them.

It put the life she was leading and her silly worrying into perspective.

That same evening, just before she went to bed, she at last got a response to her email to her parents who were again in an area with access to the Internet. They were delighted that she'd taken this opportunity to travel. They didn't add 'about time too' but they'd said to her face that she should see something of the world, said it more than once, and she could read the same words behind what they were saying now.

The message ended: *We've emailed our cousins on both sides of the family to let them know you're in the UK. They'll probably be in touch. They were very hospitable when we were over there. We're just dashing off but will phone you soon to tell you a little about our family there.*

She was glad about that – wasn't she? Her parents had wanted her to travel and meet some new people – and she wanted it too now, didn't she? Oh hell, she wasn't even sure what she wanted at the moment.

She couldn't remember any of these cousins' names, so shot off a reply to her parents asking for a list of relatives. Then wondered again if she wanted to bother. These people would probably be her parents' generation. That was fine but she'd also like to meet some of her own generation, give or take a few years.

She was going to miss Libby most of all, chats on the phone, coffee together at the shops at weekends, a sympathetic ear to life's little problems.

She was definitely not going to even hint to her daughters that she was dreadfully homesick. No way.

# Chapter Seven

The next day Simone went further afield exploring the countryside, using the new satnav. After successfully finding her way to and from a couple of picturesque villages, she ended up at the shopping centre buying another load of her own sort of food.

That took up most of the day, but she couldn't settle when she got back. There didn't seem to be anything she wanted to watch on television that evening so she looked outside. Still daylight.

After a fine day, surely it would be warm enough to sit on the patio for a while? Well, it might be if she put on her travelling jacket. It was rather similar to a sunny winter's evening at home, actually.

The Dittons had a set of outdoor furniture but it was all carefully wrapped up in what Simone supposed to be its heavy-duty winter protection. She went across to unwrap some of it. When there were no clouds and the weather was warmer she'd be able to enjoy the night sky. She'd have to get used to a different set of constellations. She'd look it up online and find out what there was to see.

Good heavens, the coverings were hard to take off! She could usually cope with outdoor tasks but this one was taxing her strength and the shaped tarpaulin seemed designed to need two sets of hands to peel it off.

She nearly jumped out of her skin when a man's voice nearby said, 'Looks like you need a bit of help with that.'

She turned and saw her neighbour standing at the border of their two properties, which had a line of sparse baby bushes planted along it. This was the first time he'd bothered to speak to her. 'Yes, I do. Would you mind?'

He moved across to join her. 'Happy to be of service. I'm Russ Carden.'

He was taller than her, with a lithe look to him that usually said that person was into active pursuits, but he was walking rather stiffly, favouring his left leg slightly. He seemed uncertain whether to offer to shake hands and she had difficulty holding back a smile when she saw his right hand twitch upwards then fall back again.

She offered hers. 'I'm Simone Ramsey.'

They shook and she asked, 'You're walking stiffly. Have you hurt yourself? I don't want to risk making it worse by asking you to move heavy furniture.'

'It's a long-term injury from a car accident. Believe me, I won't do anything to make it worse because it's well on its way to getting better, as much as it can, anyway. It aches a bit by the end of the day, especially when I've been more active than usual.'

He seemed to understand the arcane fastenings on the covers and she followed his directions. They soon had the outdoor furniture revealed and it looked fairly new.

'Do you want it set out?' he asked.

'Yes, please. I love sitting outside.'

'So do I. You must be able to do that more often in Australia, though. It's still very chilly here.'

'Yes. Mozzies can be a nuisance at home, though.'

He stepped back. 'I'll leave you to it, then.'

'Can I offer you a glass of wine as a thank you?'

'Not tonight, but another time would be nice. I've only just moved in and there's a lot to sort out.'

Or maybe he didn't want to socialise with the neighbours. She didn't know him well enough to guess his true motive. He didn't seem stand-offish, though, so perhaps he was simply telling the truth.

He turned to walk into the house, then stopped. 'Damn! The wind's blown my insect screen open. I've got to fix a better catch to it. Bye.'

She only wished the house she was living in had insect screens, as houses did in Australia.

Just as he started to hurry towards the three steps that led to his back patio, the wind blew more strongly and from nowhere a big plastic sheet came flapping at him, making him fall down the steps.

When he didn't get up, she rushed across to help him.

'Just a minute.' He clung to her for a few moments, cursing under his breath. He started to pull away from her, but still seemed unsteady and grabbed her again.

She helped him slowly into the house and he kept using her to maintain his balance.

'Thank you. I'm truly grateful. I'm going to have to do something about those steps. I have a slight unsteadiness sometimes as a result of the accident.'

'Come over to a chair.'

'I need to do some simple exercises before I sit down. They help.'

'Shall I leave you in peace now?'

'Why don't you stay? In fact, how about I offer you a glass of wine?' He gave her a wry smile as he added, 'I could certainly do with one. I haven't had that happen for ages.'

'Are you sure? You said you were busy,' she pointed out.

'I was. But I've totally lost my concentration now and I'm definitely going to have a drink. I'd be grateful if you'd get the bottle out of the fridge and pour me a glass, though. Oh, and I've only got white.'

'Happy to do that and I prefer white anyway. Do sit down.'

He moved slowly across to the nearest armchair but started doing some simple exercises.

She found the wine easily enough but didn't like to search his cupboards, so poked her head out of the doorway again to ask, 'Where are the glasses?'

'The end wall cupboard.'

After handing one to him she sat down and raised her glass. 'Cheers.' She took a sip and rolled it round her mouth. 'Very nice.'

He followed suit, but took a gulp not a polite sip,

then let out a long sigh and wiggled his leg to and fro a few times. 'So, what brought you to England?'

'A sudden whim. The Dittons' daughter offered me a house swap on their behalf. She's expecting her first child, you see, and wants them nearby. In a fit of madness I accepted, then I discovered a really great special offer on a flight cancellation website, business class. Only snag was it was leaving Perth the same night. So within a few days of accepting the offer I flew to England. I'm still a bit surprised at being here and I haven't even begun to work out what I'm going to do with myself for several months.'

'No relatives in the UK?'

'Yes, a few, but none of them close and actually, I don't know them at all. My parents have kept in touch with a couple of cousins of their own generation, but only in a casual way. I don't know whether to make myself known to them or not.' Which was more than enough about her, she decided. 'What about you, Russ? You said you'd had an accident.'

'It happened in Australia, strangely enough, but in New South Wales, not your side of the country.' He explained about the idiot driver.

She whistled softly. 'That's rotten luck. I hope he got a prison sentence for that.'

'He and his passenger were killed outright. I try to count myself lucky to have survived.'

She saw him look down at his left leg as he spoke.

He asked about her family. She told him she was a widow then on impulse tried to lighten the sombre mood by describing the dreadful school concert and how it had contributed to her decision to come here. That at least brought a genuine smile to his face and he started to relax visibly.

Wow, he was rather attractive when he smiled – and he looked vaguely familiar. Could she have seen him somewhere before? No, of course not. What was she thinking?

After she'd finished the wine, she refused another glass and claimed she was tired, because he was looking drained.

As she made her way back, she decided it was nice to know who your neighbour was. She stopped for a moment to admire her back patio, which looked attractive with the table and chairs set out on it. If she ever got to know people, she could invite them round for a barbecue. If the Dittons had a barbecue, that was.

That reminded her that she had yet to explore the garage attached to the far side of the house. The Dittons had said they didn't store their car in it and she'd not bothered to check it out yet.

She'd get round to that soon, but would wait for a rainy day. For the moment she was enjoying getting to know this part of Wiltshire.

When her phone rang the following morning, Simone snatched it up eagerly, hoping it'd be Libby or one of her daughters because it would be early evening in Australia. But they'd have spoken straight away, so she just said, 'Hello?'

'Is that Simone Ramsey?' a man's voice asked.

'Yes.'

'I believe I'm a relative. Your parents emailed my mother to say you were spending some time in England and suggested the family might like to get in touch.'

'Oh?' She still wasn't convinced this was a genuine call. 'And your name is?'

He chuckled. 'Suspicious, aren't you?'

'It's usually safer.'

'I'm Lance Mundy. My mum was a cousin of your mother's. The two of them kept in touch occasionally. I don't think your mother knew that mine was dead when she emailed about your visit.'

Simone was still not convinced by this. None of the relatives her parents had caught up with was called Mundy, she was sure. She'd have remembered it. She was good at names. 'Oh. Um, sorry about your mother.'

'Thanks. It's been a few months now so I'm used to it.'

His casual tone of voice made her even more suspicious. She was sure she'd never get used to losing her parents.

'I wondered if you'd be at home tomorrow afternoon? I'd love to pop in and say hello. I only live half an hour's drive away.'

'That'd be, um, nice. Don't you have to work?'

'No. I'm self-employed.'

'Oh, sorry if I sound dopey. I've still got a bit of brain fog from the jet lag. Yes, do please drop in. And, um, bring your wife or significant other.'

'I no longer have a wife. We divorced a few years

ago. I'm quite harmless, though, I promise. About two o'clock suit you?'

'The morning would be better, if you don't mind. How about eleven o'clock? I'll make us a bit of lunch.'

'Or we could go out somewhere. My treat.'

'It's no trouble. I have something arranged for later in the afternoon, though.' She wasn't making arrangements to spend the evening with a strange male. Maybe she was being too cautious, but there you were. Better safe than sorry.

'All right. You'll need to give me your address. I only have your email and phone number.'

'Sorry.' She gave it to him and put the phone down, wondering why she hadn't warmed to him. He'd been pleasant enough but hadn't sounded at all upset by his mother's death. Though she could have been mistaken about that. Some people could keep a stiff upper lip whatever happened to them.

Well, she'd find out about her alleged second cousin tomorrow. She prayed this Lance Mundy person would be a good conversationalist. Talking to strangers one to one could be rather awkward if you didn't take to the person. Thank goodness she'd liked her neighbour instantly. She'd had no difficulty chatting to Russ. On the contrary.

She frowned. She still had the feeling that she'd seen him somewhere before but hadn't been able to place him.

When she went out to her car, another vehicle braked suddenly in front of her house. A woman got out and hurried across to her.

'You must be the Dittons' Aussie house swapper.'

'Yes, I am.'

'Linda told everyone in the street about you. I'm Cindy and as you can no doubt tell by my accent, I'm an American.' She pointed along the street. 'That's my house with the blue curtains. If you're not doing anything tonight, how about coming round for a drink after tea? Come around seven and I'll introduce you to some of the neighbours. We're a friendly lot here, though we don't live in each other's pockets.'

'That'd be lovely.'

'Is there anyone else staying with you? If so, bring them too.'

'I'm here on my own.'

'Then just amble over around seven.' She glanced at her watch. 'Eek! Sorry, have to dash.'

The prospect of meeting people and having something to do in the evening brightened the day considerably for Simone.

And she wouldn't feel unsafe walking about fifty yards along a street to get home, even if she stayed until it was late.

When the time came to go and join the group, however, she began to feel a bit nervous and waited until she saw another couple go into the house.

To her relief the small group of people at Cindy's were all very pleasant and she enjoyed chatting to them. They stayed only for an hour or so, then one couple walked back along the street with her.

She wished there were places like this for older people in Australia. She loved Cindy's house even more than the Dittons' and Russ's places. None of the houses she'd seen here so far were tiny boxes like most Aussie retirement homes. They were very suitable for older people who didn't want the trouble of large gardens but still liked room to swing a cat.

She saw that Russ had returned but there was no sign of him at the window, so she watched television for a while then went to bed.

Maybe things wouldn't be as lonely here as she'd feared.

## Chapter Eight

Russ watched Cindy stop to chat to his new neighbour. He'd been invited for drinks to Cindy's too but wasn't going because his leg was throbbing. The fall hadn't been good for it. He hoped it would have calmed down again by the next day.

To his relief, it was fine in the morning. Must be the combination of exercises and rubbing with anti-inflammatory gel and of course his leg was getting better all the time, so setbacks would be briefer. He'd have to go more carefully in future, though, and get a handrail put up on those outside steps.

He might do some sketching. That was physically easy. He wasn't conceited enough to offer his sketches for sale, because he wasn't good enough. He was far better at filming than drawing, but he enjoyed it nonetheless and sometimes produced rough sketches to help him visualise how to film something.

He began working on a sketch he'd planned of a lively young crow pestering its mother for food. It was based on a photo he'd snapped a couple of days ago during a stroll down to the lake. It was good that there were wooden benches at intervals there. He liked to sit and watch the world go by – the animal as well as the human world.

When the phone rang, he briefly contemplated leaving it unanswered, then shook his head and picked it up. He'd promised himself to interact more with people once he got here. 'Hi. Russ here.'

A wobbly voice with a slight French accent said, 'Russ, it's me, Justine.'

His heart sank. 'Oh, hi sis.'

The only answer was a sob.

*Here we go again*, he thought. 'Is something wrong?'

'*Everything*. Can I come and stay with you? Just for a little while, till I get my bearings in the UK and work out what I'm going to do?'

He didn't want another of his half-sister's dramas dumped on him, but how could he turn her down when she was clearly deeply upset about whatever it was? 'Yes, of course you can.'

She started sobbing in earnest. 'Thank you. I didn't know what I'd have done if you'd said no.'

Camped on his doorstep until he let her in, probably, he thought. She was good at dramatic gestures to get her own way. 'When do you want to come?'

'Today. I'm in Swindon already. I caught a bus here from the airport at Heathrow. Can you come and pick me up?'

'Can't you get a taxi?'

'No. I haven't got any more money.'

He closed his eyes, upset at the mere prospect of her coming to stay. He didn't want to live with her ever again, because she was forever making scenes, but the mother they'd shared was dead and Vera was his aunt on his father's side so no relation to Justine. He didn't know much about her father's family because his mother's second husband hadn't stayed around for long after his child was born.

'I'd better pick you up, then. Whereabouts exactly are you?'

'In a café near the bus station.'

'What's its name?'

'Oh. I didn't notice. Just a minute.' There was a fuzz of voices, then she came back on the phone. Jacko's Kaf spelt K-A-F.'

'Right. It'll take me about half an hour to reach you, depending on traffic. Stay there.'

'All right. But please hurry.'

There was always some need to hurry where Justine was concerned. Was she ever going to get her life in order? He'd thought she was happy and safe with the new guy, who'd seemed to really care for her, or at least had been physically infatuated by her. It had seemed more promising than usual because two years in one relationship was a record for her.

What could have gone wrong?

Then it occurred to him that he didn't have a bed for her and he growled in annoyance. They'd have to stop and buy one on the way home. Might as well buy two while he was at it. And bedding. He would probably have other guests from time to time.

Most of all, he was doing this because just before her death, his mother had begged him to keep an eye on her youngest child if anything happened to her. He'd hoped it'd never happen because looking after Justine was no picnic. Oh well, he'd cope.

Annoyed about this interruption just as he was enjoying sorting out his studio, he locked the house and went out to his car, rubbing his aching leg.

Life was like that, hit you on the head with a problem just as you were relaxing. And make no mistake about it, Justine usually brought trouble with her.

Thank goodness she'd got off the drugs. There had been a difficult year or two when she went off to university and she'd never finished the art course.

Well, she wasn't getting into his art materials or using his studio. She was a messy worker who wasted a lot of paint and paper.

He had trouble finding a parking spot near the station, so it was more like three-quarters of an hour before he got to the café.

He saw Justine sitting at a table near the window, dabbing her eyes and staring anxiously out. She didn't smile or stand up when she saw him coming towards the café.

He went inside and over to her table. 'I've only got short-term parking so can we leave straight away?'

She grabbed his arm and said in a low voice, 'I've not got enough money to pay my bill.'

'OK. I'll do it.'

When she stood up, he was surprised to see that she was pregnant. He wasn't sure how far gone she was and she quickly pulled her coat across her belly, as if to hide it.

After he'd paid, he gestured towards the door. 'Come on. We can't discuss whatever's wrong here.'

He was about to lead the way out when she tugged on his sleeve.

'My luggage.'

There was a large suitcase, rather battered, as was the backpack she was carrying herself. 'How come you're using such shabby luggage?'

'I'll explain later.'

He picked up the suitcase and she followed him.

'Please don't be angry with me, Russ,' she begged once they were outside.

'I don't know what's happened, so how can I be angry or otherwise? Let's wait till we get home to discuss whatever's gone wrong, shall we?'

When he got her and her luggage into the car, he said, 'I've only just moved into my new house, so haven't got much furniture yet. We'll have to stop on the way there to buy you a bed, unless you've a longing to sleep on the floor?'

'No, of course not. I thought you were renting a furnished flat?'

'That had only one bedroom, so you'd have been out of luck at moving in with me there. Fortunately for you, I moved into a new house recently. I wasn't expecting guests so soon, though.'

'Well, *I* wasn't expecting to have to dump myself on you.'

'What's happened to lover-boy?'

Tears filled her eyes again and he didn't want her having one of her hysterical fits, so said hastily, 'No, tell me about it when we get home. You can help me choose some beds first.'

After a couple of minutes of ostentatious mopping of eyes, she asked, 'Do you have any spare bedding?'

'No. I've got nothing extra, hardly any crockery, either. We'll eat up at the hotel tonight and go shopping for food tomorrow.'

'All right.' She looked at him. 'Thanks, Russ.'

Which was more than he'd expected. On the few other occasions she'd descended on him, she'd acted as if she was entitled to his hospitality. This beaten-looking, pale imitation of his half-sister worried him.

Or was it another act?

Her indifference to what they bought worried him even more. Normally she enjoyed shopping and drove him mad fiddling around to match or tone colours together perfectly. Now, he quickly chose beds to suit his own taste by bouncing on them to make sure the mattresses were firm, and paid extra to have them delivered later that afternoon. They settled for cream-coloured sheets and pillowcases and flowery duvet covers. That would be enough for the time being.

She didn't say anything as he drove the rest of the way home, but at least she'd stopped crying.

When they were inside the house, he said, 'All right. Sit down and tell me what's wrong'

She started talking as she made her way across to an armchair. 'It's Pierre. He doesn't love me any more.'

'Oh? What makes you think that?'

'He doesn't want to get married.' She laid one hand on her stomach and sat down carefully. 'He wants to make his own child a bastard.'

As he'd thought, a lovers' quarrel, probably a storm in a teacup.

'Did he throw you out?'

'No. I waited till he'd left on one of his stupid business trips and then I came back to England. Only I didn't realise he hadn't paid off my last credit card bill so I didn't have access to enough money to travel comfortably. I'd forgotten how bad it is to travel cattle class and I'm *exhausted*.'

'Have you spent all this quarter's allowance from your trust fund already?' By anyone else's standards she was well off.

'Yes. I needed a few things. And my next payment from them isn't due for another month, so I'm flat broke.'

'How are you going to manage till then without any money? Sounds as if it was a stupid time to leave Pierre. He'd at least have kept you in the style to which you're accustomed.'

She gave him one of her wounded looks.

'I'm not responsible for you, Justine, so you're not staying long. I have my own problems, which you don't seem to have noticed, and I'm not, never have been and never will be rich. In fact, I'm going to need all my own money to live on. I'm still having trouble with my leg because of the accident.'

It might be a bit of an exaggeration about his finances, but it'd never do for her to think he was going to be a soft touch.

'Sorry. I should have asked how you were. I thought you'd have recovered fully by now.'

'Why break the habit of a lifetime?'

She looked puzzled. 'What do you mean?'

'I mean you never think of other people. Why should that have changed?'

Silence, then, 'That's what Pierre said when he told me about your accident in Australia.'

'Perhaps you need counselling about that aspect of your life?'

She sighed. 'He said that too. As if I'd go to a shrink! Especially one *he* chose. He's a controller, that man. I can't do anything without his permission. You've no idea.'

He wasn't going to discuss that. He rather liked Pierre.

A pause, then, 'Can I stay here till I'm solvent again, Russ?'

'Not for a whole month, no. You can stay for a day or two, though, just while you sort things out with Pierre.'

'But—'

He held up one hand in a stop sign. 'Or until you've found some other idiot to sponge off. You trained as a commercial artist even if you didn't finish the course and you're quite good. Why don't you try getting a few casual jobs and earning your own money?'

She sniffed scornfully. 'Doing boring, repetitive adverts! As if.'

'That's how most people earn a living – doing boring stuff. Money is money, however you earn it. Now, you look like you need a shower and a change of clothes. You can't have a lie-down before the bed arrives, though. I'm going to be working in my studio but when you come down, give me a shout and I'll get you something to eat.'

He took her up to what would be her bedroom, showed her the bathroom she'd be using and found her a towel. Then he left her to it, going into his studio and shutting the door. He groaned as he leant against it. Oh, hell! Looking after Justine was the last thing he needed.

Would Pierre come after her? He might. But he'd not know where Russ had moved to. Very few people did yet.

On that thought, he got out his phone, found Pierre's number and texted him the new address and the fact that Justine had just turned up. Thank goodness, Pierre had contacted him after the accident to ask how he was doing. Not Justine, Pierre!

She didn't come down to find him, so he didn't go hunting for trouble.

When the beds arrived, he and the delivery men found her curled up on the floor in the spare bedroom, fast asleep. Her belly looked bigger than Russ had expected. How far along was she?

'Pregnant women!' one of the men said in an indulgent tone. 'My wife was just the same. Kept falling asleep all over the place.'

Russ didn't correct him about Justine being his wife.

He watched her wake up, clap one hand to her mouth and hurry into the bathroom.

When the sounds of her throwing up came echoing out, the man grinned. 'My wife was like that too. Cheer up, Mr Carden. It only lasts nine months.'

Russ shuddered at the mere thought of even one week with her. He wasn't having his peace and quiet spoilt by his immature half-sister.

He prayed that Pierre would contact him quickly.

Russ watched the big van drive away then wandered into his studio, unable to settle. He stood staring out of the side window at the rear garden of the next house and saw Simone come out and shake a duster, holding her face up to the sun and smiling. What a difference there was between the two women.

He had to do something to prove to his selfish half-sister once and for all that firstly he wasn't rich and secondly he had better things to do with what money he did have than take care of her. But would that be enough to ensure that she wouldn't try to use him again?

It really ought to be up to Pierre to look after her and what was presumably his child. But did he still want her? Whether he did or not, surely he cared about his unborn child?

On that thought Russ got out his phone and checked it again, but Pierre hadn't replied to his message yet.

'Hurry up, damn you!' he muttered.

He picked up a pencil and began to doodle, which usually helped him to think more clearly. To his surprise he found himself drawing Simone's face. It came out well, too. His sketches of people didn't always do that, for some strange reason. He was better at sketching animals.

Simone had not only been kind to him, she'd made him laugh as well. He added a few more pencil strokes. He felt as if he had known her and her face for a long time. She wasn't beautiful, she was . . . *comely* . . . an old-fashioned word but then her attractiveness was old-fashioned.

'Who's that woman next door? I thought you said an older couple lived there.'

He jerked round to see Justine standing just inside the doorway. 'My temporary neighbour is an Australian. She's swapped houses with them for a while.'

'Oh. I thought she might be a close friend of yours.'

'I'm working on that.'

'But she's *fat*! How can you even be interested in her?'

She scowled at him, though what business his friends were of hers he didn't know. 'I like women with nice curves.'

'You always have been weird, Russ. Fancy being attracted to fat women.'

'She isn't fat by anyone else's standards but yours.'

'Of course she is. We know now that fat is unhealthy and thin is best.' She gave one of her elaborate, artificial shudders. 'The woman must be weird too. Who'd want to come to this dump of a place, stuck out in the middle of nowhere when they could be in a sunny country lying on a beach?'

'You, apparently. Feel free to leave at any time.'

She began to walk round, fingering his things. 'This is a lovely room. I could work in here.'

'You're not going to do that. And please don't touch my art materials. I have my own way of arranging them. In fact, please go and wait for me in the kitchen.' When she made no attempt to leave, he grabbed her, ignoring her whine of protest and pushing her gently out of the door. He shut it firmly.

Hmm. She'd be in here again as soon as he turned his back since the door didn't lock. The trouble was, this room was very important to him and he didn't want her messing around in it at all. She'd spill paint on the new carpet and mess up his supplies, and he'd hate her to get her hands on his cameras.

He remembered suddenly that he had an old lock in one of the unpacked boxes standing along one wall. He'd used the lock to secure the shed at a rented house a couple of years ago and removed it when he left. He wasn't in the habit of throwing away perfectly good items that might be useful one day.

He opened the door, checking its construction. Yes, he could fit the lock into it quite easily and he'd do it before he went to bed, because Justine had no respect whatsoever for other people's possessions.

She didn't seem to have much respect for anything, actually. How she'd managed to get Pierre to stay with her for so long was a miracle. She might be physically lovely, especially her face, and able to turn on the charm when she wanted, but she was selfish to the core and incurably untidy. Russ could never have lived with her chaos.

She ought to be wearing a sign saying *Only rich men need come near me*. She was stupid to have run away from Pierre.

Russ's phone pinged and he got it out of his pocket quickly. 'Ah.' He made sure the studio door was firmly shut before he answered, switching into adequate French as he and Pierre chatted.

'Is Justine all right, Russ?'

'What do you mean?'

'She's not, um, hysterical or anything?'

'Not hysterical but acting rather strange.'

'Can you keep her there till tomorrow afternoon? I've had a doctor looking after her and we thought she was settling down. I can hardly drag him out and take him to England in the middle of the night, though. I'll have to see him first thing and get a recommendation for a similar service in the UK.'

'Service?'

'Mental health. She'd grown more unbalanced than before because she'd been taking drugs again till I found out and stopped it.'

'Oh hell, no.'

'I'm trying to keep her calm until the child's born. She seemed to have settled down so I took the opportunity to nip across to Frankfurt for an important meeting. I thought I'd made sure she didn't have any money, but she took one of my statuettes and I should think she's sold it. I'd removed all her fancy luggage, too, but she must have found something in the attic. When I got back, she'd left and taken some of her clothes.'

Unbalanced was a good way of describing Justine. Her moods had always been up and down, and had got worse since their mother died. Had that led to her going back to drugs? Ah, who knew what motivated the silly girl?

'So, you'll look after her?' Pierre prompted.

'Yes, I'll keep an eye on her tomorrow. But she's not staying here any longer than that.'

As he put the phone away Russ nodded in satisfaction. It would all be sorted by tomorrow night. He opened the packing box he thought the lock was in and yes, there it was!

Better and better.

Before he started work he peeped into the living room. Justine didn't notice him. She was lounging in front of the television. Heaven alone knew which channel she was watching but she'd turned up the volume and was wagging her head to and fro in time to some ghastly thumping music.

He had the lock fitted in his studio door within half an hour. Piece of cake.

When he went back into the living room, the music was still blaring loudly and Justine was asleep again.

He turned the volume down and got himself a sandwich, switching to a news channel as he ate it.

Two hours later he shook her awake. 'You need to eat something.'

'Not hungry. Food makes me sick.'

'How about something light like a yoghurt with a bit of fruit?'

She considered that, head on one side, then nodded

slowly. 'I think that might stay down. And it wouldn't be fattening, well, not much.'

When she'd finished most of the yoghurt, she pushed her bowl aside.

'Time for bed now,' he said.

'It's far too early to go to bed. Are you mad?'

'This is the time I like to go to sleep and I'm not having that racket on. It'll not only disturb me, it'll disturb the neighbours. If you're staying here, you're living by my timetable anyway.' He switched off the television to encourage her on her way.

It felt like having a wild animal in the house. She'd never seemed this irrational before. Was it because of her pregnancy – or because of the drugs?

Russ didn't know her well enough these days even to guess. He'd not lived with her in recent years and only seen her at rare intervals.

Pity he'd had to bring her back here. But you had to look after your relatives when they were in trouble, even the nuisances.

Well, she wouldn't be able to get into his studio at least and he only had to keep her here until tomorrow, then Pierre would come and take her away – and hopefully, keep her away permanently.

With a bit of luck she'd sleep late in the morning.

# Chapter Nine

In the middle of the night Russ was woken by the sound of bumping and clattering downstairs. He tried to work out what the noise was, then remembered Justine and rolled quickly out of bed, grabbing his dressing gown and stuffing his feet into his slippers as he moved towards the stairs.

He shoved her bedroom door open as he passed, just in case, but of course she wasn't there.

He moved quietly down the stairs but he needn't have bothered. She was in the kitchen, taking things out of cupboards and thumping them down on the surfaces as she continued her search. She didn't even notice him.

As he watched she pushed some of the items aside impatiently and knocked them on the floor, breaking one jar. '*What the hell are you doing?*'

'Looking for where you keep your wine. It's the only thing that puts me to sleep at times like this.'

'*Wine?* But you're pregnant. You shouldn't be drinking anything alcoholic.'

'I just told you: it's the only thing that gets me to sleep. Where do you keep it?'

'I don't have any wine here at the moment. I used up my only bottle and haven't bothered to buy any more yet.'

She picked up a tin and hurled it across at him, fortunately missing. 'You stupid fool, we were at a shopping centre. You could have bought some there.'

'I'm not a heavy drinker so it didn't even occur to me. Are you telling me you can't live without it?'

'Of course I can! But I don't see why I should. Isn't this bad enough?' She jabbed one finger at her stomach then hurled another tin at him.

He ducked and ran across to grab her as she picked up a jar of jam. For that short distance, thank goodness, his leg behaved. He managed to pry her fingers off the jar so that it dropped back onto the surface. As he kicked aside the pieces of broken glass and yellow mush from what had been a jar of peaches, she started to struggle violently, scratching him with her long red fingernails and screaming mindless abuse at him.

He tried to talk softly, he shouted, he even shook her, but he couldn't calm her down or get her to listen to him.

He had to hold onto her arms to stop her hurling things about, was getting seriously worried about her state of mind and the safety of the unborn child. She kept trying to get away, even kicked him and all the time the shrill screaming and cursing continued.

What would the neighbours be thinking? She must have woken some of them by now.

Simone had been having another of those wakeful times, lying in bed wondering when jet lag would abate fully and allow her to sleep through the night. Suddenly she jerked upright as she heard a woman scream shrilly nearby.

The noise stopped then started up again, this time going on and on. It was coming from Russ's house. What on earth was going on? Simone quickly dragged on some clothes and went to investigate.

She stood at the front outside the window of his kitchen and stared in, amazed at what she saw. A woman was throwing tins from the kitchen cupboards at Russ, who was dodging them and begging her to stop.

'I won't stop till *you* stop attacking me!' she shrieked.

Only, he hadn't moved, let alone tried to attack the woman.

It was a good thing she'd come to investigate, Simone thought. It wasn't the screaming woman who might need her help but Russ if whoever this was maligned him to others.

She let out a shocked gasp as the woman lashed out at Russ. If she'd ever seen someone who'd 'gone mad' it was this woman, who was still yelling at him to stop attacking her.

She leant closer to the window because it seemed as if – yes, Russ had fresh scratches on his cheek, with blood trickling down, and still he was desperately trying not to hurt the woman.

Who was she?

She saw a light go on in one of the other houses and decided it was time to intervene, so went and rang the doorbell. Maybe her arrival would help calm the woman down.

Justine was making so much noise it took Russ a while to realise that the front doorbell had rung several times.

By now he'd realised that his half-sister was beyond reason. He kept hold of her to stop her doing further damage to his kitchen – or to herself – but couldn't think what to do next. He didn't let go of her but dragged her across with him to open the front door.

When she saw Simone standing outside, Justine immediately began screaming for help, yelling that she was being raped.

'I've been watching through the window and I think it's you who needs help, Russ, not to mention an impartial witness,' Simone said quietly to him.

'Did you hear me?' Justine screeched. 'Make him let me go!'

She ignored the woman.

Russ looked at her in obvious relief. 'Oh, I do need help! I'm so grateful. Please come in and close the door. I don't want her getting away or waking the whole street.'

Panting with the effort, he dragged the woman back into the living area. 'This is my half-sister, Justine, who turned up suddenly today. She's always been – um, volatile – but I've never seen her like this before.'

The ongoing moans and accusations of being attacked cut off abruptly and Justine yelled again. 'Save me from him. He's raped and abused me! That's *incest*.'

His grip slackened, he was so shocked at this and she at once snatched up a vase of flowers and raised it in the air as if about to smash it on his head. But he grabbed her arms before she succeeded in doing anything except shower them both with water.

Simone grabbed the vase from behind the hysterical woman and put it quickly out of reach on the windowsill. 'What on earth has set this off, Russ?'

'You might well ask. She woke me by pulling things out of my cupboards and throwing them about. She claimed she was looking for a bottle of wine to calm herself down so she could sleep. Then she began screaming.'

'Why is she here?'

'She rang earlier to ask if she could stay with me, said she'd run away from the man she's been living with for nearly two years in Paris.'

'I had to run away!' the woman yelled. 'He's been ill-treating me. You're all against me, every last one of you.' She began sobbing loudly like a child, burying her face in her hands, swaying back and forth.

Russ kept an eye on her and held onto her arm, continuing to speak to Simone in a low voice, 'I think she must be an alcoholic – or maybe even on drugs – she's behaving so irrationally. She doesn't seem to care about the baby at all.'

'I never wanted this damned baby!' Justine yelled at him. 'Never, ever! It was an accident. He's *paying* me to carry it to term, but I'm not going to do it any longer. I can't bear looking like this.'

She glared at Simone, then let out a mirthless laugh. 'If I'm not careful, I'll get as fat as you are, you interfering bitch.'

They both goggled at this unjust accusation, then she jerked away from Russ, picked up a cushion and tossed it at him. 'Will you stay away from me?'

He didn't move but once again she jerked back as if someone had hit her and began screaming for help.

'I think we'd better call an ambulance,' Simone said. 'She's beyond reasoning with, and she may harm the baby.'

'I hope I do!' Justine yelled at them.

'Can you call them, Simone, while I keep an eye on her?' he asked. 'My phone's over on the breakfast bar.'

'Yes, of course.'

Simone dialled the emergency number and spoke to someone who said it would be at least an hour before anyone could get there.

Justine began to shriek for help and yell that she was being raped.

'Is that her?' the emergency officer asked, sounding shocked.

'Yes. There's no one near her and Russ hasn't touched her. We're worried because she's pregnant, quite a good way along, we think.'

'Do you know her?'

'No. I only just met her a few minutes ago when I

came to help my neighbour. She's his half-sister and he's not touching her, but we're worried sick that she'll hurt the baby.'

'If there's a baby involved, we'd better get someone there as quickly as we can.'

Justine began laughing hysterically. 'I heard that. They'll be arresting you by the time I've finished laying charges of rape and incest, Russ bloody Carden.'

He didn't even attempt to answer, just continued to keep a wary eye on her. He murmured to Simone, 'I hope the ambulance will come quickly.'

So did she. This was like a nightmare.

Time seemed to pass slowly, with occasional outbursts of yelling from Justine, and it was over half an hour before the ambulance turned up. When the paramedics found themselves confronted by a violent, screaming woman, they insisted on calling in the police to help them subdue her on the way to hospital.

By that time there were lights on in a couple of nearby houses and the security officer at the hotel had phoned to ask if everything was all right.

The police arrived quickly and took over the task of keeping Justine from attacking Russ. By that time the paramedics had phoned the duty doctor for guidance on dealing with a violent pregnant woman.

The police officer questioning Russ kept her voice low but she was looking at him rather suspiciously. Simone couldn't bear to see it and moved to stand next to him, linking her arm supportively in his.

The thankful look he gave her made her stay by his side while the paramedics managed to coax Justine to go with them quietly.

In the end Russ agreed to accompany the police, first to the hospital to give them Justine's details then on to the station to make a statement about what had happened.

'Can I phone the baby's father in Paris first?' he asked.

'You're not the father?'

'I told you: I'm her half-brother. What sort of man do you think I am? She turned up here today, saying she was running away from Pierre. And she keeps saying she's going to get rid of the baby.'

'I heard her say that more than once in this short time,' Simone put in. 'And I saw her arrive. She wasn't here before.'

'I phoned the father earlier and he's coming here tomorrow – no, it's today now, isn't it? But she's grown so hysterical he needs to find a way to deal with her more quickly if he wants to protect his unborn baby.'

The officer looked from one to the other, shaking her head as if dubious about a phone call, so Russ said, 'I'll put the phone on speaker and you can hear everything we say. Hell, you can record it if you want. I've nothing to hide.'

It took three consecutive phone calls to wake Pierre.

Russ told him quickly what had happened and asked him to stick to English so the police would know what was being said.

'Police?'

'I had to call for help. She'd gone berserk, shrieking

that I'd raped her, for heaven's sake. I thought she might harm the baby. They've taken her away in an ambulance.'

'*Mon dieu!* I've been worried sick since you phoned earlier but this is beyond my worst imaginings. I'll be there as soon as I can, Russ. With some form of medical help. I can't allow this to go on.'

When he switched off his phone Simone asked him, 'Do you want me to come with you to the police station, Russ?'

'I have no right to ask it, but would you?'

'Yes, of course. I'm probably a useful witness.'

The police officer, who had been keeping an eye on them both, said quietly, 'It'd be better if you followed us to the hospital in your car, madam, then you can drive Mr Carden back from the police station later once we've got his account of what happened.'

'Good idea. Give me the name of the hospital first, though, because I'm new to this area. I've only been in England for a few days. I'm Australian.'

She gave her a friendly wag of the head. 'I guessed that from the way you talk. You've dropped right into the thick of this situation, then.'

'Tell me about it. I've never seen anything like how she was behaving. I'll just nip next door for my handbag and keys.'

She drove out of the hotel grounds behind the police car, amazed that this had happened in the peaceful rural England the Dittons had promised her.

Simone arrived at a huge hospital just as Justine was being persuaded to leave the ambulance on a stretcher.

She started screaming as soon as she saw Russ get out of the police car.

The two officers frowned at him, looking even more suspicious, but they waited for Simone to join him before escorting the two of them into the A&E department into which Justine had already vanished.

One of the officers went with him to the counter to give information about his half-sister and Simone stood to one side.

'Are you sure you don't know the other details about her?' the clerk asked Russ. 'Not even her address?'

'I'm certain. I hadn't seen her for well over a year till she phoned me from Swindon yesterday afternoon. I'd had an accident in Australia, you see, and I'm only just recovering from it.'

'Is that what caused the limp?' the police officer asked. 'She told my colleague she had to kick you to stop you attacking her and that was why you were limping.'

'*What?*'

Simone moved forward. 'Mr Carden has been walking stiffly because of the accident in Australia and a fall the day before yesterday in his garden. When the screaming started I went out to see what was happening. I watched him and his half-sister through the window before I knocked on the door.'

'What were they doing?'

'She was screaming for help and saying he was attacking her but he was nowhere near her. I think she must have been hallucinating. He didn't even touch her till she attacked him, then all he did was try to hold her still.'

They had to hang around under the watchful eye of the police until a doctor had seen Justine and given her a sedative.

The doctor came out to see Russ. 'Does your partner take drugs?'

'She's not my partner; she's my half-sister. And the man she's been living with said he'd got her off drugs. I don't know whether she managed to get hold of something or not. It's been over a year since I've seen her. She has taken drugs a couple of times that I know of in the past, though I don't know what exactly.'

When they'd finished admitting Justine and taken her away, Russ turned to leave but was intercepted by the police officers.

'If we could go to the station and take statements from you both, it'd save you coming to see us later today,' one officer said to them.

Russ shrugged. 'Why not? I'm certainly not going to sleep easily. Is that all right by you, Simone?'

'Fine by me. I'll probably have trouble getting to sleep again, too.'

By the time they were allowed to leave and Simone started driving back to the leisure village, the sky was full of pre-dawn greyness.

'I can't thank you enough for your help tonight,' Russ said quietly. 'The suspicious way those officers were looking at me made me shiver.'

'I only told the truth.'

'Very quietly and convincingly.'

When she pulled up in front of his house, he said, 'Come in and I'll make you a hot chocolate. I don't know about you, but I'll never be able to sleep now without something soothing.'

'Sounds good to me. I'm a bit wired up by it all, too.'

Once the drinks were ready, they sat side by side on his small sofa, watching a glorious dawn gradually colour the sky and sipping the hot drinks. They didn't say much but he felt himself gradually calming down.

When she leant her head against his shoulder and didn't answer his question, Russ turned his head to look down at her and smiled. She'd fallen asleep between one sentence and the next. He took the mug away from her with his free hand and put it down next to his on the side table.

The warmth of her body against him and her soft, even breathing seemed to soothe him still further and he let his own eyes close, just for a few moments of peaceful rest.

# Chapter Ten

The doorbell woke them both with a jerk and they looked round in surprise at where they were.

'I can't believe we fell asleep!' Simone stated the obvious, more because she needed to get her head round that than because he wasn't already aware of it.

The doorbell rang again.

'I'd better answer it.' Russ glanced automatically at his watch. 'Hell, it's nearly ten o'clock.' He stood up, moving very stiffly, and went to find out who it was.

As she listened to the conversation, Simone stood up and ran her fingers through her hair to tidy it as she waited for him to return.

There were no mirrors to check her appearance. What must she look like? Thank goodness wavy hair didn't show untidiness as much as smooth hairstyles did.

\* \* \*

Russ opened the door. 'Pierre! How on earth did you get here so quickly?'

'Hired a plane, then a helicopter.' He gestured to the man standing beside him. 'This is Alain Chevret, the doctor who's going to be looking after Justine from now on. Can we come in?'

Russ moved away from the door. 'Yes, of course. Sorry. I've only just woken up. This is my neighbour Simone, who drove me to and from the hospital. We didn't get back till dawn.'

'Hospital?'

'They admitted Justine, had to sedate her, and she's still there, I'm afraid. She was in a wild mood and seemed likely to damage the baby, besides accusing me of attacking her.'

Pierre exchanged glances with the doctor. 'She's getting worse, then. I thought we'd calmed her down.'

'Sounds as if she got hold of some drugs,' the doctor said. 'We've already found out that she can be very cunning, *n'est-ce pas?*'

'Unfortunately, yes.' He turned back to Russ. 'Sorry. You were saying?'

'We were so tired, we sat down for a rest and must have both fallen asleep soon afterwards. You woke us ringing the doorbell.' He yawned again. 'Sorry. After so little sleep, it may take me a few minutes to gather my wits together. Would you like a cup of coffee or tea?'

'*Non, merci.* We need to see Justine as soon as possible and start on the paperwork for taking over her care. How exactly was she behaving?'

'Screaming, shouting, throwing things – and accusing me of raping her when I wasn't even standing next to her,' Russ told him.

'I saw that you were limping. Did she hurt you?'

He was getting very tired of explaining about his limp. 'No, no. That's the result of an accident last year. I had a fall at the weekend and hurt it again, just slightly.' He gestured towards Simone. 'Thank goodness my neighbour heard the screaming and came round. She saw how Justine was behaving and was able to bear witness to the police that I'd not been touching her.' He hesitated. 'Justine was acting as if she really believed someone was hitting her yet no one was even near her.'

'Hallucinating, probably,' Alain said.

Pierre shook his head. 'Damn. What exactly started her off?'

'She said she needed a drink of wine to get to sleep. I've only just moved into this house and I hadn't any to give her, nor would I have done in her condition. She went mad about that.'

'She must definitely have been getting some drugs, in spite of all our care, if she's reverted to that behaviour.' Pierre looked at the doctor. 'That settles it, don't you think, Alain?'

The doctor nodded. 'Yes. She'll have to be admitted and watched carefully for the baby's sake as well as her own till after it's born. The poor thing might have been damaged already by what she's been taking, I'm afraid.'

Pierre looked sad and whispered, 'I pray not.'

'When is she due?' Simone asked.

'Next month.'

'That soon! But she looks so thin.'

'She's trying to avoid eating. She's been obsessive about food and staying thin for as long as I've known her. We've been persuading her to take vitamins and small amounts of highly nourishing food. A couple of times she had to be admitted and fed intravenously because she grew so listless and pale.'

He looked distressed. Simone's heart went out to him.

The doctor turned to Russ. 'I presume you were the admitting relative at the hospital?'

'Yes.'

'I know it's asking a lot but could you please come with us and officially hand her care over to Pierre and myself? It'll make things easier, though my clinic is well known in Europe as a leader in this field so I'll be quite credible.'

'Yes, of course I'll come.' He turned to Pierre. 'She seemed furious that you weren't going to marry her, and one has to wonder why you're making such an effort to look after her.'

He shook his head. 'All she cares about is my money. I'm definitely not going to marry her and give her the chance to come after it as a divorce settlement. Sorry if that sounds mercenary but she's money-hungry. I'll look after her, of course, but what sort of life would I lead with her as a wife? As for the baby, if he survives, I'll make sure I'm the one with custody of him.'

'Do you have other children?'

Pierre shrugged. 'No. I have a low sperm count and thought I was unlikely to father a child, which is why I've tried so hard to take care of this one. I have wanted a son very much.' He let out a deep sigh. 'I'm sorry, Russ, but your sister seems hell-bent on destroying herself. I tried to get her off drugs, I really did. She can be such fun when she's on a more even keel.'

There was a silence, then Simone said firmly, 'I'll drive you to the hospital again, Russ.'

'No. I'll manage. You must be exhausted.'

'Why don't you both come in our car and let the chauffeur drive?' Pierre gestured towards the front of the house where a huge limousine was parked. 'I'll send you home in a taxi afterwards. I'm sure you're both too tired to drive safely. I wouldn't ask you to come as well, but I think it will look better if you're with Russ, Simone. A group of men trying to take a woman away forcibly might raise a few eyebrows.'

Russ looked at her hesitantly.

She nodded. 'Yes, I can understand that. I'll help if I can.'

Pierre cleared his throat to get their attention. 'I don't know anything about your relationship, or even if there is one, but could you please tell them you're partners?'

Russ opened his mouth to protest but Simone got in first. 'Of course. The police already took Russ's denial of hurting his sister more seriously because of me being there with him.'

He mouthed the words, 'Thank you!'

She linked her arm in his. 'Let's get this done, eh?'


As they sat in the ultra-comfortable limousine, Simone marvelled at how well she'd coped with an unpleasant situation. She didn't usually poke her nose into what the neighbours were doing, but you couldn't let a series of screams go unchecked, could you?

Her daughters were so wrong about their estimation of her capabilities, as she'd just proved again.

She'd been stupid to let them treat her like an inferior being, but she'd not been herself after Harvey's sudden death. Grief took you in strange ways and you didn't get over losing someone in a few days, or in her case, even a few months. She wouldn't accept that sort of over-protective treatment from them any longer, though, however well-meant and loving it was.

She looked sideways. Poor Russ! He sounded to have had a bad time in the past year and from the way he absent-mindedly rubbed his leg, it must be hurting. He'd fallen heavily down those stupid steps the other night. She was glad there were none at the Dittons'. Their house was on a more level block of land.

He seemed to sense her looking at him and turned sideways, smiling at her.

She returned the smile instinctively. For some reason, it felt as though she'd known him for ages. It was like that with some people. You got on well with them from the very first meeting.

She saw him getting stiff and tense again as they walked into the hospital, so linked her arm in his once more.

He laid one hand on hers. 'I hate these places. I spent a lot of time in them last year.'

They waited for Pierre and Alain to speak to the person at the desk, which seemed to be taking a long time.

'The people here will have known what to do for your sister, at least,' Simone said in an attempt to comfort him.

'I expect so. I thought Pierre had dealt with it while

they were living together. He's very rich and if anyone should be able to find the right resources to handle such a problem, it's him.'

'The doctor guy said people using drugs can be very cunning.'

A short time later Russ said absent-mindedly, 'Must be nice to be rich.'

'Yes, it must. I'm reasonably comfortable, thank goodness, because Harvey had good life insurance. But then I don't have expensive tastes.'

'How did your husband die?'

'He simply dropped dead one day and couldn't be resuscitated. Sometimes there's nothing you can do. No warning, just . . . gone.'

'How long ago?'

'Four years.'

'It must have been hard to lose him so young.'

'Yes. But you move on, don't you? Well, most people do. They don't have any choice. You can't bring people back from the dead, however much you love them.'

'It sounds to have been a happy marriage.'

'Yes, very. But I'm not unhappy now – at least I won't be once I've found something more meaningful to do with my life – and once my daughters have learnt that I'm not merely a glorified babysitter.' She smiled ruefully. 'That sounds awful, doesn't it? It's not that we don't love one another, or that I mind babysitting occasionally. I'm as much at fault as they are, too, for not saying no to them more often.'

They realised Pierre had come across and was standing next to them waiting to speak. 'Alain has been taken to speak to one of the specialists here. He'll probably get on better in an expert-to-expert situation than if I were with him. Apparently there's a cafeteria somewhere. Maybe we could buy a coffee?'

Russ grinned at him and Simone could guess why, if hospitals here were similar to those in Australia.

'Trust me, Pierre, unless something here is very different from other hospitals, you won't even recognise what they serve as being coffee.'

He grinned. 'That bad, eh? Then perhaps we could try the fruit juice from that dispenser? I'm quite thirsty after all that explaining.'

Simone took the first mouthful from the cardboard carton he brought over to her and grimaced. 'Doesn't taste much like real apple juice, but it's wet, at least.'

Half an hour later, Alain returned, accompanied by an older man wearing a doctor's white coat.

Simone was very conscious of how closely this other man was scrutinising her and Russ, but they must have passed some sort of visual test, because he led them back to his office and all the paperwork was brought there by his secretary.

Alain took out his phone. 'You permit? I need to make arrangements for transferring Justine.'

'Of course.'

He made a phone call, speaking in rapid French, said, '*Bien!*' and put it away. 'I had a private ambulance waiting. It will be with us in about an hour.'

## Chapter Eleven

Just over an hour later, Simone and Russ said goodbye to Pierre and Alain then got into another limousine which had been summoned for them.

'Very posh taxi, this is,' he joked.

'He needn't have gone to this length, but it *is* very comfortable.'

They each sighed tiredly as they settled back to be driven to the leisure village, then exchanged smiles at the coincidence, hardly saying a word for the rest of the journey.

Once they'd been dropped off at home, Russ looked at her apologetically. 'It's past lunchtime. I'm sorry it's taken so long to sort this out.'

'It was needed. What an extraordinary night! I hope that poor baby will be all right.' She couldn't hold back a yawn. 'I think I'm just going to grab a bowl of cereal, then catch up on some sleep.'

'Good idea. I'm tired too. I hope you'll allow me to treat you to dinner at the hotel tonight, as a thank you?'

'There's no need.'

'We both have to eat and I doubt either of us will feel like cooking. Besides, I enjoy your company.'

'Oh, well, I enjoy yours too.'

'I can't thank you enough for helping me, Simone. I'll look forward to our meal. I'll book a table before I go to bed. Sleep well!'

*What a strange way to make a friend*, she thought as she got a quick snack. While she was eating it, she noticed a blinking light on the main phone unit. Someone must have called while she was out.

She was tempted to leave answering it until after her nap, didn't think her family would have called. Then she suddenly remembered that she'd arranged for her relative to come and visit her this morning. Oh, no! Lance must have turned up and found no one there to greet him. She'd completely forgotten the arrangement.

Feeling guilty she phoned him and he picked up after the second ring. 'Lance, I'm so sorry to have missed you.'

His voice was stiff. 'Yes. Bit of a surprise not to find you there, I must admit.'

'Russ next door had a medical emergency with his sister and needed my help in a hurry. We had to call out the ambulance and the police. I went to hospital with them.'

'Oh. Friendly with him, are you? That was quick when you've only been here a few days.'

She was so surprised by this sour remark she didn't

know how to respond. What business was it of his who she was friends with anyway?

His voice became soft, cajoling. 'Sorry. It was just that I'd been looking forward to meeting you.'

'Mmm.' Why was he making such a fuss? Why was he so eager to meet her?

'How about I come tomorrow instead?'

She felt guilty but didn't want to tie herself down. 'I'm afraid I've already got something arranged for tomorrow. Look, I have to go now. I didn't get any sleep and I'm far too tired to think straight. I'll phone you and arrange another time to meet once I've caught up on my sleep. Bye.'

She ended the call without waiting for him to say anything else.

Why was he being so pushy? His tone of voice had annoyed her. He wasn't proving any more to her liking than he had the first time they'd chatted. In fact, rather less. How strange! She'd never taken a dislike to anyone by phone before.

She went upstairs and lay down on the bed. Then she wondered whether she might sleep too long and upset Russ by not being ready this evening, so sat up and fiddled around until she'd found out how to set the bedside alarm clock. She smiled and gave it a pat as she finished. Russ was much more likeable than Lance. She definitely didn't want to miss spending time with him.

After that the world went away until her alarm rang.

As she got into the shower, she realised she was humming, feeling happy at the thought of seeing Russ.

*Be careful!* she told herself. *This is only a temporary*

*holiday break. He and I live at opposite ends of the world the rest of the time – and so do our families.*

But every relationship didn't have to end in marriage, did it? Some you could simply enjoy for a time and then move on. She'd never had the chance to try shorter relationships, having married so young.

She might enjoy a fling with an attractive man. Which Russ definitely was.

Why shouldn't she? She wasn't exactly in her dotage.

She enjoyed the evening even more than she'd expected. They had a pleasant meal together, finding shared interests and differences as well as being amused by the same things in this crazy world.

One of his main interests was wildlife, not the big stuff but the smaller species that lived cheek by jowl with human beings, often unnoticed. She hadn't been particularly interested before, though she'd enjoyed feeding birds in her garden, but he made it sound fascinating and she wanted to find out more.

'I'll show you what's nearby over the next few weeks, if you like.'

'I'd enjoy that.'

The food was good, but she was still tired and declined a dessert, suddenly desperate for sleep. When the server had left them, Russ yawned in the middle of saying something, unable to stop himself, and that made them both smile.

'We're still sleep-deprived,' he said. 'Let's stroll home.'

She didn't say that this wasn't her home, didn't say much

of anything, but she enjoyed the star-lit sky above them
and it was good that he didn't try to force a conversation.

When she stumbled, he took her hand. That felt
nice too.

It was ages since she'd been out walking after dark,
something which, like most women, she didn't usually
risk doing on her own.

Inside her house the light was blinking to show a
missed telephone call, but she didn't check who it had
been. Even if it was one of her daughters, all she wanted
now, and that quite desperately, was to lie down and
sleep. She turned towards the stairs.

The following day, Simone got up late, checked the missed
phone call and saw that it had been from Lance. She
frowned. Again? He was getting to be a bit of a nuisance.
Annoyed, she deleted it without listening, then felt guilty
but forgot about him and prepared some breakfast.

As she ate a leisurely meal of a banana followed by
scrambled eggs on toast, she wondered how to spend the
day. She'd maybe look for another pretty village and go
for a stroll round it. Not as much fun on your own, but
those she'd seen so far were lovely.

When she checked her emails, she found one from
a stranger, so opened it cautiously. To her relief it was
from a cousin of her father, the one her parents had gone
to see when they visited England. It ended:

*Would you like to come over for lunch on Sunday
next and meet some of your UK relatives? It's my*

*wife who is the relative – she's Fern Pennerton,
has kept her own surname – but she's asked me
to contact you because I'm the one who's into
genealogy.*

*She and I have some old family photos we can
share with you. I've attached a couple of your
parents as teenagers. They both lived near here and
our families knew one another.*

*If you've already got something arranged, no
worries. We can meet another time.*

*Joe Harton*

She opened the attachments and smiled to see what
her father had been like then. He'd always had that
wayward tuft of hair at the front, it seemed. It had
vanished now, together with the rest of the hair on the
top of his head, but she remembered it clearly and his
fruitless attempts to persuade it to lie flat. His grin had
hardly changed over the years.

Her parents weren't interested in old photos and were
unwilling to discuss their family histories as well. She'd
often wondered why. Her father was particularly dismissive
of that sort of thing. Had he not got on with his relatives?
No, he couldn't be at odds with them because he'd gone to
see this Joe and Fern when they visited England, but hadn't
elaborated on their surnames. And if she remembered
correctly, they'd been to see a few of her mother's relatives
too, those living in the same village, anyway.

Well, unlike her parents she was looking forward to
finding out more about her ancestry on both sides while

she was here and Sunday would provide her with a good opportunity to start doing that.

She replied to the email straight away, saying she'd be delighted to meet some of the family and would be there for lunch as he'd suggested.

Thinking about that, she looked up the village where her parents' families seemed to have mainly lived. An online trip planner said Pennerton, same name as Fern's, was about forty minutes' drive away from the leisure village, and Upper Pennerton, where this cousin Joe lived, was a mere couple of miles beyond that. The distances were so small here compared to those in much of Australia.

She decided on the spur of the moment to go a bit early and check out Pennerton today, maybe take a few photos. Her mother had saved a few old papers and letters from her father's ruthless clearing out by hiding them in her sewing box and had given them to her, in case she ever went back.

'But don't tell your father. And I don't want to talk about this again.'

One of the letters had been from an Aunt Henrietta and there were a couple of smudges on it as if tears had fallen. She hadn't dared ask her mother what that was about.

There was a Christmas card from her mother's maternal grandparents, too. Rather a posh card it was, with the address printed on it. Her mother had said she'd lived with them for part of her childhood but hadn't said why.

When she'd looked at them again, Simone had realised this was the same address as the letter from Aunt Henrietta: Pennerton House.

Strangers would be living there now, she supposed – if it was still being lived in at all, that was, and hadn't been demolished. But if it was still there she'd be able to look at the outside of it, at least, and take a couple of photos to show her mother after she got back.

There was no sign of Russ as she went out to the car. Probably a good thing. She didn't want to grow too dependent on his company or make him think she was pestering him.

She pulled a face. Who was she kidding? She might not want to be thought a pest, but she'd be very happy to spend more time with him, found him a very pleasant companion. The upset with his half-sister seemed to have brought them together more quickly than usual with a new friend.

Taking her time, she drove through beautiful scenery and picturesque villages to Pennerton. The village centre consisted of two main streets, with a few shops and cafés, and a small church. She parked in the first available space so that she could walk up and down. Quite a few older buildings seemed to have been carefully preserved and were built in beautiful golden stone, but unfortunately the church was locked. She'd have liked to look round it during opening hours. One or two of the buildings had thatched roofs, a style she'd only seen on television or in films before.

She stopped for a coffee and cake, sitting near the

window of the café, happy to watch people ambling past, making bets with herself as to which ones were tourists and which were locals.

When she got into the car again she followed the satnav's instructions and came to Pennerton House. She'd thought it just a fancy name for an ordinary house, using the family surname. But it was in no way 'ordinary'. Indeed, it surprised her how big the house was, three storeys high, three windows wide and set in a large garden behind high wrought iron railings that looked old too.

She took a few photos but there didn't seem to be anybody around to ask who lived there now and the gates were closed so she couldn't even poke her nose into the garden. Her relatives might be able to tell her whose house it was now when she had lunch with them.

As she drove back through the village centre, she noticed that one beautiful old pub was called the Pennerton Arms. Was this called after the village, or had everything been named for the family in the big house? She'd have to research it.

Her mother had always claimed she knew very little about her family history. Now Simone came to think of it, she'd seen her mother look at her father pleadingly the couple of times when she'd pressed for more information about their family. He'd taken over the conversation each time at that point, saying firmly that neither of them cared about that boring old stuff.

Did he really find it boring or perhaps . . . could there be something to hide? No, what was she thinking of?

Her parents were ordinary people who'd worked hard all their lives and were now enjoying their retirement. What could they possibly have to hide?

And yet the house where her mother had spent part of her childhood was the sort to be lived in by the minor gentry, unless she had her understanding of history wrong. So who were her distant ancestors on that side of the family?

On the way back, just before she left the village, she stopped at a garden centre. She loved to visit such places back home in Australia and enjoyed wandering round this one. As she was leaving she saw some flowers for sale, so bought herself a bunch.

On impulse she asked the friendly woman at the till, 'Do you know anything about that big old house with the same name as the village?'

'Pennerton House? Been there since way back when, that old place has. My gran used to clean for the Pennertons – family has the same name as the house. There's only one of them left now, a nice old lady by all accounts. Does a lot for the village. Miss Henrietta, folk call her, last of the direct family as far as I know. She has a great-nephew who works in London and he comes down to see her regular. Buys her a bunch of flowers from us if we're open. Nice chap. Proper townie. He's not a Pennerton, though, from the name on his credit card.'

A person standing there coughed, wanting attention.

'Anyway, I must get on. Have a nice day.' She pushed the flowers across the counter and turned to serve the next customer.

Simone walked slowly back to the car, wondering if this Henrietta was the same lady who had looked after her mother. It wasn't a common name.

Just imagine your family living in the same house for centuries. It wasn't like that in Australia, which was a young country. The west had fewer old houses than the east because it had been much slower to be settled. She'd look up stately homes online and find some to visit while she was here.

She liked old places and antique furniture, would have bought some herself, but Harvey hadn't liked 'old rubbish'. She might pick up a few small pieces while she was here, now that she could please herself, things worth the expense of shipping back to Australia.

She felt good as she pulled up outside her house and got the flowers off the back seat. Altogether it had been a very satisfactory outing.

She looked next door as she walked from the car to the house, and saw Russ moving about the room he called his studio, which had a window on the side of his house facing hers.

She wondered if he'd care for a glass of wine, since he apparently had none. Unless he'd done some shopping today.

No, what was she thinking about? She mustn't bother him.

Russ got up late on the day after their visit to the hospital. He was pleased to find a message from Pierre waiting for him to say that Justine had been safely lodged in a special clinic near Paris and would be carefully looked after, both before and after she had the child.

Good, he thought. That was one problem off his hands.

The best thing about it was that he'd got to know his new neighbour better. What a nice woman she was! And how kind she'd been to him. He didn't know what he'd have done without her.

As he ate a leisurely brunch, he couldn't help wondering where she'd gone. Pity he hadn't caught her before she left. He'd been going to offer to take her to a fresh food market that she'd probably not find on her own, and then to a small, ruined castle you could walk round.

He mustn't keep pestering her, though. She'd helped him greatly yesterday but she would have things of her own planned, a lot of sightseeing no doubt, relatives to catch up with.

He went out shopping and when he was about to start the car to set off back from the market, his phone rang. He looked at who was calling and smiled. His agent. About time he got back into some work again.

'Hi, Sally!'

'Hi, Mr Elusive.'

He chuckled. 'Not true. I've been busy moving into my new house and setting up a proper studio again. I was going to contact you tomorrow.'

'Did the house turn out as well as you'd hoped?'

'It's even nicer – or it will be once I've got everything in order.'

'Can we start thinking about a new series with

book links, then? They've been putting out feelers about your recovery.'

'That's great. I'd love to do another one. I was worried I'd miss out on following up on my success with the last series.'

'If you make them money, they don't drop you unless they have to. Have you got any definite ideas?'

'Possibly. I'd like to stick to the UK for the time being while I continue to recover. I know we talked about how popular Australia is but I don't want to go back there yet. It doesn't have good memories.'

'How's the leg going? You were only limping when you got tired last time I saw you.'

'I'm mostly past even that now, just a bit of stiffness.' He wasn't going to tell her about his fall. To his relief his leg seemed to be recovering well. Give it another few days and there'd be no stiffness showing, if he could help it, because those strengthening exercises the physio had given him seemed to help a lot.

'Go on, then, Russ. What do you mean by "possibly"? What's the new idea?'

'I'm living in the beautiful Wiltshire countryside with a lake nearby. I did wonder about a book *and* series of programmes about what's in the back gardens and nearby countryside round here.'

'Like your Lancashire series?'

'Yes, fairly similar, except that the countryside is very different from the Pennines, lush, you might call it, and picture-book pretty, instead of the breathtaking open spaces of the moors. So in a sense we'll be focusing on more accessible species.'

'Sounds good. Can you do me a brief preliminary proposal? Maybe include a few takes of the wildlife in action?'

'Yes. Give me two or three days to organise my thoughts and do some wandering round the countryside for inspiration.'

'How about I come down to visit when it's ready? Next week, maybe?'

'Don't push. I'll try to do it by then, but I've got other things to sort out here as well.'

'*Carpe diem*, remember! Don't be too long. Oh, and there's another bit of good news. It's still to be confirmed but it looks as if we might sell the series to the States.'

'Wow, that'd be great.'

As he ended the call, ideas suddenly began bouncing into his mind, which sometimes happened and he knew enough to take notes of them while they were fizzing away in his brain. Not a simple overview of the species and plants this time, but a series of activities designed to introduce townies to their tiny close neighbours, and especially to help parents show their children what was hopping, crawling or flying nearby.

He'd make lists for readers to print out and tick off when they'd seen the creatures or plants. Children loved the achievement of completing a list and he suspected many adults did too. There was something very satisfying about hunting down every last creature.

He went into his studio and switched on his laptop, then scowled at how it felt to sit there at the rickety fold-down card table. The room was so lovely and spacious, he wanted a permanent desktop computer in here. Laptops were useful for taking out and about, but he was a lot more comfortable at a desktop when working long hours. He'd have to go out and buy one. Not today, though. He wanted to get his preliminary thoughts down straight away, planting seeds in his imagination, he always thought of it as, then sorting them out and firming the patterns up later as the ideas blossomed.

He had trained himself to take regular breaks, for his body's sake, but today these consisted only of brisk walks round the house, a couple of climbs up and down the stairs and a few arm exercises. He worked hard until nearly half past five, by which time he'd had enough and was ready for a good, hearty meal.

Just then he heard a car draw up and watched Simone come back. He almost went out to ask her in for a drink. Then he remembered that he hadn't bought any wine, only visited the fresh food market set in the middle of nowhere. He really ought to have gone to an off licence on the way home, or bought a bottle from the hotel, but he'd got so tied up in ways of making a new series interesting in a different way that he'd just wanted to get back to work.

He could invite Simone up to the hotel for a drink. Unfortunately, just as he was debating this, a car drew up outside her house and a tall, thin chap got out. There was something about the way he stood looking at her house, *calculating* was the word that came to mind. He didn't like the look of that fellow, Russ decided abruptly, moving forward to see better what was going on.

She opened the door, but didn't invite her visitor straight in. She came further out, still barring the way. Unless he was very much mistaken, she'd looked surprised when she saw who it was and not pleased to see this guy. There was no sign of her lovely smile.

Russ went out at the front and pretended to weed the nearest section of his small front garden bed, half hidden behind some shrubs, unashamedly eavesdropping.

'Simone?' the caller asked the minute she opened the door.

She recognised his voice immediately and instinctively pulled the door closed behind her, keeping him outside. 'You must be Lance.'

'Yes. I was passing and thought I'd call in on the off-chance that you'd be free now. How about we go up to the hotel for a drink and a meal, get to know one another as relatives should?'

She wondered why he was pursuing her so relentlessly and what to do about it.

He gestured towards the house. 'Aren't you going to invite me in?'

*Cheeky devil!* she thought. *You're pushing your luck, fellow.* But she had no real reason to deny him entrance. 'Only for a minute or two, I'm afraid. I really do have something arranged for tonight.'

As she gestured to him to come in, she had a sudden idea because she knew Russ was home. 'I'll just have to nip next door and tell my friend that I'll be a few minutes later than planned.'

She saw annoyance flicker briefly on Lance's face then he took on what she always thought of as a 'shuttered look' when she saw someone with that expression. It was as if he were guarding his real feelings. And his smile didn't reach his eyes. You could nearly always tell when smiles weren't genuine.

'Do sit down for a minute.' She fled next door.

Russ stood up from near his little garden just before she reached him and she came to an abrupt stop. 'You look as if something's wrong.'

'There is.' She looked over her shoulder as if to check that she'd not been followed. 'That man who just arrived – he seems to be a sort of cousin and well, he keeps pestering me. I told him on the phone yesterday that I had something planned for today and he tried to call me again yesterday evening. And now he's just *happened to be passing* and popped in to ask me out.'

'Bit pushy.'

'A lot pushy. Um, I told him I'd agreed to go out with you tonight. Would you mind? Could I buy you a drink at the hotel and, um, pretend that we'd already arranged to go up there?'

She'd tried to speak calmly and confidently, but she looked at him as if worried she was asking too much.

He grinned and dusted his hands. She cheered up even before he spoke because his smile *did* reach his eyes.

'I'd love to go out with you, Simone, any time, no excuses needed. Let's have a meal there again, and if this guy persists we can even pretend we're in the process of getting together.'

'You're sure you don't mind?'

'Of course not. Did you mind helping me with Justine?'

'No. That's what friends do. Great. I'd better dash back and get rid of him.'

'I'll be ready in a couple of minutes and come across to hammer on your door like an impatient lover, if you like.'

'Wonderful. Do I swoon at the mere sight of you?'

'Oh, yes, please. At the very least, we could kiss one another. If you don't mind.'

'I don't mind at all.'

She walked slowly back, her smile fading. Once again they'd found humour in a situation. Why hadn't she taken to Lance? She'd taken to Russ immediately.

When she went in, she said apologetically. 'Russ and I have arranged to go out together in a few minutes, I'm afraid. I've told him I'll be a little late.'

'Then can you and I arrange to see one another tomorrow?'

'Don't you have to go to work?'

'I have flexible hours and what's more important than making a cousin from Australia feel welcome?'

The old Simone would have given in to this pressure, the new one said, 'I'd rather not, if you don't mind. Russ and I have been planning a few days' sightseeing. He and I are just – you know, quite interested in getting to know one another.'

The sour expression reappeared briefly on Lance's

face but was quickly replaced by another glassy-eyed and patently false smile.

She couldn't get rid of him fast enough, was wondering how to nudge him to leave when she heard the door at Russ's house shut with a bang.

Lance leant back, making no attempt to stand up. 'How are you planning to spend the rest of your time here?'

Russ rushed round getting ready. He grabbed a light jacket and locked up the house, then banged his door shut as loudly as he could. He forced himself to slow down and tried to stroll casually next door but he wanted to hurry. Oh, he did. She was such a nice person. Very nice. And he wasn't going to let this guy whose face he didn't like go on annoying her.

On impulse he didn't knock on the door and wait for it to be opened, but walked straight in. 'Ready, Simone love?'

She had a wooden expression on her face. 'Almost. This is a distant cousin of mine who's just leaving. Lance – Russ.'

The two men nodded to one another and Russ continued to follow his impulses, going across to put an arm round her shoulders and kiss her cheek, pleased when she stayed close to him.

Lance studied them, eyes narrowed.

Simone reached up to kiss Russ's cheek in return, then said as cheerfully as she could manage, 'Nice to meet you, Lance. I'll be in touch when things have settled down.'

It wasn't until she held the door open that he even stood up. She closed it quickly behind him, not waiting to wave goodbye as he drove off. When she went back inside, she found Russ peeping out of the window, so joined him.

'He hasn't set off yet, Simone. Why is he just sitting there? Look, shall we move closer to the window so that I can kiss you while he's watching?'

'I'd be delighted if you did.'

She looked towards the window and saw Lance still peering into the house, so when Russ swung her round and put a lot of effort into the kiss, so did she.

Which took her breath away.

As they started to pull apart the car drove off. She moved away from Russ with reluctance and it was a moment before she spoke. It had been an excellent kiss. 'Phew! You saved my life. He's being very persistent. I wonder why.'

'Who can tell? I didn't like his face. However, I'm grateful that he gave me the opportunity to kiss you. You can ask me to help you out that way any time.' He chuckled. 'I don't know why you're blushing. I merely followed your lead. I have to say, you're a red-hot kisser, Simone.'

Her blush deepened. 'So are you.'

He took hold of her hand again. 'Come on. Let's stroll up to the hotel. I'm ravenous. I've hardly eaten anything today, I've been so busy. I'll share my news when we're settled at our table.'

She stopped to study the hotel car park before they went in. She wouldn't put it past Lance to be watching and checking she had meant what she said. But she couldn't see any sign of him, thank goodness.

\* \* \*

When they'd disappeared into the hotel, Lance moved from behind a tree and got back into his car, which he'd parked behind a large van.

Damn! She'd hooked up with this guy quickly.

He'd wondered if she'd been making it up but they looked to have been chatting away happily as they strolled up to the hotel. And they'd been holding hands.

He wasn't giving up. He wanted to keep an eye on her one way or another. He didn't want her charming old Henrietta, not after all the work he'd put into the old bat. He'd had to be particularly careful with the old lady because she'd once worked for the government in a secret capacity. She would never talk about it.

Why did the women in his family live so long?

And who had Henrietta left the big house and her other possessions to? She had been very tight-lipped about it all when he tried to find out.

# Chapter Twelve

Simone and Russ were shown to a table in the corner of the hotel restaurant, and he suggested a glass of wine while they looked through the menu. 'I could get a bottle.'

'I think one glass will be enough. I know it's been a week but I'm still a bit jetlagged.'

They clinked glasses then sipped appreciatively as they studied the menu and discussed their favourite dishes.

Before the waiter could return to take their order, a woman came across to them. 'Excuse me, but I'm not mistaken, am I? You're Russell Carr, surely?'

Simone was surprised by this and wondered why he didn't immediately correct the woman about his surname. In fact, he looked rather embarrassed and as the woman stood waiting, he muttered, 'Yes, I am.'

'I thought so. I adore your nature programmes. Well, my whole family does, even my teenage son. I'm so glad you've recovered from the accident. I wonder if you'd be so kind as to give us your autograph?'

'Um, yes, of course.'

'I'll have to go and ask at reception for a piece of paper. Won't be a minute.'

When the woman walked away, Simone stared at him. 'What was all that about? You told me your name was Russ Carden.'

'It is. My real name is, anyway, but don't tell her that. I work as Russell Carr.'

She stared blankly. The name clearly wasn't familiar to her.

He grinned. 'I do nature programmes on the telly. My first series was set in Lancashire, about the local fauna there. And I shan't take offence if you don't recognise me. I was only just taking off, so to speak, when I had the accident. I'd treated myself to a trip to Australia to celebrate, part holiday and part to suss out the possibilities for future programmes.'

'What was your series about?'

'What's living in your back garden or the nearby park. I'm planning to feature the smaller scale wildlife of the various regions in the UK. My first one was about Lancashire and the Pennines. My next will probably be about Wiltshire.'

The woman who'd accosted him returned, beaming and brandishing a piece of paper and holding one of the hotel's giveaway pens out to him.

'Here you are, Mr Carr. My son will be thrilled to have your autograph.' She spoke so loudly, other people turned round to stare and to Simone's amusement Russ blushed.

He took the paper and pen, asked for the son's name and wrote a few words before signing the page.

'Are you filming round here, Mr Carr?'

'No.'

She opened her mouth to ask something else and he interrupted, 'Look, no offence, but I'm trying to have dinner with a new friend.' He gestured towards Simone.

'Ah, sorry!' The woman winked at him and walked off, waving the paper at the group sitting round a table on the other side of the room and calling, 'I've got it!'

'You really are a celebrity!' Simone exclaimed.

'Only a very minor one and only in the UK. You didn't know about that side of me at all and I was so glad of that.' He glanced quickly round the room, but no one was looking at them now, thank goodness. 'It's annoying to be interrupted by people wanting autographs, however pleasant they are.'

'I'm sure her son will be delighted.'

'You're not into nature programmes?'

'I've lived in Australia all my life. I've seen a few but they're not my favourite viewing, I must admit. My husband was into the ones showing big animals killing and eating smaller animals. Sorry, but I covered my eyes at the gruesome bits.'

'Don't apologise. That's not my favourite viewing either. But just for the record, my programmes are more about the social life of small creatures, and the way they interact with humans. They're just starting to be shown in other countries, so it's looking quite hopeful.'

'I'm glad for you. I must look out for your programmes.'

He leant forward and took her hand. 'You don't have to, Simone. I've really enjoyed you treating me as a real person not a celebrity. Actually I was going to tell you what I do later when I told you my good news.'

'Let's place our orders, then I'm all ears. Who doesn't love to hear a friend's good news?'

After the waiter had left them, she waited for Russ to speak, smiling happily at him across the table. He loved her smile.

'I had a phone call from my agent today. The company who did my first TV series was expressing interest in a new one and they've waited patiently for me to recover. Hopefully there will be a linked book as well. So I've started working out what to offer them.'

He added, 'But the good news isn't that. My agent thinks we're going to sell the original series to the US. The money for that would be rather nice.'

'Well done, you. I'd be interested to see gentler nature programmes, especially what's in the garden here. This being my first visit to the UK, I don't recognise everything.'

'Just ask me. I promise you instant personal service.'

'I'd like that. I'm enjoying the differences here.'

'I must say I'd like to go back to your country. I was enjoying the differences there too. But I don't want to go anywhere near bushfires.' He couldn't help shuddering. 'I can still remember the black smoke and the red sky, not to mention the roaring sound the fire made. It sounded like a monster coming to devour us.'

'It's horrible the destruction it can cause.'

'The firefighters were wonderful, and the police. We tourists would have got away safely if it hadn't been for that idiot.'

He closed his eyes for a moment, then pushed the memory of the accident away, glad of the waiter's arrival with the food.

When they'd eaten a few mouthfuls he said, 'Go on. You were talking about the differences here. I'd be interested in what's struck you.'

'Well, I've got one question for a start. Some of the creatures I've seen have the same names as similar ones in Australia but they aren't exactly the same, so are they the same species or not? The wagtails, for example. They're my favourite birds in Australia and I've seen some here. They're not quite the same but they're just as cute, and they do wag their tails.'

'Yes, but the Aussie bird wags its tail from side to side and the English one goes up and down – and our bird is more delicately built.'

They concentrated on the food for a while, then she asked, 'How long will it take you to film a new series?'

'Depends. I think I'll just stick to filming creatures during the warmer months. I have to get cracking on that to catch the spring activities. There's far more going on from now onwards than there will be in winter, and I've already got quite a lot of footage from round here. Every time I came to see how my house was going on, I took a walk on the wild side as well. I always keep my eyes open.'

'I shall keep my eyes open for you creeping through the undergrowth, acting the sleuth.'

He chuckled. 'If I didn't creep they'd fly or run away. If I see anything interesting near the houses, I'll try to call you out to watch it with me. I must get a bird table set up soon on my back patio. Anyway, that's enough about me. What do you love doing? You must have some hobby or passion.'

Her smile faded. 'I have all sorts of small domestic activities that I quite enjoy, but no great passion like yours. It's one of the reasons I broke free of my family for a while. Since we lost their dad, they've been smothering me, and also using me to support their lives. They haven't exactly encouraged me to develop a new life of my own. Don't get me wrong, I don't mind doing some family support jobs like baby-sitting, because I love my grandchildren dearly, but I need to find something for me to *achieve*.'

'I'm sure you'll find a focus. The fact that you're even thinking of it says something positive about you.'

'I hope so.'

After their plates were taken away, they decided to indulge in a dessert and both chose cakes from a small trolley, sharing them as they continued to chat and exchange views of the world.

He didn't know when he'd enjoyed an evening so much. He loved watching the emotions play across her face. She was so pretty and vivid, though she didn't seem to realise it, didn't give herself credit for anything except being a wife and mother.

He felt as if he'd known her for ages. They might have different backgrounds and skills, yet they communicated easily and shared a similar sense of humour.

He hadn't been lying when he'd told her unpleasant visitor that he wanted to get to know her better. He did. Very much.

He was sorry when the evening ended. It had been a long time since he'd fancied a woman so much.

In fact, his body had come back to life with a vengeance since he'd met her. He had worried about his lack of that sort of feeling after the accident. Clearly he needn't have done. All it had taken to wake him again was a very short time spent with Simone.

He would have to tread carefully, didn't want to seem too pushy about that. She would be worth waiting for, he was sure.

That night she featured in his dreams, of course she did. He hoped he featured in hers too. Unless he was much mistaken she was attracted to him as well.

All too soon it was Sunday, the day Simone had arranged to meet her relatives. She had mixed feelings about this. Joe sounded very nice, judging by his emails – if you could judge a stranger by email – but she was worried that Lance might be there. His attentions had felt distinctly creepy and she didn't want anything else to do with him.

She arrived at Joe's two minutes exactly after the specified time and sat in the car for a few moments, studying the house. It was another older dwelling, detached and built in red brick but the same size as its neighbours, unlike Pennerton House. The garden was tidy but not especially pretty and there were several cars parked in the street nearby.

What was she doing, sitting here staring at it? She took a deep breath and got out, carefully undoing the seatbelt that had held the bunch of flowers and bottle of wine safe on the rear seat. She pondered who exactly were her hosts? Joe had told her a little about his relationship to her part of the family, but not which family members would be his other guests.

Just as she lifted her hand to ring the bell, the door opened and a man smiled at her. 'I saw you coming. You must be Simone. You look a bit like your father, but like the Pennertons, too, especially the curly hair.'

'I'm pleased to meet you. These are for you.' She thrust the flowers and wine at him and he took them.

'Thank you.' He glanced quickly at the label. 'Australian wine. We love it. I think we'll save this one to enjoy at our leisure. Come in, do. They're all looking forward to meeting you.'

As a woman came along the hall to join them, he gestured, 'This is my wife, Fern. As I said in my email, she's the relative and I'm the genealogist.'

The two women nodded at one another and he added, 'Look at the lovely flowers she's brought, Fern.'

'Gorgeous. Thank you, Simone. You go and put them in water, Joe, and I'll start introducing Simone to our other guests.'

He pretended to tug a forelock. 'Yes, ma'am.'

Fern linked her arm in Simone's. 'Come through. I'll

stay by your side to begin with, because you're bound to get confused. Joe has me well trained and I can tell you which branch of the family tree each person is from.'

'I'm afraid I don't even know what the different branches are. My father is an appalling communicator about his family, always has been. He says the past should stay there.'

'And your mother? Didn't she tell you anything? Her family is also connected to the Pennertons.'

'She won't say much about it either, I'm afraid.'

Fern stopped moving and frowned. 'When they came here, they seemed to have got over all the fuss their getting together made, but admittedly they came for a flying visit only and asked me not to have any large family gatherings.'

'It was you they came to see?'

Fern looked at her in surprise. 'They didn't tell you anything at all, did they?'

'No.'

'They came mainly to see Henrietta, who's a sort of great-aunt, the oldest family member. Your mother was very fond of her, stayed with her grandparents a lot when she was younger, and Henrietta is her grandmother's younger sister.'

'Someone told me she's still alive.'

'Yes. And she'd like to see you, if you have time. Come to think of it, her lawyer wanted your mother's current address as well. I think there's going to be some sort of small bequest for her. Henrietta is ninety now and she's tidying up what she owns.'

*Curiouser and curiouser!* Simone thought.

Joe called out from the kitchen, which sounded like a plea for help with something that was cooking, and Fern shouted, 'Coming.' She turned to Simone. 'Everyone here is friendly and happy to let the past go, so I hope you'll enjoy yourself. You and I will get together another day and I'll bring you up to date on . . . well, certain rather delicate family matters. Then we'll arrange a visit to Henrietta, if that's all right.'

'Why don't you and Joe come across to lunch one day next week?'

'It'd be better if I came on my own, if you don't mind. Joe's a bit like your father, would rather let the past stay in the past. He's only interested in the family genealogy in an academic way. And he doesn't always see eye to eye with Henrietta, who can be a trifle autocratic. Well, more than a trifle, actually, because she had rather an important job back in the day.'

'Then come on your own. Any day will be fine with me. I don't have any firm engagements. This whole house swap opportunity blew up quite suddenly and I don't know anyone over here.'

'You do now.'

'Yes. I do now.' But one encounter didn't make a friend and she was still missing Libby dreadfully.

Of course she knew Russ now, but wasn't sure how that was going to work out, whether it would turn into a long-term friendship. It had been less than two weeks of occasional meetings, but it felt as if she'd known him longer.

Fern didn't come back for a while, but people introduced themselves to Simone, so she was never left standing awkwardly wondering who to approach. Some of them said they had Australia on their bucket lists, or they'd visited Sydney during a world cruise. Typically, none of them had visited Western Australia. Not nearly as many tourists ever did.

These were not poor people, she soon decided. They were treading carefully and studying her as warily as she was studying them.

To her relief, there was no sign of Lance today.

When lunch was served, she was taken to help herself at a buffet table before the others as 'guest of honour', which embarrassed her. She didn't pile her plate, just chose a few things she could eat easily. She had given enough luncheon parties for Harvey's work colleagues to know which foods could slip and slide about your plate.

A short time later she turned from chatting to one person to see Lance standing in the doorway. Damn!

'Who invited *him*?' the woman next to her muttered.

Simone gave her a quick look and risked asking, 'What's his connection to the family? He's been pestering me for days to get together.'

'You must have money,' the woman whispered. 'Don't believe a word he says and keep your distance. If he wasn't related, he'd not be joining this party. Look at Fern's expression. She can't stand him. You know what? I bet she didn't invite him. But I suppose she can hardly turf him out now without embarrassing everyone. He'll be counting on that.'

Simone felt relieved that she wasn't expected to welcome Lance with open arms. She tried to keep away from him, but he worked his way skilfully round the room and eventually trapped her in a corner.

'I thought you'd be here,' he said cheerfully. 'We must arrange that get-together before we leave.'

She was glad the woman whose name she couldn't remember had been so frank with her. It gave her the courage to say, 'Maybe after I get back from my trip. Russ and I are going to be taking a holiday together for the next week or so.'

His expression hardened for a moment or two, then he said with an attempt at lightness, 'He certainly got in with you quickly.'

*In with her?* What a strange thing to say! That wasn't how you approached making friends – well, not how she did.

Fern reappeared at her side, threaded an arm through hers and said, 'There's someone else I want you to meet. Do get yourself something to eat, Lance.'

Relieved, Simone went off with her out to the garden. 'Thanks for rescuing me.'

'I can tell a damsel in distress at three paces,' her companion said lightly. 'What day would suit you for me to come and visit?'

'Tomorrow, the day after, whenever.'

'I thought I just heard you say you were going away with some guy.'

'That's my neighbour. He and I get on well, but I've only just met him and we're not – you know – close.

Yet. He kindly pretended we were getting together when Lance dropped in on me.'

'Well, keep up the pretence. There's a reason for you to stay away from Lance. I'll tell you tomorrow, if that suits you.'

'That'll be fine.'

Half an hour later, Simone again avoided Lance and went to say goodbye to Fern and Joe. 'I wonder if one of you could walk me out to the car, so that I don't get waylaid?'

'I'll do it,' Fern said. 'You go and head Lance off, Joe. He's been pestering poor Simone.'

'You must have something he wants. Leave it to me.'

At the car, Fern said, 'Tomorrow then. Give me your address. Oh, bother. I should have brought something out to write on.'

'I have a notebook.' Simone scrawled her details on a page and tore it out. 'About noon?'

'Fine by me. You need to know: I'm a coeliac. I can't eat—'

'I have a friend who's got that condition. Unless you have any other food problems, you can trust me to cater safely for you and not offer anything with gluten in it, or even anything cross-contaminated by gluten.'

'Thanks. Being coeliac causes trouble with some people who can't be bothered to learn how to deal with it. As if it's hard to provide a simple salad and protein.' Fern looked towards the house. 'Lance is looking out of the window. Oops, he's moving across the room. Better get away quickly. I'll intercept him if he escapes from

Joe, who doesn't like to be blunt with a relative.' Almost to herself, she added, 'Most of the *women* here would have no trouble whatsoever being blunt with Lance.'

When Simone had left, Fern went back into the house and found Lance waiting for her in the hall.

'Thank you for having me.'

She nodded and would have continued on her way, but he put an arm across to stop her. 'And by the way, you'll not keep me away from her for ever.'

'I don't know what you hope to gain by pestering her.'

'I need to know what she and her mother are going to be left.'

'That's Henrietta's business.'

'And mine. I've been cheated before by people in this family and you damned well know it.'

'I don't happen to agree. It was you trying to cheat your half-brother, if I remember correctly. Only, your mother was too smart for you.'

'That's not what my lawyer thinks.'

'Been gambling again?' Fern said. 'Is that why you're so desperate?'

He didn't answer but she reckoned from the way he scowled that she'd hit the target with that.

'You'd better go now. And don't come to my house again. I won't hold back on throwing you out another time. I'd have plenty of willing helpers in the family to do it, too.'

He shrugged and walked out to a rather old car.

She was thoughtful as she stood watching him drive

away. She'd really like to find out what was going on with Lance and Henrietta's legacies. But for that, she'd need to speak to Henrietta and the oldest member of the family was playing her cards very close to her chest.

Fern didn't want to speak to him again, not ever. He was the sort of man who didn't know how to be polite to women, still treated them as sex objects. Ugh! She hated the way he looked at her. He'd once tried to grab her, pretending it was a joke, and she'd had to kick his leg hard and threaten worse to make him let go.

She'd never told Joe, who'd have made a fuss and drawn attention to the incident.

## Chapter Thirteen

The following morning Simone was standing at the kitchen window when Russ came out of his house. He waved as he got into his car and drove off, looking happy. She hoped his plans for the new project were going well. She knew he'd had a sudden request to go and see his agent in London tomorrow. Where was he going today?

As if that was any of her business!

Later that morning Fern arrived for lunch bearing a gift of home-made strawberry jam. She looked round the room. 'Nice place, this. You must tell me about leisure-village living arrangements another time. I have a recently retired friend looking for somewhere to live.'

'Come and sit down. I'll serve lunch in a minute or two.'

'How about a cup of coffee now and lunch later? Today we really do need to talk frankly.'

'OK by me. I particularly want to know what's going on with Lance. Why is he harassing me?'

'Harassing? Is it that bad?'

Simone shrugged. 'It feels like harassment. He gives me the shivers the way he looks at me, so calculating and sexist in an old-fashioned undress-you-with-his-eyes way.'

'Good description of him. It's not only you. He gives me and half the women in the family the shivers, too. His wife left him years ago and he hasn't really got together with anyone since. He mainly ignores women of his own age and tries to chat up women who are far too young for him. Now, let's start with your parents and come back to Lance after I've painted the whole picture – well, as far as I know it.'

'Fine by me.'

'First, I have a message from Great-Aunt Henrietta, though she prefers just Aunt as a title and she certainly doesn't act like an old lady. She rang me yesterday evening with what we call one of her 'royal commands'. She wants to meet you and asked me to invite you to go for lunch with her on Wednesday or Friday at Pennerton House, whichever suits you best. I think you'll like her.'

'I'm sure I will if you say so.'

'She's ninety now and is doing well physically for someone that age, and she's as shrewd as they come. We try not to upset her when she has her mind set on something and at the moment she's set on making a will that's fair to everyone – and that includes you now. So if you wouldn't mind going to see her?' Head on one side, she looked at Simone.

'I'd be happy to do that. I looked at her house from outside last week and was surprised at how big it is, like a small stately home. I'd love to see inside it. Would she show me round, do you think?'

'She'd probably get her secretary to do that because she has mobility problems with stairs and hates people to see her struggling. You'll like Elizabeth. She knows as much about the house as Henrietta does and watches over her employer like a mother hen. You've described exactly what the house is: a small stately home.'

'I didn't realise we had that sort of upper-class ancestor. When I found a Christmas card from her with an address on it, I assumed it was just a fancy house name.'

Fern shrugged. 'Well, the upper-class element seems to have been dying out of our lot for a while now. No one on my side wants to inherit the house because it would be such a burden to try to keep it going. Henrietta has spent a fortune on maintenance over the years. She's talked to the closest relatives and told them she's going to hand it over to the National Trust when she dies. They've expressed an interest. Everyone's relieved.'

'It would be hugely expensive to maintain.'

'Tell me about it. The National Trust has agreed to take it on because it's a little gem and has some rather special historical features from World War Two.' She gave a wry smile. 'Lance, of course, feels the house should come to him as the closest male relative, but he wasn't even asked if he wanted it. Anyway, he'd only sell it and gamble away the money. Henrietta knows that.'

Simone was surprised at how negatively Fern always spoke of Lance. What was it about him? She realised her companion was waiting for her to pay attention.

'Sorry. My mind wandered for a moment or two there.'

'I'm not surprised. There's a lot to take in.'

'Yes. I wish my parents had told me more.'

'You can ask me any time you want to know something. Now, back to Henrietta. She does want to leave small bequests to various family members, items she feels should stay in the family. I doubt Lance will get any of those either unless he can change his habits. Henrietta doesn't approve of gambling.'

'Can't she just leave him out of her will completely?'

'She may do that, but he does have a son, and Kit is a nice chap. It'll look so bad if he's left something and his father isn't.'

'Oh.' Simone waited, feeling a bit bewildered to have so many relatives.

'Your mother used to be married to Lance's father, Ralph, so—' Fern broke off and stared at her companion. 'You didn't know that either?'

For a few moments Simone could only gape at her. 'I had no idea Mum had been married before, no. What was this Ralph like?'

'I didn't see him till he was older, but he was good-looking still, though a bit of a cold fish.'

Fern paused again, as if to give this time to sink in and Simone gestured with one hand for her to continue.

'The marriage didn't last long and in case you're wondering, she and Ralph didn't have any children. She left him after six months and skipped off to Australia with your father while she was still married. Brits could just go and live there in those days. It was a couple of years before Ralph started looking round for another wife and everyone assumed he was waiting for a divorce to come through.'

'Do you know why she left him?'

Another hesitation, then Fern said, 'People weren't certain but they suspected that he'd started thumping her. A couple of them saw suspicious bruises apparently. Anyway, she ran off with your father to Australia and it was years before she got in touch again. She didn't come back to visit till after Ralph was dead and even then she and your father only caught up with a couple of people, Joe and me among them, because she'd been close to my mother – and Henrietta, of course.'

'Wow. It's – hard to take it all in.'

'I'm not sure when they got divorced, no one is. And if you didn't know she'd been married before, you won't be able to tell us. Not that it's any of our business.'

Simone could only shrug. She doubted she'd even ask her mother about it after she got back. It could be best to let this sleeping dog lie.

Fern went on with her tale. 'When your parents came back, your mother *said* she and Ralph had got a divorce almost immediately, but I'm not sure the rules allowed that then. No one pursued it but we've never been quite sure. Lance's father simply turned up with a brand-new young wife one day so probably something had been done. The new wife left him too a few years later.' She looked at Simone sympathetically. 'Confusing, isn't it?'

'Very. No wonder my parents always refused to discuss the past and their family history with me. I'd have appreciated some information before I came here, only, to be fair, they didn't know I was coming until after I'd left. They've been travelling round Australia in a caravan for the past couple of years.' She frowned. 'But I don't see how that affects Lance or why he's pestering me.'

'My guess is that he thinks you might be coming into money taken from what he considers his share from Henrietta ought to be, so he wants to keep an eye on you, but who knows what goes on in that man's twisted little mind?'

Simone shrugged. 'My husband left me reasonably well provided for, so I don't *need* Henrietta to leave me anything. Any items she's distributing should go to the people who've helped keep an eye on her over the years, surely?'

'She'll do as she sees fit, as usual. Let's leave it at that for today, shall we? I'll get Joe to email you the basic family tree. You need time to take all this in and I'm getting hungry, so can I be cheeky and ask you to feed me now?'

Simone stood up. 'Yes, of course. I have everything ready in the fridge. And I've remembered that you're a coeliac. I checked the ingredients in the wraps carefully and there are no wheat or other gluten-containing grains in them, but you might like to check them yourself.'

'I would, if you don't mind. Can't be too careful.'

She did that while Simone got the various salads and a frittata out of the fridge and they were soon sitting, eating and chatting about the leisure village.

When they'd finished their meal, Fern said she had to go.

'Thanks for telling me so much,' Simone said. 'It's better that I know given I'm staying here for a few months. Will you be at Henrietta's if I go on Wednesday?'

'No. She wants a cosy chat with you, as she calls it. There will just be her and Elizabeth. I'll let her know you're going.'

Simone stood at the door waving goodbye to her visitor, then looked regretfully towards the next house. The car still wasn't back yet.

She went back indoors and finished clearing up, feeling a bit lost as to what to do until teatime. She thought of phoning her daughters for a chat but wasn't ready yet to tell them what she'd found out and it was likely they'd be alseep already.

A few times she caught herself glancing next door.

'Oh, you fool!' she muttered. 'Stop thinking about him. He's a busy man.'

Unfortunately, she wasn't busy, wished she were. And her thoughts were in a tangle after Fern's visit.

That's when it occurred to her to get online and join one of those organisations that allowed you to research your family history. Maybe she'd find out something more about her parents and ancestors there.

While she was doing that an email arrived from Fern with what was known of the family tree attached. It was a bit of a jumble, with some branches researched and others mostly ignored.

Dealing with all that kept Simone nicely occupied for the afternoon.

\* \* \*

She decided to watch television that evening and have some of the leftovers for a late meal. There was a knock on the door as she was just about to get something to eat and when she opened it, she found Russ brandishing a bottle of wine.

'Fancy a drink? You Aussies call it a sundowner, don't you? I replenished my stocks of wine on the way home and I haven't tried this one before. You could help me test it.'

Her spirits rose immediately. 'I'd really enjoy some company. And actually, I have enough leftovers from providing lunch for my cousin to feed you, if you don't mind miscellaneous bits and pieces. Come in, do.'

He beamed at her. 'That sounds great.'

As they ate, she told him about Fern's visit and the shock revelations about her parents and he whistled softly as the tale ended.

'Bet you didn't expect that.'

'Definitely not.'

He was such a good listener she shared her puzzlement over what to do about it.

'I don't think you need to do anything about it at the moment. If they'd wanted you to know, your parents would have told you, and after all, it all happened a long time ago.' He changed the subject. 'I wish I could be a fly on the wall when you go to see the old aunt, though. It's like a modern gothic tale, isn't it, disposing of the family bits and pieces? I'm looking forward to hearing the next instalment.'

'Thanks for listening. That's enough about me. Tell

me about your day. You looked full of yourself when you came home.'

'I had a great day, checking locations where I can find various animals living peacefully in the wild, with a guy from a local nature lovers' group. Afterwards I went shopping, not just for wine, but for bits and pieces of equipment so that I can start filming.'

'What you do sounds interesting.'

'Then I wonder . . . would you mind reading my proposal through? I've jotted down a rough draft, to see if the idea sounds, well, attractive? This series would be partly for children. You'd bring a new view to it, since you've not seen my other programmes, but you know about young children. It's only a couple of pages.'

'I'd love to.'

'Here it is.' He grinned. 'I didn't think you'd refuse.'

She read it quickly and nodded. 'Sounds interesting and with fun activities.'

They continued to chat until she yawned suddenly and they realised how late it was getting. His company ended the day nicely, especially as he stopped at the door and reached out to touch her lips with one very gentle fingertip. 'Would you object to me giving you a goodnight kiss?'

'I'd like it.'

It was very nice, too, and she was sorry when it went no further than a couple of kisses. She hadn't wanted a man in that way since rat man, but she did now.

No, what was she thinking of? It was too soon. She wasn't going to rush into a relationship with anyone ever again. Look what had happened when she had rashly allowed rat man to move in with her.

When she went to bed, her thoughts turned once again to her parents. Why had they never mentioned her mother's first husband? Lots of people got married more than once. There was nothing to be ashamed about in that.

The thought of her mother having been married to Lance's father made her shudder, though. Ugh. She didn't want to be connected to him in any way.

In the morning she watched Russ set off again. This time he was smartly dressed. Well, you would be if you were having lunch with your agent, wouldn't you? She hoped everything would go well for him.

She might go up to London a few times while she was here, only it'd be more fun to do that with someone.

Determined to do something useful with her day, she made a careful list of items she considered essential, mainly food, and went out shopping. But she got seduced into buying a rather pretty skirt and top at the shopping centre, a younger style than she'd been wearing lately. Well, she wasn't antique, was she? Didn't need to dress like an old, past-it woman.

After she got back, she put everything away in a kitchen cupboard she'd cleared for her own use, then went out for a brisk walk round the lake. She hadn't done much exercise since her arrival and it was a fine day, if a little cool by Aussie standards.

But the rest of the day dragged, she had to admit.

And Russ didn't get back until much later than she'd expected. She heard his car and saw him stop in front of next door from her bedroom window.

She felt better to have him back. There was a house on the other side of hers but its occupants were away. Her fellow residents seemed to do a lot of coming and going.

And a lot of the leisure village area was still a work in progress, with streets but no houses along them yet and piles of building materials in some parts.

# Chapter Fourteen

Russ arrived at his agent's office in London a little early, but you had to allow extra travelling time in case of delays because rail services weren't always reliable.

Sally's secretary looked up as he walked in. 'Oh good, you're early.'

She knocked on a nearby door, stuck her head round it and said, 'He's here,' then gestured to him to go in.

Sally came from behind her desk to give him a hug. 'You're looking like your old self again.'

'Am I? That's good.'

'No walking stick needed now?'

'Not for a while, thank goodness. They're such a nuisance to "park" when you sit down.'

She gestured to two comfy chairs over by the window and then got straight to the point. 'I read your brief outline and loved the basic idea so I sent it to the guy at the production company.'

He was startled. 'But it's only a brief summary. I was going to write a proper outline after I'd discussed it with you.'

'Well, you can do that later. Clement and Baines are interested. They've made a nice lot of money from your first series and they won't mind making more, believe me.'

'Wow.'

She gave him a motherly smile. 'No one could accuse you of having an inflated ego, Russ, and yet, you're a known TV identity in the UK these days.'

He shrugged. 'The fame side of things isn't nearly as important to me as sharing my love of nature and doing my bit for the environment.'

'I know. But money is nice too. I'd rather we stayed with Clement and Baines, if that's all right with you, because they're the best for nature programmes and they have a very good rapport with your publisher.'

'I hope the publisher likes my idea too, then.'

'They love it. Everyone does. In fact, we're having lunch with a couple of their staff today because they want to go to contract and for you to deliver your live shots and basic narrative as soon as is humanly possible.'

He was startled. 'They decided so quickly?'

'Well . . .' she grinned at him. 'It's a question of *carpe diem* again, because with your agreement, I'm just about to sign up the sale I mentioned for American rights to your first series, and your book is going into reprint. So the TV people want to grab you while they can.'

He cheered loudly and pulled her up to waltz her round the office. She always felt to him to be more like an honorary aunt than a business associate.

She pushed him away, laughing. 'I'm too old for that sort of thing.'

'No one's too old to show their happiness.'

She gestured to the chair. 'Enough of your blarney. Let's think about dates. How soon can you do this?'

'Not sure. It takes time. Animals don't always come out to play just because you want to photograph them.'

'But it *is* spring now, Russ.'

'Early spring. Luckily I've already got some shots that I can use. I never let a cute animal go to waste.'

'Well, you said this is coming up to the best time of year to film them.'

'It is. Now the move is over and I'm living in Wiltshire, I can check out the local conditions more carefully. I've had a preliminary look round a few places already.'

She cocked her head on one side. 'Not interested in how much money is on offer for advances?'

'As long as it's not less than last time.'

'Wash your mouth out! As if I'd allow that. It's going to be a lot more, actually.'

'Good. Go ahead and sort it out, Sally. I'll go with what you think is OK. I needn't have come up to town today, really, could just have left it all to you, O clever one. Though it's always a pleasure to see you, of course.'

She shook her head in mock dismay. 'You don't like coming up to London, do you, Russ?'

'Not really. Too many people pushing past you in the street, lots of fumes from all the vehicles and all those grey buildings towering over you. And going on trains below the ground makes me feel distinctly uncomfortable.'

He stared into space for a moment then realised she was waiting patiently for him to continue. 'I do enjoy the museums sometimes, especially the Natural History Museum.'

'You would.' She looked at the clock. 'Let's walk to the restaurant. I suggested your favourite eatery.'

He didn't need to ask which. They both loved its ambience, not to mention reasonable prices and delicious food in reasonably sized helpings. He hated places where you had to navigate pretentious food towers or other arty constructions teetering in the centre of your plate in order to obtain a few meagre mouthfuls.

The television people were fun, the food was excellent, but by the time he parted company with Sally and got on the train to go home, he felt utterly drained. It had been great to catch up with Sally, he was thrilled with his new contract and he was desperate for some fresh country air but someone he didn't have to watch every word with.

It wasn't late. He hoped Simone hadn't gone out this evening, because he wanted to share his good news with her.

Simone saw him come back and when he waved to her, he was smiling so broadly she guessed something good had happened in London.

'Come and celebrate!' he called and raised a bottle of what looked like champagne in one hand as he clicked to lock the car with the other.

She grabbed her handbag and ran out to join him, not

forgetting to lock the door. She'd never once forgotten that since she lost Harvey.

'What's happened?' she demanded as she joined him.

'Come inside and I'll tell you. But first I have a desperate need to open this bottle and sample its contents.' He took her hand and tugged her into his house and across to the kitchen.

'We have to stop meeting over glasses of wine or we'll turn into alcoholics.'

'This news deserves a drink.' He found some champagne glasses and started to fumble with the bottle.

She took the glasses from him and tutted, then found a tea towel and polished them carefully. 'What are we drinking?'

He showed her. 'English sparkling wine. We're not allowed to call it champagne nowadays. And anyway, who wants to?'

The top popped suddenly out of the bottle and with a laugh he poured the foaming liquid into the glasses then thrust one into her hand.

'Today I signed a provisional agreement to go to contract for a new TV series and associated book.'

'Wow! Well done. Here's to your new venture, whatever it is.' She clinked glasses with him then sipped appreciatively. 'Lovely.'

'Come and sit down. I'm exhausted underneath it all. London does that to me. I'm a country boy at heart.'

'Is the new book going to be about what you said?'

'Yes. Trouble is, the TV people want it like yesterday, so I'm going to have to hire some help.'

'To do what?'

'A bit of everything. Manage the details, take notes, hold the camera, hold a creature if necessary, to stop it running away. General factotum, I think you'd call it.'

'That's a bit like what I used to do for my husband – well, except for the animals.'

'Aren't you on holiday, not to mention retired?'

'I'm bored already. I like to keep busy. You wouldn't like to give me a try-out, would you?'

He grinned. 'I'd love to.' Then he saw tears trickle suddenly down her cheeks and put his glass hastily down. 'What's wrong?'

'I'm so happy!'

He sagged back in relief. 'Do you always cry when you're happy?'

'When it's important. I've been a bit down about not having much to do.'

He picked up his glass and clinked it against hers. 'You're hired, then. When can you start?'

'Day after tomorrow.' She beamed at him.

'Aren't you going to ask how much I'm paying?'

She shrugged. 'I'm sure you'll treat me fairly and having something interesting to do is far more important to me than the money.'

'Can't you start tomorrow?'

'I'm afraid not. I've arranged to have lunch with my great-aunt Henrietta.'

'What a magnificent name.'

'Isn't it? She's apparently the one who has to be obeyed in my English family. She summoned me to visit her because she wants to check me out. She lives in Pennerton.'

'One of my favourite villages. There's an unspoiled wood there where I've taken some of my favourite photos.' He snapped his fingers. 'Hey! How about we drive over together and then I'll go off to check out the wood while you have your luncheon party? You can phone me when you're ready to be picked up.'

She clinked her glass against his. 'You're on. I'll enjoy that.'

His expression softened. 'You're not a solitary type, either, are you?'

'No. And you?'

'I like to be on my own sometimes, but I like to be with people. Or creatures. I love animals, beetles, birds, you name it. They fascinate me. I grew up roaming the English countryside and my biggest ambition is to save enough money to buy myself a fairly big slice of it and keep it safe from developers.'

'Maybe if your new series is successful, you'll be able to do that, or at least put down a deposit on somewhere suitable.'

'From your mouth to God's ear!' He raised his glass again, then took the empty glass from her and put it down. Pulling her into his arms, he said huskily, 'I've been dying to kiss you. I love it when your hair gets all ruffled and bouncy. It's not wildly curly but it has a very nice bounce, as if it has a life of its own.'

He ran his fingers through it and she shivered, reacting to his touch but also feeling shy. 'It's starting to go grey.'

He chuckled. 'Who cares? You're what? Mid-fifties?'

'Fifty-six.'

'And you have only faint streaks of greyish hair at the temples. I think you're doing very well for someone so decrepit.'

'Your hair is the same.'

'Ah, but I'm younger than you.'

She frowned at him and he grinned at her. 'I'm only fifty-four.'

She gave him a mock punch in the arm. 'Decrepit indeed!'

'When I was involved in the accident in Australia, I felt past my use-by date for a while. I'd only just got there too. I was going to suss things out for filming a series there, but I'm not in a hurry to go back now that this other project has turned up. I still get nightmares about that bushfire. I've recovered most of my physical functions, I've found myself a home and I've met you. What more can a man want?'

She stilled and he looked at her thoughtfully. 'Now, why are you looking so wary?'

'Because I've vowed not to rush into any more relationships. I did that once a couple of years after my husband died, and it was an utter disaster.'

'I'm not rushing you into anything.'

'And – I definitely don't want to get married again.'

'Have I asked you to marry me?'

'No. But I want to make it clear from the start.'

'How about a nice love affair? Would you be against that?'

'No. As long as we take it slowly. I'm not very

experienced, Russ. I got married young and the other guy only lasted a few months.'

'Suits me to take things slowly. We can have an office romance – without an actual office most of the time because we'll be out and about.'

He could see how tense she still was, so plonked a kiss on her cheek. 'Lighten up, Simone. Let's just enjoy some time together.'

'All right. That I can do.'

When he'd walked her to her door, he went slowly back into his house. Phew! She was very wary of commitment as he'd noticed before, and rather lacking in self-confidence where men were concerned. What had her life been like with her husband? Quietly, happily domestic, from the sounds of it. They didn't even sound to have travelled outside Australia. And what had the other guy done to her to make her so reluctant to commit?

He picked up the bottle and poured the last of the fizzy wine into his glass, raising it and murmuring, 'To Simone. I might have to wait to marry you, my love, but I'm very likely to do it.'

He just *knew* she was right for him.

He hadn't told her yet that he too had lost a spouse. He had vowed at the time never to marry again – until he'd met Simone and suddenly experienced the same sort of feelings as had led him into marriage with Poppy.

Oh, yes, he had plenty of experience and he knew for certain that Simone was right for him.

It had surprised him, he had to admit, because the two women in his life were nothing like one another. But the feeling was the same and made him just as willing to follow his instincts a second time.

His marriage had been very happy until poor Poppy died.

For some reason, he had high hopes that life with Simone would be happy too.

He'd take it slowly, but he could be very determined when he wanted something.

# Chapter Fifteen

Russ stopped the car in front of the gates of Pennerton House. 'Ready to enter the lion's den?'

Simone smiled. 'Yes, of course. Someone's even opened the gates so maybe they're friendly lions today. The gates were firmly closed on the world last time.'

He set off down the drive and stopped the car in front of the double doors. 'You've got my number. I'll only be ten minutes or so away.'

'I know. You've said that three times.' She got out of the car.

The right-hand part of the front door opened before she reached it and a woman of about her own age stood smiling at her. She smiled back then turned to wave goodbye to Russ. She doubted she'd need her personal Sir Galahad to rescue her but it was nice to know Russ was going to be nearby.

'Welcome to Pennerton House, Simone. I'm Elizabeth, Henrietta's secretary.'

'Lovely to meet you.'

'Don't you have a car of your own? We'd have sent one for you if we'd known.'

'I do have one, but my neighbour was coming to this district on business, so we decided to travel together and perhaps explore a little more later this afternoon.'

'He must be a nice neighbour. Now, Henrietta is waiting for you impatiently. Just one thing, if you don't mind me saying it: please don't treat her as if her brain is slower than yours just because she's old and physically slower. She's as quick-witted as anyone I've ever met.'

'I'd never do that.'

'Some people do. They speak slowly and clearly to her, using simpler words as if she's an idiot and it absolutely infuriates her. Give me your jacket and I'll hang it up before I take you through.'

They went into a cosy little sitting room. 'Oh!' Simone stopped in surprise because her hostess bore a distinct resemblance to her mother, or what her mother might look like in another ten years.

'Is something wrong?' Henrietta asked.

'No.' She explained what had surprised her and got out her phone to show a photo of her mother and prove it.

'You carry a photo of her around with you?'

Simone smiled. 'I've got all my family with me, which includes two daughters and four grandchildren.'

'May I see them?' Henrietta patted the sofa beside her.

Simone sat down next to her and went through a few of her family photos.

'I like that you carry them with you. I envy you your big family. I never had the chance to marry, spent a lot of my later years looking after my parents and then my brother. Now I'm the last of my generation and have only distant relatives.'

'That must be lonely, to have no one who shares your early experience of life, I mean.'

'It is. However comfortably one is cared for, and I can't fault my dear Elizabeth for that, some shared childhood memories would be enjoyable.' Henrietta smiled across at the woman who'd let Simone into the house as she spoke. 'Perhaps you'll tell Jane we're ready for lunch now, dear?' She turned back to Simone. 'Jane's my cook-housekeeper. She's been with me a long time.'

When Elizabeth came back, she helped Henrietta to stand up and passed her a walking stick, then let her lead the way into the next room at her own speed.

Just then a bell gave a double chime and Elizabeth said, 'Oh dear. I'd better check that.' She went across to a small screen on a side table and tapped it to bring up an image.

'We've set up a protected area at the far side of the grounds to encourage some of the rarer birds to nest,' Henrietta explained. 'We keep a careful eye on it, though we don't often get people invading the wood since we fenced it off.'

'Modern technology can be marvellous.'

'Those birds are marvellous, too. My favourites are

the lesser spotted woodpeckers. There are several nesting pairs there this year. Go closer and have a good look. Can you see the red cap on their heads? Gives them a cheeky look, don't you think?'

'Oh, my!' Simone suddenly realised who the man on the screen was. 'Elizabeth, that man is my neighbour, Russ. I'm sure he won't hurt your birds.'

Indeed, Russ was already backing away carefully from the nests, camera raised to photograph the birds as he moved.

Henrietta joined them. 'I wonder why he's taking so many photos.'

'He's a wildlife photographer, specialising in smaller species of the UK, not just birds but other creatures too,' Simone explained.

'It's Russell Carr! Why didn't I recognise him?' Elizabeth suddenly exclaimed. 'Is he going to do another telly series? If so, it'd be better for him not to mention the location of those birds on his programme or people might try to track them down.'

'I'll tell him. I'm sure he'll understand the need to protect them.'

'We'll make sure he understands,' Henrietta said. 'When he comes back to collect you, we'll invite him in and I'll tell him.'

'Is he on your land? I thought from what he said that the park was public land.'

'It used to belong to the council but I bought it from them for a bird sanctuary last year. It's got caveats on what can be built on it and I'm not allowed to sell it to developers, but then I wouldn't want to.' Henrietta smiled at Simone. 'You were quick to defend him. You must like him.'

'He's been very kind to me and I'm going to be working for him as general factotum on his new project, doing anything and everything needed for his new series.'

'Could be interesting – or boring,' Elizabeth said.

'Or both. Most jobs have tedious patches and tasks.'

Conversation flowed easily but nothing was said about Henrietta's will, to Simone's relief.

Elizabeth kept an eye on the screen but the tone didn't sound again and there was no further sign of Russ near the nesting area.

After a leisurely lunch, Henrietta said, 'Why don't you call your friend now and ask him to join us for coffee? We can check that he won't reveal where the nesting area is and there are other parts of my land where he's welcome to look for creatures to film as well, the grounds of this house, for example. I've let a lot of it grow more naturally again.' She gestured towards the windowsill where there was a pair of binoculars. 'I spend hours watching my little visitors.'

Simone got out her phone and called Russ. 'I'm still with my great-aunt and Elizabeth and you're invited to come round to the house and join us for a cup of coffee.'

To her relief he must have picked up on the hint she was dropping about Henrietta being nearby and didn't ask anything which might have upset her hostess.

'That'll be nice. I'll be about fifteen minutes.'

As the call ended, Henrietta said abruptly, 'While

you're waiting, Elizabeth can show you round the ground-floor rooms.'

Simone noticed Elizabeth shoot a quick, assessing glance at her employer but what she saw must have reassured her, because she turned to Simone and said, 'We'll make it a quick tour today. You can come back another time and have a full tour, if you're interested.'

'I'd love that.'

When Russ arrived, Simone watched in amusement as he charmed Henrietta with tales of his adventures filming animals – and sometimes his misadventures where the creatures were definitely the winners. She liked that he didn't mind laughing at himself.

In fact, the better she got to know him, the more she liked him. Too much. She'd better be careful. Rat man had seemed charming at first.

'You certainly seem to know your business, young man,' Henrietta said after a while.

'One can never know enough about the world around us. You certainly know a lot more about the local wildlife than most people, if you don't mind me saying so.'

'I know about the creatures living close to me. I've enjoyed watching over my world, been lucky to live here during my retirement and have access to so many different creatures and their habitats. If you like, you're welcome to come here and photograph what's going on in the grounds.'

'Really? That would be wonderful.'

She sighed and leant back. 'I've enjoyed chatting to you, Russ, but I'm going to have to throw you out now because

I'm tired. One could do with shorter days as one gets older, because one's energy doesn't last as long as it used to.'

Elizabeth showed them to the door. 'I hope you'll come again, Simone, and you too, Russ. She's thoroughly enjoyed your visit.'

'Did she mean it about me photographing the wildlife in the grounds?' Russ asked. 'I'd love to come and do that, but the grounds are big enough for it to take me a week or two at least to do them justice. It's getting increasingly difficult to find somewhere undisturbed by bustling hordes of sightseers.'

'Yes, of course she meant it. There are parts which haven't been disturbed for over a decade. When the National Trust takes over, things will no doubt change and that'll be a pity. But it's the only way we can think of to preserve the house and grounds, given the lack of a willing and suitably rich heir. I'll phone you soon about another visit, Simone.'

'Just a thought, but would Henrietta like to come and have lunch with me one day, do you think? Does she have one of those mobility scooters? There's a lovely lake nearby and the paths are designed to be wheelchair accessible.'

'I'll ask her. She doesn't go out much these days.'

'I can fit in with her.' Simone shot a teasing look at Russ. 'I think my boss will give me time off. He wants to keep on her right side.'

'You can phone me when you find out,' he said.

As they drove away, he added, 'I ought to put you on the books today. I can't thank you enough for introducing me to your aunt. The grounds of Pennerton

House will make a wonderful place to find creatures to film. And besides that, I really like Henrietta. She's a feisty old girl, isn't she?'

'Yes. I like her too. She isn't at all old in the head, is she?'

'On the contrary.'

On the way home he stopped at a big garden centre. 'I want to buy a couple of bird tables. Well, it will be a couple if you'll allow me to put one at the back of your house as well as outside mine.'

'It's not my house, but I can email the Dittons and check it out with them.'

'I'll buy two anyway. Tell them you'll leave it behind for them and I bet they'll say yes. A lot of people enjoy birdwatching.'

When they got back, she phoned the Dittons who answered, though it was late, and agreed, and he immediately started assembling the bird tables, which came in flat packs. He seemed to have forgotten that it was teatime as he altered one to make it higher, with a protected ledge underneath it.

'Some birds like chaffinches can be a bit timid,' he explained.

'I don't think I know what a chaffinch looks like.'

He fumbled in his pocket for his phone, which he always seemed to have at the ready, and flicked through the images. 'There you are.'

The bird he showed her was delightful, small and fluffy, with the males brightly coloured.

'I'd love to attract some of those!' she exclaimed. 'They're so different from our native cockatoos, which are larger and can be so noisy and cheeky. Though we do have little honeyeaters. I love to watch them sip the nectar from flowers.' She stopped with an embarrassed laugh. 'I don't need to explain about them to you, though, do I?'

'I know a fair amount about Aussie birds. I was considering making a programme about them when I was involved in the accident.'

'You were in the eastern states, I think. They're a bit different from the west. Well, they're two thousand miles away from Perth, aren't they?'

He let out a blissful sigh and beamed at her. 'So much to explore and see in the world. I do hope I continue to be successful.'

'I must get hold of copies of your first two series.'

'I'll give you the DVDs.'

'Thanks.'

They continued to work with no mention of getting something to eat but she'd had a late lunch so she could wait. She was enjoying herself, passing him tools, and finally filling the dishes with water for the birds. She was sorry when they'd done all they could for the moment. It had been lovely to have a busy day.

When they'd finished they made some sandwiches and sat outside chatting for a while. They'd been together for most of the day and conversation hadn't faltered once, she thought in wonderment. She did enjoy his company.

And she enjoyed his kisses, gentle as these were. He

was holding back, not rushing it, which suited her. There was such a comfort in not being on your own.

Even so, she intended to tread very carefully with Russ.

Did he have the same sort of reservations? A couple of times he'd broken off what he was saying and changed the subject slightly, as if they were heading into something he didn't want to discuss. Had a past relationship upset him too?

When they said goodnight, she found the phone light blinking to show that someone had called. She hadn't noticed it ringing, but there had been occasional hammering sessions.

She studied the caller ID, not recognising the number. Oh dear, she hoped it wasn't Lance pestering her again.

Should she see who it was now, or wait until morning?

No. She'd better find out who'd called or she'd lie awake worrying in case it was bad news from her family in Australia. She pressed the buttons and found that it wasn't them, thank goodness.

Her relief turned to anxiety, however, when she found out that it was Kit Mundy who'd called. Fern had mentioned Lance's son, though she'd said Kit was a nice guy, not at all like his father. Only Simone didn't want to get involved with that branch of the family at all, because she didn't want to meet Lance again.

She listened to the recording once more, half inclined to delete it.

*Hi. Kit Mundy here. Sorry I missed you at the family barbecue. I hope you don't mind me being cheeky but I wondered if we could get together for a chat? It'd have to be quite soon. You see, my company has just offered me a posting to Australia for a couple of years and they want a quick answer. The job's in Western Australia and my wife's a bit nervous about us making such a big change. You could come to visit us or we'll visit you. I'd really appreciate your advice. Give me a call when you have a moment.*

Oh dear! Now what was she going to do? She felt it would be rude to refuse to see them and talk about her home. But somehow she was sure that Lance would push his way in as well if he heard of a visit. She wondered how often he got together with his son. Did she dare tell them outright not to bring Kit's father with them? No, that'd be so rude.

She'd read about people doing some sneaky and even illegal things when it came to family inheritances. She could imagine Lance being suspicious if he heard she was going to be spending time with his son.

Fern shared her dislike of him, though, which reassured her a little about her own judgement.

She got ready for bed but couldn't settle, kept worrying about what to do about Kit Mundy.

Just when everything had been going so well!

# Chapter Sixteen

Simone was woken abruptly by someone ringing her doorbell. She glanced at the bedside clock-radio and groaned. Not quite six o'clock and it had been after midnight when she finally got to sleep. Who on earth could that be at this early hour? The post didn't come until much later.

Muttering, she threw the covers back and peered out of the bedroom window. It was Russ. He was jogging up and down on the spot, looking as if he'd been up for ages and was about to run a race. The sun was shining brightly, barely above the horizon still. It was the start of one of the lovely longer days they had here in England.

As she went down, the doorbell rang again and she flung the front door open, pretending to be angry. 'What do you mean by waking me up at this hour, Russ Carden?'

She realised she hadn't put a dressing gown on and he was eyeing her flimsy nightdress appreciatively. She should have been annoyed about that but she was decent enough – barely! – and it had been ages since any guy had looked at her like that.

'You, um, said you were an early riser.' He was still staring.

'I am. Sort of. I had a phone message that worried me and it took me a while to get to sleep.' She watched in amusement as he tore his eyes away.

'We'll sort out whatever your problem is later, Simone. For now, I'd really appreciate your help as quickly as possible.'

'OK. I'm awake now.' She was much more inclined to help Russ than try again to figure out what to do about Lance's son, that was certain. He was staring at her feet now and she had a hard time not chuckling.

'After I left you last night I was a bit restless, thinking about my new series, so I went out for a stroll down to the lake. I got talking to a local guy there, who said he'd seen some willow warbler fledglings in a nest near the fence by that bit of woodland on the far side of the water. He thinks the mother bird is encouraging them to fly so today could be the day it happens. That could make for some brilliant shots.'

'Put the kettle on and I'll get dressed.'

He grinned and held out an insulated mug. 'I've got a mug of tea ready but you're not getting it before we set off. Hurry up. I don't want to miss a single move.'

And suddenly it felt like fun, something unexpected to start the day, something she'd never seen before.

'Five minutes.'

'Three, or I'll come and drag you out, ready or not.'

She laughed and raced up the stairs, coming back in four minutes precisely to find him holding the door open. She took the mug from him as they set off at a brisk pace, then took a welcome gulp on the move.

That was another thing that had been missing for a long time: giving in to a sudden impulse. What fun!

Russ was pleased at how briskly she walked but couldn't forget the sight of her in that nightie. Phew! He had to forget about her long, bare suntanned legs, though, because he might catch some great shots this morning.

Adjusting his backpack which was full of equipment, he forced himself to concentrate on the task in hand, explaining what he was planning to do as they walked.

'The guy I talked to tried to describe the spot and if it's where I think, there are some bushes nearby. We can crouch behind them to check whether something's going on. We don't want to intrude on the birds unnecessarily.'

'What do we do if something is happening?'

'We'll try to stay out of sight and I'll move forward slowly, hoping to get some shots, however long that takes. Did I mention there's sometimes a lot of hanging around when photographing animals?'

'Why do you need me, though? Sounds as if the fewer people there are to upset the birds, the better.'

'I want to get a shot of you watching them as well. If you can look excited and say so, I'd be grateful.'

She stopped for a few seconds to gape at him and he gave her a quick tug to get her moving again.

'I didn't sign on to become an actress, and I didn't put any make-up on. Anyway I'm no good at pretending to feel excited about something when I'm not.'

'I don't like make-up, would much rather have you without it. Why women want to put gunk all over their skin beats me. You won't have to pretend, believe me, Simone. It's one of the most adorable sights there is, seeing little bundles of fluff learning to fly.'

'Well, don't blame me if my part of it comes out badly. It'd be better for me to film you explaining exactly what people are seeing.'

'No. I can do that any time. I want to try the effect of someone to whom it's all new sharing their excitement. Trust me, you really will be excited.'

'Hmm.'

She supposed she'd quite enjoy it, but she'd never got wildly excited about birds before, so why did he want to film her watching them now? She stared into the distance as she walked, and it occurred to her that she hadn't got wildly excited about anything much in the past couple of years, had settled into a pleasant but uneventful life after she got rid of rat man.

She'd been stupid. She should have *looked* for something exciting or fascinating to do.

Russ touched her arm to stop her moving, then whispered, 'Aaah! I think we're going to be lucky.' He indicated where she should stand, dropped his backpack and got his camera ready.

She stared at the birds. Russ was right about one thing.

The tiny creatures were adorable. They were sitting in a row on the branch next to their nest with a bigger bird, presumably the mother, keeping a watchful eye on them.

They were so small to be venturing out into a big, dangerous world, mere balls of feathers with bright eyes peeping out cautiously. They weren't rushing to start flying.

She was a bit the same about her new life, she realised, sucking in a sudden breath – not rushing into anything. At that moment she began to feel truly glad she'd taken this opportunity to come to England, glad Libby had pushed her into it.

And whether anything came of her friendship with Russ, she was glad she'd met him too.

It had all brought bright new colour into her life.

She continued to watch the birds. If such tiny creatures could face the world and dive out into it, so could she.

Russ raised his camera and began filming, turning a couple of times to catch shots of the emotions playing across his companion's face. 'What were you thinking of just then, Simone?'

She turned to him, clearly forgetting she was being recorded. 'I'm thinking how brave those tiny creatures are. Could you fly out into a world full of giants as they do?'

'I think I could give it a go. Why not?'

Why not, indeed? 'Oh, look!' She gestured towards one little, bright-eyed bird and for a moment didn't speak, just let its fluttering dive off the branch speak for itself. Then she added softly, 'They're beautiful as well as brave. I shall never forget this moment.'

He encouraged her to continue commenting as another little bird nerved itself to fly awkwardly to the ground.

When all the birds had safely flown the nest and were fluttering about practising their flying, he said, 'That was perfect. Come on. There are a couple of other things I want to get shots of before too many humans start intruding on the scene.'

He set off, turning the camera onto the lake, then stopping again at a meadow full of wildflowers, masses of delicate colour, some just opening up. That section had been fenced off with a sign saying, *Please enjoy the flowers but don't trample on them.*

Simone didn't even notice when he turned to film her once more because she was staring at the meadow, clearly entranced. He waited, hoping she'd share her feelings again.

'I didn't know how beautiful wild flowers could be, Russ. There are so many different types here, some of them so tiny.'

'There are too few meadows like this one these days.'

Her expression was radiant. 'This is another sight I shall never forget.'

'It's gorgeous, isn't it?'

She turned back to look at it, whispering, 'So beautiful!' her whole face alight with joy. 'I love flowers anyway, but the mass of these, the colours, their rippling movements in the breeze – it's absolutely stunning.'

When they got home, he took her inside his house and replayed his recording.

She smiled at her own enthusiastic face. 'It lit me up, didn't it, Russ? You were right.'

'It lights me up every time I see something beautiful,' he said simply. 'Which is why I try to share my love of nature. Will you let me use those shots?'

'What? Put me in your programme?'

'Yes. Your joy shines through. It's far better than a commentary could ever be.'

She spread her hands in a helpless gesture. 'If you're sure anyone will want to see me.'

'I think they will. I loved watching your reactions and the camera likes you, too.'

She gave him another glowing smile. 'Well, thank you for sharing it with me.'

'My pleasure. And we'll share a lot more important moments with the people out there before we're done filming this series.'

He put his arms round her and gave her a hug, rocking slightly. 'We're going to make a brilliant team, you and I.' Then he pushed her to arm's length. 'Now, I've been very selfish this morning. Tell me what upset you last night.'

He hated to see the joy fade from her face as she explained about Kit's phone call.

'You've really taken a dislike to this guy's father, haven't you?'

'Yes. I don't trust him. Fern can't stand Lance either. I didn't take to him at all.' She gave an involuntary shudder.

'So what are you going to do about his son? Perhaps you should give him the benefit of the doubt until you've met him.'

'Yes, I've just about decided to invite him and his wife

to come here so that they can ask me about Australia. It's good to help people, don't you think?'

'I do.'

'But what if his father tries to join us? That's what worries me.'

'My advice is to be honest with Kit about his father. Tell him you and Lance didn't get on and he isn't welcome at your house.'

'I can't do that. It'd be so rude.' She broke off and frowned. 'Yes, I can do it and I will. It's my life and my house, after all.'

'That's my girl. Now, I'm absolutely ravenous. Let's go and have breakfast at the hotel, a great big buffet meal. My treat.'

When they got back from the hotel, Russ said he wanted to download his shots and fiddle around with them and she needed to phone Kit, so she went into her own house.

She checked the time and rang the number he'd given her. A voice said, 'Kit Mundy.'

'It's Simone Ramsay here. Sorry I missed your call yesterday. Is this a convenient time to talk or do you want to call me back?'

'Now is fine.'

'I'd be happy to chat to you and your wife about Western Australia. Would you like to come round here?'

'Yes please. Would today suit you? The HR people want me to decide about Australia as quickly as I can, you see, so I'll have no difficulty getting away from work for a couple of hours.'

'I'm free any time. Why don't you contact your wife and get back to me?'

'That'd be good.'

He called back five minutes later. 'How about we pop over to see you around eleven this morning? Mags can take an early lunch break.'

'That's fine. Do you have my address?'

'No. I was about to ask.'

Only when she put down the phone did she realise that she'd forgotten to mention his father. Well, she could do that when she saw them. It would be stretching coincidence too far for Lance to get in touch with his son during the couple of hours or so before Kit came to see her.

But she would tell him then that she didn't want to see his father at any time.

She was annoyed at herself for forgetting to mention that. It was important to her to prove she could stand up for herself.

She hadn't always been good at doing that. Hadn't needed to with her husband.

# Chapter Seventeen

To Simone's dismay, when a car drew up outside her house, three people got out of it: two strangers who were, she assumed, Kit and Mags, and – no, it couldn't be – but it was: Lance!

The look Mags shot at her father-in-law as they got out said that she wasn't pleased to have him there any more than Simone was. He was wearing a bland smile and didn't seem to notice how anyone else was feeling because he was too busy studying Simone.

As she went out reluctantly to greet them, he gave her a sneering smile which seemed to say he'd gained an advantage over her. That added fuel to the anger mounting inside her.

The younger man moved forward, hand outstretched. 'Simone? I'm Kit and this is Mags. I think you know my father already?'

'Pleased to meet you, Kit. Mags.' She looked at Lance,

who moved forward and held out his hand to her.

'Nice to see you. I said we'd meet again, didn't I?'

She ignored his hand and took a step backwards, turning to the younger man. 'I thought you and Mags were coming here on your own today, Kit.'

Lance moved closer. 'Oh, I promise not to take up much space, Simone.'

It was his smug smile that was the final straw. That smile seemed to be declaring that he'd won this round and would win any others.

'You aren't going to take up any space, Lance, because I don't want you in my house at all. We aren't friends and we aren't going to be. Perhaps you could wait for your son over at the hotel?'

Three people gaped at her, then Mags began to smile.

Simone was surprised at herself. Had she really spoken so bluntly? Well, she'd tried polite refusals to spend time with Lance and they hadn't worked, so why not? She still felt the same instinctive distaste at being anywhere near him, so she had to do this to make sure he didn't try to butt into her life and affairs again.

She also wanted to prove to herself that she could act decisively. She'd let people take advantage of her for too long, in big ways and small, for loving reasons and out of timidity. When he didn't move, she added, 'It's only a two-minute walk and they serve good coffee at the hotel.'

His expression thunderous, Lance turned to his son. 'I think we all need to leave if that's how this woman is going to treat me.'

Kit didn't move but threw a panic-stricken look at his wife, and it was Mags who said firmly, 'You can do what you want but I'm not leaving. It's very important to me to find out more about Australia.' She turned her back to him and raised one eyebrow at her hostess. 'Is it all right if I come into your house?'

Simone nodded and gestured to the door with one hand.

As Mags passed her, she whispered, 'I can't stand him either, but my Kit is a dear, not at all like Mr Slimey. You'll like him, I'm sure.'

There was the sound of a man's voice raised in anger, so Simone and Mags stayed where they were to listen.

'Are you going to let that woman treat me so rudely?' Lance demanded.

'I did tell you she hadn't invited you but you insisted she'd be happy to see you. Only you were lying to me again. There's a hidden agenda to this, isn't there? As usual with you, Father.'

'What the hell do you mean by that?'

'My guess is you're sniffing around her in case she gets between you and your supposed inheritance.'

'That's telling him!' Mags nudged Simone and gave her another quick grin.

'Well, you can leave me out of your machinations, Father. I don't need anyone else's money and Henrietta can do what she wants with hers. I'm perfectly happy to earn my own way in the world.'

'Look here! As your father I must insist—'

But Kit had turned away from him and was moving towards the door. The two women moved further inside and he followed them, shutting the door quickly behind him. He looked apologetically at Simone. 'Sorry about that. I didn't realise he was pushing his way in where he wasn't wanted. I should have done. You're not the only one who doesn't enjoy his company.'

He moved towards the nearest window so that he could watch what his father was doing. 'Oh good, he's going across to the hotel.'

'What did he do to upset you, Simone?' Mags asked.

'He kept pestering me to meet him when I'd made it plain that I didn't want to. I don't know why I don't like him, I just don't. He even gate-crashed a family gathering at Fern's so that he could corner me there.'

Mags rolled her eyes. '*She* doesn't get on with him either. She'd never have invited him, I'm sure.'

'She said she hadn't. I did as much as I could to make my feelings plain to him while staying polite but today was the final straw.'

'Politeness doesn't work with him anyway,' Kit said bitterly. 'He only sees what he wants and doesn't mind who he tramples on to get it.' He turned to his wife. 'I hope you like the sound of Australia, Mags darling, because what he did today only makes me all the more eager to go there.'

Simone liked the loving way he spoke to his wife, as well as his open expression. 'Do you want a coffee while we chat?'

'No, thank you. Mags is on an early lunch hour so we have to be quick.'

'Sit down then and ask away. I'll tell you anything you want to know.'

They asked all the usual questions as if it was a colony on the moon. How did you deal with hot weather? What sort of social life was there? Mags wanted to know what the houses were like. She was tired of living in a flat, it seemed, however conveniently situated.

As the conversation continued, Simone could tell that Kit was nothing like his father. Well, the way he smiled lovingly at his wife had told her that right from the beginning and the way he truly listened to what she told him only confirmed it. As for Mags, she was a delightful, lively person with a gurgling laugh. The two of them would probably fit in well in their age group in Western Australia.

Once she felt fairly sure she'd got their measure, Simone offered to introduce them to her daughters and their families in Perth and they eagerly accepted. They were about the same age, she'd guess.

In the end, she asked, 'What makes you hesitate to go to Australia, Mags?'

'The fact that I'd have to give up my job.'

'What do you do?'

'I'm in IT. I know it's supposed to be easy to find jobs in my area, but I really like the project I'm working on at the moment and I get on well with my colleagues.'

She mimed holding her nose because of a bad smell and added, 'Mr Slimey has changed my mind today, though. Now, what I want more than anything is to get away from him and never live anywhere near him again.' She turned to her husband. 'I think you should take the job offer, love. And if we like it, we might even stay there. If we're allowed, that is.'

He let out a happy yell, pulled her towards him and plonked a smacking big kiss on each of her cheeks, then on her lips. 'I'll do all I can to make sure you don't regret it, my darling.'

It was lovely to see them together, Simone thought, and waited quietly for them to turn back to her. Who'd have thought *that man* could have produced such a nice son?

Seething with fury, Lance walked across to the hotel, unable to believe how that ghastly woman had just treated him. Did she know nothing about good manners? Clearly not.

And his son had let her get away with it. If Kit had any family loyalty, he'd have left in support of his father. Well, he was going to regret that, by hell he was! There would be a way to teach him a sharp lesson. There was always a way.

But he'd not regret it as much as *that woman*. She was going to be sorry she'd come to England to try to steal the inheritance that rightfully belonged to Lance.

He smiled at one thing. He'd fooled his son again and been able to come here with them. And his daughter-in-law hadn't been able to prevent it. Not the brightest spark in the fire, Mags. Her company must be employing some real thickos, if they'd promoted a woman like her. Well, fancy promoting a woman anyway. Didn't they have any good men? Political correctness had gone too far, much too far.

He'd been amazed a couple of years ago when Kit turned up with Mags and introduced her as his wife.

He'd said they didn't want a fussy wedding but why the hell had they got married so secretly? She must have pretended to be pregnant. Women still did that, however liberated they claimed to be.

It was letting the side down to bring such a woman into the family. Not only ugly but brought up by a single mother who didn't even have her own house to leave them one day. With his good looks, Kit should have waited and found a woman with money and good family connections to help mend the Pennertons' fortunes. As Lance had told him several times.

Things had to be worse financially at Pennerton House than Henrietta would admit, damn her, or she'd not be planning to hand it over to the National Trust. If she wanted to hand it to anyone, she should hand it to him.

He stood in front of the hotel, scowling at the row of houses with more new homes being built at the far end. It was the longest street and this place was in the middle of nowhere. How the hell was he going to get home? There would be no public transport out here and a taxi would cost a fortune. Unfortunately Lady Luck hadn't been on his side and he was short of money this week. He'd even hit his credit card limit.

He'd have to go and beg for help from Henrietta. She'd told him last time there would be no more money from her and he was to consider that he'd had all his inheritance in advance. Ha! She'd said that before and he'd always managed to charm some more cash out of her. He'd find a way to do it again.

He still had to get home today, though. He wondered if Kit would simply drive past him if he stood near the hotel entrance and pretended to thumb a lift? Surely not? He'd have to try it. He was too old to hitch-hike.

How long would those two spend with *that woman*? He glanced at his watch. He'd have time for a quick drink, surely? After that, he'd have to go and wait near the entrance to the car park to waylay Kit.

He didn't think his son would have the nerve to drive straight past him. Mags might, the hard-faced bitch, but not his soft touch of a son.

He sorted through the change in his pockets. He'd have to limit his drink to a measly half-pint of beer, not his usual tipple. And he had to make it last for half an hour while he flicked through a crumpled newspaper someone had left lying around because there was no one to chat to in the bar at this time of day. The guy behind it was busy stacking up the shelves and hardly looked at him.

After half an hour had passed Lance walked outside again, moving slowly across the nearly empty car park to wait near the exit to the road. Good thing it wasn't a hot day. It was muggy, though. He wiped his forehead. Weather like this always gave him a headache.

So did spending time with his damned daughter-in-law. And he'd have to be polite to her on the way back. That would make the headache worse.

As they drove away from the house after their talk, Mags said suddenly, 'There's your father. I bet he's going to have the cheek to try for a lift back with us. Don't stop for him! Leave him there. For once, let him face the consequences of trying to trick people.'

Kit slowed down at the near end of the car park. 'I can't do that this time. We did bring him here, after all. Why did you even mention our visit to him, Mags?'

'I met him in the car park at work when I nipped down to get my sunglasses.'

'What was he doing there?'

'Who knows? That didn't occur to me till afterwards. I assumed at the time he was going to see someone in the building. There are people coming and going all the time in a ten-storey building. I tried to get away with a quick hello but he was in affable mode and fooled me . . . *again*. He asked if I'd met the long-lost Aussie relative and I said I was going to do that later this morning. You know how information just seems to slip out when you talk to him.'

'Don't I just! I've always been glad he mostly didn't pay me much attention when I was a kid. No wonder Mum left him.'

'How a man like him fathered a son as nice as you, I'll never understand.'

He'd often wondered how he came to have such a father. He gestured to Lance, who was still standing waiting, staring across at them with a near-pleading expression on his face. 'I'll have to give him a lift back.'

'You're too soft-hearted. Don't chat to him. He'll try to worm out what Simone told us. Not that she told us any of her family secrets, but still, it's none of his business. And *don't* tell him we will be agreeing to go to Australia. I want to just vanish. End of.'

'I'm happy to keep quiet. I don't want to speak to him at all.' He set off across the car park, muttering, 'How does he manage to upset so many people?'

'It's his one skill.'

At last! Lance watched Kit's car set off again and come towards him through the hotel car park. They must have been discussing their visit. He'd like to hear how it went.

As he'd expected, when he stuck out his thumb, his son stopped the car.

'Can I get a lift back with you, Kit? I, um, forgot my credit card, so I've no way of getting home again if you don't take me. After all, you did bring me here.'

Mags scowled at him from the front passenger seat, but he ignored her and concentrated on his son. He saw by his change of expression that Kit was going to do it.

'Get in, then.'

'Thank you.'

As they drove along, Lance couldn't resist asking, 'Have a nice time with Mrs Dumbo Down Under, did you?'

'You'd better speak politely about her if you want to stay in this car,' Mags said sharply. 'She's a very nice person. Actually, I'd be happiest if you kept quiet altogether from now on if you want to travel in a car with me. You never have anything positive to say about anything.'

So Lance didn't speak, though only because he desperately needed this lift. Hen-pecked, his son was, which meant he'd do as Mags said if she demanded he chuck his father out of the car.

When they got to his block of flats, Kit still didn't say anything to him.

'Thanks for bringing me back, son. See you soon.' Lance waited for a reply but none came so he sighed and got out. He was tempted to leave the car door open but it would be stupid to anger them further, so he closed it quietly and walked towards the entrance to the building.

He stopped when he was inside and out of their sight. They hadn't set off yet. What were they doing?

He watched them sit talking for a few moments, then drive away again. He could tell they'd been arguing. There was no mistaking the body language, hands waving, heads wagging.

Good. He wished they'd argue themselves out of the marriage altogether.

After Lance got out of their car, Mags and Kit watched him stand, look back at them for a few moments, then turn and walk into the block of flats.

Kit didn't set off immediately. 'You did mean what you said, didn't you, Mags?'

'About what?'

'About us going to Australia.'

'Yes. It's the best way I can think of to get away from *him*.'

'I agree.' He gave her a high five and she slapped his hand then shoved him in the shoulder, so he did the same to her.

'Stop grinning!' she said.

'I can't help it. I really, really want to go to Australia. I've always liked the sound of it, ever since we studied it at school. And with my mother and stepfather living mainly in Spain, there's nothing much to keep me here. Except you.'

He glanced sideways and said quietly, 'There's still time to change your mind if it's too much to ask, though. Your happiness is more important than anything else to me, as I hope you know.'

'I meant it, darling. We might try for a baby while we're there. It'd fit in quite well, don't you think?'

'Brilliant idea! A little girl who looks just like you.'

'Our baby had better not take after its grandfather, though.'

'We won't let him.'

'Or her.'

She laughed and added provocatively, 'Or *them*. You do know that twins run in my family?'

'If they're all like you, I don't mind having triplets.'

She shuddered. 'That'd be a step too far, thank you very much.' Then she smiled at him in that special way she had as she added, 'I do love you, darling.'

# Chapter Eighteen

After her guests had left, Simone sat down to eat some lunch, smiling as she thought about the meeting. Kit and Mags' love for one another had shone out so clearly. She'd really enjoyed helping them. How could Kit be so utterly different from his father?

She felt a small surge of pride at the way she'd refused point-blank to let Lance come into her house. Her friend Libby would be proud of her. She was making progress in one of the main outcomes she wanted from this stay overseas: learning to stand on her own feet and say no, even to people she loved.

Her husband would have thought it very bad manners to treat Lance like that and would have winced at what she'd said. She'd never heard Harvey speak sharply to anyone, whether they deserved it or not. He hadn't been demonstrative in public like Kit, either, but he had been loving in private, as well as steady and dependable, always there when she needed him.

Had he been too protective of her? Yes, maybe. And she'd settled down too easily into a quiet life. Libby had frequently pointed both those facts out to her over the years. But it had been a very pleasant and stress-free way of life. Simone had always asked her what was wrong with that. After all, Harvey hadn't been a control freak, just a very caring person whose home was his castle.

She still missed having someone to love as much as she missed being loved by him. Maybe that was why she'd rushed into a relationship with rat man. She shuddered at the memory. That had been a horrendous mistake and she'd vowed afterwards never even to think of marrying again.

And now? Well, she was definitely attracted to Russ, she admitted to herself, and the more time she spent with him, the more she liked him. He seemed to return her feelings, too. How would it work out with a man like him if she let things go further? He was very different from her late husband and yet she was quite sure he faced the world just as honestly, treating other people just as decently. Two very important qualities, in her opinion.

She'd been thinking about him and the possibilities of a relationship during the night, one of the reasons she'd slept so badly. She'd come to the reluctant conclusion that she shouldn't let herself get too deeply involved. His life was firmly based in England, not only for the small birds and animals which he loved and about which he seemed to be an amazing expert, but for his increasing success as a television presenter, and the good he did by communicating a love of the countryside to other people. Not just the countryside but the often hidden urban wildlife habitats.

The trouble was, her life was just as firmly based in Australia, because no way was she prepared to leave her family for ever to move to the other side of the planet. She might not want to attend school concerts and she definitely wasn't going to do that again. She was even able to smile at that memory now. But she did want to be there with her daughters and grandchildren to celebrate birthdays, Christmases and other happy family events.

So the sensible thing was not to let anything serious get started between her and Russ. He was too nice a person for a mere holiday fling and anyway, she didn't do flings.

Life didn't always give you what you wanted and as you grew older, there were other things to worry about than yourself. Responsibilities. Family ties. Even when your children left home and started their own families, you still felt emotional responsibilities towards them, wanted to stay *attached*, for lack of a better word.

Russ didn't seem to be nearly as close to his family, though he'd helped his half-sister when she needed him. He'd mentioned a brother once or twice but not said much about him, let alone spoken of nephews and nieces.

What's more, with a job like his, Russ would be away from home as much as he'd be there. Another problem for her. You got used to being lonely when your life partner died, but she didn't think she could get used to an on-again, off-again relationship with a man who hopped round the world for a living.

So that was that. She was going to be sensible. Absolutely.

Did that mean she should stop working for Russ?

No, that would be a step too far. She'd loved this morning's outing and apart from needing company and something to occupy her time, she now wanted to learn more about the little animals and birds who shared this part of the planet.

She tidied up the kitchen and went next door to find out whether he needed her that afternoon, fixing a calm expression firmly to her face as she rang his doorbell. Well, she hoped she looked calm.

When she obeyed a yell to come in, Simone found Russ sitting amid utter chaos, eyes on the computer screen. He didn't even stop to say hi, so she went across to see what was so absorbing. He seemed to be editing his takes from their early morning walk.

He pointed to the screen. 'You know, you're very photogenic.'

'Am I? That's nice.' She changed the subject, not wanting to get too personal, frowning as she looked round the office. 'Did you just dump everything when you got back today? And before that?'

'What? Oh.' He followed her gaze. 'I suppose so. I was excited about what I filmed this morning, wanted to see how it had turned out.' He grinned. 'You don't cope well with compliments, do you? You changed the subject when I said you were photogenic, but you *are*, not just slightly but extremely photogenic. Doesn't that please you?'

She shrugged. 'I'm a practical sort of person, not into glamour and – and such frivolities. You asked me to work for you.' She gestured around them. 'I can't do that if there's nowhere for me to work.'

He looked round the room again, seeming surprised to see no other desk in the room. 'Ah. Yes, I see.'

'You need to buy some office furniture as a priority but instead, you've dived into working on the new series. I bet things will just get worse as you grow more absorbed in it, so if you want my help, it really would be better to get things organised *before* you start, Russ.'

He gave her a rueful smile, took his fingers off the computer keyboard and leant back, rolling his shoulders. 'I don't suppose I can pay you to do that as part of your job?'

'I would if I could but only you know what sort of cupboards and desks you'll need long-term. I'm just going to be a temporary employee. When the Dittons come back, I'll go home to Australia. So, you need to buy furniture *you* will be comfortable with.' She gestured around them again. 'This is a big space, so I presume you were expecting to need it all.'

'Yes. I see what you mean. Good thinking. Let's go out and buy some office furniture straight away. If we get it over and done with, I can concentrate on my work again.' He gestured towards the door.

She held her ground. 'Where exactly are we going?'

He froze. 'Ah. I don't know. I thought you did.'

She gave him an incredulous look. 'I'm from Australia!'

'And I'm an idiot.'

'True.' She grinned at him. 'Let's get serious about the basic details before we decide where to go. Do you intend to buy all new stuff, or do you want to look at second-hand office equipment? Or doesn't price matter?' She watched him sag slightly as that sank in.

'Price does matter at the moment, I'm afraid. I'm doing quite well, but payment is often in arrears, as it is for authors of books, especially for the extra sales that sometimes follow a series' first outing. Some of the money is paid only twice yearly.'

That surprised her. 'Then how can you afford to employ me?'

'I can't afford not to if I'm to supply what the TV company is asking for in the time frame they're suggesting. My accident did have some repercussions on that. I've got some cash reserves, because I'm not a spendthrift, but I have to manage them carefully.'

She watched him run one hand through his hair, leaving it ruffled up, and found it hard to resist a sudden urge to smooth it down again.

'With an offer like the one they've made, Simone, I have to show them I can produce work in a timely manner as needed.'

'Then let's find a second-hand furniture shop and get what you need as cheaply as possible. You can always replace it later if it gets on your nerves.'

'I don't know where the nearest place would be.' He snapped his fingers. 'I bet Molly who manages this leisure village will know. She told me to call her if I needed help with anything.'

He phoned the hotel and Molly suggested they pop into her office on their way out.

She was waiting for them and when she found out exactly what they needed, she directed them to a second-hand furniture shop near a village on the outskirts of Marlbury.

Simone enjoyed the drive. She kept being surprised at how many pretty villages there were nearby.

The shop was on a farm and a big signpost directed them to a rambling barn which seemed to have been extended more than once. It had a couple of large sheds nearby and there were several vehicles parked in front of the complex.

They wandered inside and were told where to look for second-hand furniture, then left to get on with it in peace. To their delight, they found two huge desks as well as some really solid old cupboards and chests of drawers at the rear of the huge, echoing space. And the prices were significantly lower than new stuff.

It didn't take them long to find what Russ would need initially.

'I enjoyed that,' Simone said happily as they got back into his car.

He didn't start off straight away. 'You're certainly a demon bargainer, Simone. *And* you charmed that woman into getting the stuff delivered straight away.

Can you really fix the drawer handles on that second chest of drawers?'

'Easy-peasy. Harvey and I didn't have much money when we first married. He taught me how to do up old pieces and to bargain for money off here and there when we were buying. It was fun doing that again.'

'Is there no end to the skills you're producing when I need them?'

She looked at him in surprise. 'I'm not really *skilled* at anything, Russ.'

'You genuinely believe that, don't you?' He pulled her towards him, framed her face with his hands and plonked a kiss on her nose. 'Simone, my love, you're extremely capable, as good an organiser as I've ever met, judging by how quickly you got things sorted out today. Yes and look how easily you nudged me into doing what's necessary before we start working together.'

'Oh well, thanks.'

He studied her for a few moments longer, shaking his head as if baffled. 'You should have more faith in yourself, my girl. Now, let's get home and prepare my studio for the deliveries. I'm sure you'll be equally good at arranging the furniture.'

She could feel herself flushing. 'You'll make me conceited if you go on like this.'

'You're one of the least conceited people I've ever met.'

She tried not to show how much pleasure this compliment had given her and focused on making a mental list of priorities and practical needs as he drove them home.

She was starting to feel more confident, though, she really was. But it was hard to keep her cool when Russ was so close to her in the car or simply standing next to her in his home office.

And that kiss on the nose, a simple friendly gesture, had sent shivers down her spine. She couldn't help reacting to him.

Oh dear!

Russ pulled a pizza out of his freezer around six and they slung it in the oven, then ate it on the run.

When Simone next looked at her watch, it was going on for ten o'clock at night.

It had been hard work but now the furniture was in place and arranged into a pattern in which he would be happy to work, and a lot of his papers and paraphernalia had been sorted out and stowed in permanent 'homes'.

She moved away from him and stretched. 'I need to get some sleep now, O slave driver. I bet I sleep well tonight.' She couldn't hold back a big yawn.

He stood at the door to watch her across to her house and she paused very briefly to wave goodbye, then went inside.

A light was blinking again on the answering machine at one side of the big open-plan kitchen. She went across, wondering who it was, smiling when she realised her elder daughter must have called.

She checked the time and worked out that it'd be early morning in Western Australia. It'd be great to end her day with a chat to Clo and see how the family were.

For that, she could hold out a little longer before she went to bed.

Someone picked up after only two rings. 'Ma! How are things?'

'Brilliant.'

'Oh.'

Clo sounded surprised and even a bit disappointed. Why? Simone wondered. Had she thought her mother wouldn't be able to cope?

'That's, um, good. I was worried you'd be feeling lonely or – or homesick on your own.'

'No, darling. This is a delightful place to live. I've met some of the UK family connections and I've even got myself a temporary job.'

'*A job!* Goodness. What as?'

'General factotum.' She heard the sniff. Clo always sniffed when she didn't approve of something.

'That just means an odd jobs person. There's no need for you to demean yourself like that, Ma. You don't even *need* to work. *You* don't have a mortgage.'

Simone stiffened. She and Harvey had got rid of their mortgage by the time they were forty, because they hadn't built a lavish house and had stayed in it with only the addition of a games room. She still found it perfectly adequate for her needs because they'd updated the kitchen just before he passed away.

Clo, on the other hand, had had to go back to work as soon as she could after each child was born in order to service their huge mortgage.

She couldn't understand why her daughter was being

so negative about her new job. Was she still trying to control her mother's life at this distance?

Simone wondered what had got into Clo lately. In the past month or two her temper had been decidedly edgy, and clearly still was. 'I'm working for a TV producer, actually, helping him organise the practical details of shooting his next nature series. What's demeaning about that? It's going to be fascinating.'

'A TV producer! Oh. Sorry. That's not mundane at all.'

'Is something wrong, darling? You don't sound at all yourself.'

'Well, actually, I wanted to tell you my news. I'm pregnant again.'

'*What?*'

'We were a bit surprised by it and I feel such a fool. I was going to tell you before you left, but you dashed off to England so quickly there wasn't time.'

'You told me after Vicki was born that Bob was going to have the snip. You were both sure you only wanted two kids.'

'He was going to, but we never got round to organising it. He was involved in an important project and we were so busy with me going back to work. Childcare doesn't get the housework or shopping done, does it?'

No, but mothers can help a lot in that, Simone thought. They'd always relied on her too much. She could see that now.

'Well, the truth is we got a bit careless, Ma. It was only one night too, so it's rotten luck that it should turn out like that.'

'Well, congratulations anyway. If you produce another child as gorgeous as Tommy and Vicki, it'll all be worth it in the end. When's it due?'

'Early August. You will be back by then, won't you?'

'Probably. I'm not sure yet.' She wasn't going to tie herself down. Clo had already had two straightforward pregnancies and easy births. It wasn't as if there were likely to be any complications. And anyway, if help was needed, Bob's parents could step in, for once. About time they did a bit more to help.

When she ended the call, Simone stood frowning at it as she remembered the last birth. Clo's husband was a nice guy but Bob didn't pull his weight in the house. Why would he when his mother-in-law always stepped up to the plate to help out in crises? Like Clo bringing the new baby home a couple of days after Vicki's birth. He'd been too busy at work to help with that.

Simone had picked Clo and the baby up from the hospital, then stayed with them for over a week. What with ferrying Tommy to and from nursery, and stocking up the house with food, she'd been exhausted by the time she moved back to her own house and left them to it.

That had all happened only a few months after Harvey's death and she'd been feeling low at times, still crying herself to sleep some nights, trying to hide that from her daughter on top of everything else.

Life had been very different when she'd had her own children. She'd spent one night in the birthing unit at the local hospital then come home, feeling terrified at being responsible for a human life.

Her mother had popped in and out a couple of times to help her, doing the shopping and some of the washing. Apart from that, Simone and Harvey had had to manage on their own. She'd only ever gone back to work part-time.

She felt a bit guilty thinking like this about Clo and Bob, but she felt that looking at everything somewhat differently from this distance was doing her good.

Clo would be fine. She was a normal, healthy young woman and had already proved how easily she bore children.

What Simone needed to do now was figure out where her own future path lay.

# Chapter Nineteen

Henrietta let Elizabeth check that she was strapped into the front passenger seat properly, then make sure her little scooter was equally secure in the back of the big four-wheel drive. As they set off, she settled down to enjoy the outing. It would be lovely to go somewhere new. She'd become a bit of a stay-at-home lately.

Simone greeted them with her lovely smile and Henrietta was interested to walk round the ground floor of what was, to her, a little house and out onto the back patio, where there was a bird table. 'What a clever idea, swapping houses. What are your neighbours like?'

The younger woman pointed to the right. 'The ones to that side are away at the moment. The owner used to be on telly, Cassandra Benn. Have you heard of her?'

'I certainly have and I've watched her many times. She's a very incisive interviewer.'

'Russell lives on that side.'

'How lovely. He's such a nice man. Are those bird tables for him?'

'Yes. Most people like watching birds, don't they? One of my neighbours in Australia has a shrub called a grevillea outside a side window that looks onto a blank wall. It flowers all year round, so she's put a bird bath under the shrub and all sorts of birds come to drink there or feed on the nectar. They get a lot of pleasure watching them instead of staring out at a fence. I've sat and watched with them a few times, too.'

'What a good idea,' said Elizabeth.

'I'd love to chat to him again. He knows so much about wildlife. Do you think he'd have time to join us if we go to the lake?' asked Henrietta.

'He'd be delighted, I'm sure. I know he's in. I'll go and see if he can come with us.'

Henrietta saw Simone look at Elizabeth for confirmation that this was OK, then she nipped next door. It was nice that they cared about her but an annoying part of extreme old age to be guarded all the time.

'It's good to get out occasionally,' she said firmly to Elizabeth. 'I'm going to enjoy today. And if I get tired, too bad.'

'As long as you take it easy.'

She rolled her eyes. 'I'm not stupid. Anyway, that scooter won't let me go mad – it doesn't exactly go fast.'

She turned round as Simone and Russ came in. They made a lovely couple. He was good-looking, not what she called indoor good looks, but an outdoor type, casually dressed.

He was as easy to chat to as the last time and best of all, he didn't talk down to her. Ageism people called it. They had a lot if 'isms' these days. Sheer bad manners was at the root of most of them, she always thought. She hoped the idiots who patronised her would get treated the same way themselves when they grew old. If they did grow old. If someone didn't strangle them first.

Russ seemed happy to accept Simone's invitation to stay to lunch and Henrietta enjoyed watching him tuck into his food. Well, it was a nice spread, healthy and delicious, just the sort of things she liked to eat.

As they finished the little iced fancies that formed the afters, Russ said, 'I saw you had an electric scooter in the back of the car, Henrietta. We could go right round the lake together, if you like. The path is designed for wheelchairs and has been well maintained. I'll probably be able to point out creatures you might not notice otherwise. And if you get tired, I can easily nip home, then drive round by the road and pick you and your scooter up from the car park on the other side of the lake.'

'I'd love to go right round the lake. I don't think it would be too tiring but we'll see how we go.' Henrietta pulled a face. 'I fought against getting that scooter, but it's been a godsend, I must admit. I should be able to manage the whole circuit on it.'

'I'll just get my camera first, if you don't mind. You never know what you'll see. Will you let me film your reactions for my show if we come across anything interesting?'

'Me?' She gaped at him. 'Who'd want to see my wrinkled old face on their screen?'

'Other people who also have wrinkled faces, or who love their own wrinklies.'

What a nice way to put it. He winked at her, so she winked back. She did enjoy being teased by a cheeky young fellow.

'Actually, I got very good comments from viewers about my last series for showing a range of people of different ages reacting to the world around them,' he went on.

'Did you now?' Henrietta was secretly delighted at what he wanted her to do and shot a quick, happy smile at Elizabeth. 'That'd be a first for me, to appear on the box.'

The walk was slow, but no one seemed to mind, because Russ brought so much of what they saw to life by his explanations. By the time they got back, however, Henrietta admitted to being tired.

'But I enjoyed it, so don't try to stop me doing things like that again,' she said pointedly to her secretary.

'As if I could.' Elizabeth turned to their hostess. 'If you don't mind, Simone, I'll take Henrietta home now.'

'You open the car door. I'll help her into it.' Russ scooped her up in his arms. She squeaked and clung to him, laughing. He put her carefully into the passenger seat and laughed back.

'*Voilà!*'

She leant back in the car seat, inclining her head regally. '*Merci beaucoup*, Sir Galahad.'

He swept her a mock bow. '*Un plaisir, madame.* My leg is a lot better now. We must do it again.'

'Yes, please. Actually, you might like to come to my house and have a better look round the parts that I've left completely alone for many years. They're inhabited only by birds and small creatures these days, but maybe you could film some of them for me. The ground is too rough to get my scooter there.'

'I'd love to come and explore properly.'

He went round to the back of the big four-wheel drive, took the little electric scooter from Elizabeth and soon had it safely disassembled and fastened in.

While he was doing that, Simone went across to Henrietta, whose car door was still open. 'Thank you for coming.'

'I enjoyed it. I don't get out very often these days.'

'You're welcome to come here any time. It can get a bit quiet when you don't have a network of friends.'

Henrietta leant forward, glanced sideways to make sure Russ wasn't listening and whispered, 'You've got your neighbour to cheer you up now though. I like that man of yours. You should grab him with both hands and hold on tight.'

'He's not my man in that sense.'

'Rubbish! The way you both look at each other gives the lie to that. Don't waste a chance of affection, Simone. You don't meet too many men you can love in this life. You already made one man happy from the way you speak of your late husband and I think Russ is lonely underneath that smiling exterior – as you are. You'll excuse my frankness, I hope. One of the privileges of old age.'

'I don't mind your frankness at all. But you're still wrong about Russ and me.'

She chuckled. 'I've been watching people for ninety years, my dear. I'm never wrong about that sort of thing. You'll see.'

Elizabeth came round to get into the driving seat, so Simone stepped back, closed the car door carefully and waved them goodbye.

Russ came to stand beside her. 'Thanks for inviting me to join you. She's a feisty old dame, that one. Fun to spend time with and still got all her marbles.'

'And a few extra marbles thrown in, if I'm any judge.'

'Yes, her intelligence shines through, doesn't it? And she's photogenic too. Why don't you come in and have an early sundowner with me, Simone? I'll get no more work done today and you're looking tired now.'

'I'd better not.'

'Oh, and why not?'

'We shouldn't—'

'You can try to hold me at arm's length, but you won't succeed. And today I'm not taking no for an answer.'

He followed up his words by picking her up almost as easily as he had done Henrietta and with his face close to hers, he said, 'She told me to take no nonsense from you, so I'm obeying her orders and sweeping you off your feet.'

'Russ, I—'

But his lips cut off her protests and when the kiss ended, she stopped complaining and let him carry her inside and plonk her down on a chair.

'A glass of wine?'

'Oh, all right.'

She tried to summon up her determination to keep him at arm's length, but it refused to come out of hiding.

She enjoyed his company, the wine was good and the conversation interesting. He explained about the next stages of his work and how he wanted her to help, then she told him about some of the birds who visited her garden in Australia, including several varieties of parrot and cockatoo.

When she set down her empty glass she forced herself to say firmly, 'I really do have to go now.'

'Another glass? With some cheese and biscuits?'

'No, thank you, I have a few things to do.'

'Running away?'

She gave up trying to be polite. 'Yes. And so should you.'

'I enjoy your company, so I'm not running anywhere.' He paused and added, 'I can't stop you leaving. But unless you're taking the coward's way out and resigning, I'll see you tomorrow morning.'

'Why on earth should I want to resign? I enjoy the job.'

She didn't wait for his response but walked out quickly. By the time she closed her own front door behind her she was wishing she'd stayed longer.

She was a fool.

She got herself a snack but the evening seemed to go on for ever and there was nothing worth watching on television.

She really should have accepted his invitation. Who knew where it might have led?

What had happened to all those sensible resolutions she'd made the previous night? They'd vanished, that's what. The main question now was whether she should even try to resist temptation. Henrietta had urged her to give in to it.

But as the slow minutes passed, Simone began to worry about Clo as well as herself and that affected her decision too. Her daughter hadn't sounded as sharply confident as usual. And having an unexpected extra baby would upset their careful budgeting.

She'd help them sometimes with babysitting, of course she would, but she wasn't going to bring the child up for them.

You only got one life and even that could be cut short unexpectedly, as poor Harvey's had been. She needed to do more with the rest of hers before it was too late. Look how much she was enjoying exploring this part of the world.

She'd been right to come here, but this was only temporary. She would have to find something more permanent to focus on long term, something in Australia that didn't separate her from her family.

# Chapter Twenty

Lance was worried. Life had never been so bad financially. Never. He was not only short of money for the basic everyday expenses like food and petrol but he also needed to pay something off his gambling debts if he didn't want some rather nasty people coming after him heavy-handedly.

Given his run of bad luck, there was only the old hag left to turn to. He'd have to see Henrietta soon and beg her for help. If he acted repentant, he ought to be able to coax a little more money out of her. She'd not see him go hungry, surely? Not that he had much of an appetite these days. Which was useful, because he didn't have to waste much money on food.

It would probably be a good tactic to call on Henrietta the first time and just chat nicely about other things before paying her a second visit. That would be the time to mention how bad things were. Yes, that should do it.

The sooner he got started with the first visit the better.

While he was there, he might be able to pocket one of her little silver pieces and pawn it. That would buy him food for a few days at least. She left some quite valuable stuff lying around, he could never understand why. He'd seen her pat pieces absent-mindedly, so they must be her favourites. He'd remembered which they were and would be careful not to take one of those.

She had to pay her maid to polish it all. Was that a ridiculous waste of money or what?

He'd stolen pieces a couple of times over the years, though only when he was desperate, and no one had said a word about them going missing. The trick was to find one that was half hidden behind something else. And not to do it very often. That old maid couldn't be much good at her job if she hadn't noticed the gaps.

He'd quit his last job when he was on a winning streak and hadn't left them happy about his work. Well, he hadn't been happy with their lousy wages, either.

He wouldn't be able to get another job easily without recent references, but who wanted to spend their life selling used cars? Not him! He'd been born into a good family, destined for better things if his parents hadn't spent all their money before dropping dead on him. The main thing he'd inherited from them had been debts that ate up nearly all the money he got from selling their house and possessions.

He hated work, hated the boredom of it most of the time, not to mention the forms you had to fill in so that the government could steal your money by calling it tax.

And as for the idiots you had to be polite to, well,

there weren't just stupid customers to deal with in the car sales business but equally stupid colleagues.

He called round at Pennerton House the following day only to be told that the mistress was out.

'I'll pop in and write my aunt a note, then.'

The elderly maid shook her head. 'Sorry, sir. I have orders not to let anyone into the house while Miss Henrietta is away.'

As Jane started to close the door in his face, anger boiled up in him and he shoved the door backwards as hard as he could, causing the old servant to stumble helplessly back with it. 'I only want to write a damned note!' he yelled.

Upon which she screamed at the top of a very loud voice and lunged for something which turned out to be an alarm bell.

It shrilled out so loudly it hurt his ears, going on and on. He hadn't intended shoving the door to be more than a gesture. He started backing away. 'Sorry. Didn't mean to push so hard. Don't know my own strength sometimes. Tell your mistress I called.'

He saw her pull a walking stick out of the hallstand and brandish it at him, so moved more quickly towards his car. Only he couldn't move all that fast these days. He really ought to get fitter.

By that time a rusty van had come screeching round the corner to join Jane. The grim-faced old gardener got out of it, waving a cricket bat threateningly in Lance's direction.

Damn! As he leant against his car to catch his breath, the old man joined the maid on the stone steps and the two of them stood holding their impromptu weapons at the ready and glaring at Lance.

He got in, started the car and drove off as quickly as he could.

What would Henrietta do next, for heaven's sake? There hadn't been an alarm bell there before, surely? She must be getting senile. Surely she didn't expect burglars to try to break into the house through the front door in broad daylight?

He was angry with himself for giving way to his temper, but honestly, what was a chap without a steady income to do? He was her closest male relative, after all, even if he wasn't called Pennerton. He would be living here if the old bat had died at a reasonable age and treated him as their relationship deserved. Or at least, not living here but living on the proceeds of the sale of the ugly old ruin. You needed bigger money than he had to win really big.

He was *not* going to try to claim social security payments, however broke he was. Those officious types poked into every aspect of your life before they'd give you any money and he wasn't putting up with that.

A lawyer friend said if Henrietta didn't leave him anything, it would be worth having a go at suing the estate for his rightful share of the inheritance by showing he'd been partly dependent on her. That sounded like a long shot to him and Lance wasn't at all sure it would work. From what he'd seen, it was lawyers who got rich on lawsuits not their clients.

His stupid son might say Henrietta was welcome to leave her property to whomever she wanted. Kit had always been too soft to grab an advantage, even if it hit him in the face. And he was so very wrong. It would be bad enough for her to leave it to someone else in the family, but it wouldn't be right to simply give it away to the National Trust.

It could be that Russ Carden also had an eye to benefitting from her will in some way via Simone. Lance wasn't sure how he might do that but he was going to keep his eyes open.

He went into his grotty little flat and scrabbled round for something to eat, cursing as he found that the last few slices of bread had gone mouldy because he'd forgotten to put them in the freezer. And he was nearly out of jam.

He had to dip into his emergency coin jar, then go out to the old-fashioned corner shop and pay for another loaf and a jar of jam.

He bought a scratchcard while he was at it with his last pound. Special offer. Chance to win £5,000. Something to hope for.

He walked slowly back to his flat. He was *not* going to let go of Henrietta and her money, whatever it took to hang in there.

As for that chance comer from Australia, he was onto her tricks. Simone was already ingratiating herself with the old lady, judging by what he'd heard from other members of the family. He'd find a way to come between her and Henrietta.

He set the scratchcard on the mantelpiece next to his lucky Buddha. Never scratch them immediately was his rule. Give yourself some time to dream first.

He'd go round to Henrietta's house the next day and apologise. He'd not scratch those numbers until he got back.

When Henrietta got home she went upstairs into her bedroom-cum-sitting room and put her feet up in the recliner rocker with a happy, tired sigh. She rang the bell for her maid and Jane answered it almost immediately, asking how the visit had gone.

Jane had been with her for years and was as much a friend as an employee. Henrietta could tell that something had upset her so asked straight out, 'Who's been ruffling your feathers?'

'That Lance turned up while you were out.'

'Oh dear! He must be short of money again.'

'Well, I hope you won't give him any this time. He tried to push his way in even though I said you weren't at home. Nearly knocked me over, he did. Said he wanted to write a note to you. Ha! Wanted to pinch another piece of silver, more like. You should have reported those other thefts to the police, you really should.'

'I couldn't do that to a relative. Luckily they weren't pieces I cared about. They were showy rather than valuable. He has no taste. How did you get rid of him today? He can be horribly persistent when he wants something.'

'When he shoved the door open I thought he was going to force his way in and I got nervous, so I rang

the emergency bell. Gavin came straight away and
Lance was quick to drive off. Gavin's twice his size and
he may be nearly eighty but he's still a strong chap. It's
comforting that he keeps an eye on security round the
estate, though there isn't usually much to worry about.'
She paused to think about it, head on one side. 'I don't
think Lance can be eating properly, mind you, he's got
so scrawny these days. He looked like a shrivelled yellow
prune this afternoon.'

'I do wish he'd move away from the district. I worry
what he might do next.'

'Who can tell?' Jane let out a snort of disgust. 'He
apologised, pretending he hadn't meant to push the door
so hard but he nearly knocked me over and that doesn't
happen by chance. Does he think I was born yesterday?'

'He thinks the whole world was born yesterday except
for him. He's rather a stupid little man, really.'

'Very stupid.' Jane blew out another angry breath
then clicked her tongue in annoyance at herself. 'What
am I doing nattering your head off? What did you
want, miss?'

'Could you please bring me a nice pot of green tea?
I'm not hungry because Simone gave us some lovely
food, but I would like something to drink.'

She waited quietly in her big recliner armchair in the
bay window for Jane to return, using the binoculars from
the small table beside her to see what was happening
outside in her beloved grounds.

Elizabeth had left her in peace, knowing she'd want
to think about the outing and her new relative. Her

secretary more than deserved some time to herself anyway. She was a lovely person. How lucky Henrietta was to have such kind people to help her during this last phase of her life.

She wasn't lucky to be related to Lance, though. She had to work out what to do about him. He wasn't going to get any more money out of her but how was she to persuade him she meant that? He only believed what he wanted to.

He must have been gambling again. He'd promised to give it up last time she helped him, but it wouldn't be the first time he'd broken a promise.

Oh well. Things would work out and she'd probably not be here to see the worst of it where he was concerned, thank goodness.

She could feel herself slipping towards a quick nap so let it happen.

# Chapter Twenty-One

The doorbell rang the following day and Jane opened it to see Lance standing there again, this time with a bunch of flowers in his hand.

'These are for you, as an apology for pushing the door too hard yesterday by mistake.'

When he held them out she took a hasty step backwards, her hands going instinctively behind her back. 'No, thank you.'

He breathed deeply and the smile vanished for a few seconds then returned again. He had the most pitiful excuse for a smile she'd ever seen.

'Then I shall give them to Aunt Henrietta.'

'*If* she wants to see you. Wait there and I'll ask her.'

Jane shut the front door quickly before he could try to push his way in and locked it too, before hurrying to find Elizabeth.

'Lance is at the door. He wants to see the mistress. The cheek of it!'

'Oh dear, I wish he hadn't come today. She's still a bit tired after yesterday's outing, though she won't admit it. I'll check with her.'

'I've locked him outside the front door.'

'Good. I'll speak to him in a minute. How about you invite Gavin in for a cup of tea in the kitchen in case we need help removing Lance?'

'Good idea.'

Elizabeth ran lightly up the stairs and found Henrietta using her binoculars to watch what Russ was doing in the little grove at the far edge of the lawn. He'd phoned this morning to ask if it was all right to come today.

She pointed. 'He's moving around very carefully checking the area. No fear of that man hurting or trampling on any of the creatures who live here.'

'That's good. Look, I'm sorry to disturb you but you have a visitor.'

'I thought I heard the doorbell. Who is it?'

'Lance.'

'Oh dear.'

'Shall I tell him you're not well?'

'I'm tempted but I suppose I'd better see him. Don't leave me alone with him, though.'

'I wasn't going to.' She shot a quick glance at her companion. It wasn't like Henrietta to show any weakness and that worried her.

'Give me time to take the lift down to the small sitting room. I've got my favourite pieces of silver in here and I'm not risking him getting near them.'

Elizabeth saw her safely into the room downstairs, then peeped out of a window before she opened the front door.

Lance was walking slowly up and down the path in front of the house, looking aggrieved.

When she opened the door, he turned with one of his false smiles and started back to join her. She was surprised at how slowly he was walking and his clothes looked loose, as if he'd shrunk.

'You can come in, Lance, but only for ten minutes. Henrietta's tired today and I'll send you straight out again if you upset her.' As she was far bigger than he was, she was sure she could handle him if necessary until Gavin came to help her.

Lance came back up the stone steps to the front door and followed her inside, puffing a little as he walked across the hall.

She turned to study him carefully. 'You're not starting a cold, are you? Because if so, you'd better not see Henrietta until you've recovered.'

He stopped when she did. 'Why do you ask that? I wouldn't have come out of the house if I had a cold. You know I have a weak chest.'

'I asked because you're puffing and panting.'

'Going up stairs makes me puff, always has done.'

He'd only come up four steps, for heaven's sake! 'You should get a check-up with your doctor, just in case there's a problem.'

'It's not a check-up I need; it's some financial peace of mind.'

'Not at Henrietta's expense.'

She led the way across the hall, opening the door to the small sitting room. 'Lance is here. I've told him just ten minutes.' She gestured to him to enter.

Henrietta stayed in her chair, watching the usual sickly smile settle on Lance's face as he moved forward, holding out some rather droopy flowers.

'For you.'

She didn't take them. They were a poor bunch and she wouldn't be surprised if he hadn't pinched them from a grave at the cemetery.

'I'll see to those.' Elizabeth dumped them quickly on a side table, gestured to a chair then sat on the one between him and Henrietta.

'I wonder if I could speak to my aunt in private?' he asked her.

'No. I prefer to keep an eye on you.'

Henrietta managed not to smile at the irritation which came and went on his thin features. He looked rather like a plucked, underfed chicken today, but Jane was right. His skin did have a yellowish tinge. She decided to take the initiative. 'If you've come to ask me for money, Lance, I haven't changed my mind. As I thought I'd made clear last time, I'm not giving you any more money – not a single penny.'

'But I don't even have enough to buy food.'

'You should stop gambling your quarterly dividends away, then.' He only had those because his parents had left him a small fund set up with strict rules.

'I don't gamble. I've given that up.'

'And pigs will fly over the moon.'

His smile faded completely. 'Henrietta, I'm your closest male relative. Surely I have a right to a teeny share of the family money? Or will you watch me starve to death?'

She didn't want to watch him at all. Suddenly she'd had enough of him. Today, as she'd watched that shifty expression settle on his face when he began speaking, the one he got when he was telling lies, it had made her feel literally sick. She was too old to put up with it and she wasn't going to.

She spoke slowly and emphatically, 'Unfortunately it's true that you're my closest male relative, Lance, which just shows how weak our family line has become. But that doesn't mean I have to give you money, or even invite you into my home.' She turned to Elizabeth. 'My dear, I don't have the patience to deal with him any longer. Could you please see him out and tell Jane not to let him in again? Never. I get more pleasure from watching the birds and the bees than I get from looking at his miserable face.'

She managed not to chuckle as he let out an indignant yelp of protest at that.

Elizabeth stood up. 'Come along, Lance.'

He hesitated, then let out a long, fake sigh and stood up. 'I'm sure you don't really mean that. I'll come and visit you when you're feeling better, Aunt Henrietta.'

'Didn't I just tell you not to? I *never* want to see you again, Lance. I mean it.'

'But—'

'Go – *away!*'

He was surprised into a genuine glare, then turned towards Elizabeth, who was holding the door to the hall open.

'Make sure he doesn't pinch anything on his way out,' Henrietta added loudly. 'I'll report it to the police if there's any silver missing this time.'

Trying not to smile too obviously at Lance's outraged expression, Elizabeth led the way across the hall. She opened the front door and when he hesitated, put her hand on his back and shoved him through it, making him squeak in shock. She shut and locked it immediately.

When she turned she saw Jane peering at her from the rear of the hall. 'Henrietta just told him she doesn't want to see him again. She actually said "never". He was going to plead with me just now, so I shoved him out.' She raised her clenched fists in a gesture of triumph, a gesture echoed by the maid.

'What did he do to upset her that much?'

'Same as usual, started trying to beg money from her only she's completely lost patience with his lies.'

'About time too. I'll keep him out, don't you worry.'

'Just a minute. There's something that needs throwing away.'

She went into the small sitting room and picked up the bunch of half-dead flowers, holding it out at arm's length.

Jane chuckled as she took it. 'He tried to give these to

me first – in apology for bumping me with the door, he said. I refused to take them.'

'Not his day, is it?'

Lance went home, grimaced and used his teabag for a second time, then ate a slice of yesterday's bread and jam, wishing he'd spent his money on some butter rather than the scratchcard.

He might as well see if he'd won anything on it. Where was the damned thing? Surely he'd put it on the mantelpiece?

He looked round, felt in his pockets and still couldn't find it, growing angrier at himself by the second for such carelessness. Then he noticed a brightly coloured corner of what looked like card sticking out from under his armchair. Aha! It must have blown off the mantelpiece in the draught from a closing door. That was the trouble with living in such a small flat.

Bending, he picked the card up and sat down at the table, pulling a coin out of his pocket. He began scraping half-heartedly at the little square of dull silver coating, then stiffened and sat up straighter. Hello! That was the second £500 he'd uncovered.

He'd never been lucky with scratchcards before, well, he didn't count winning £5 as lucky. Was it possible that this time he was going to win something worthwhile? Excitement rose in him and he waited a few moments before continuing. He always liked to take time to enjoy the bright feeling of hope.

As he scratched again, he blinked in shock and delight

as another £500 icon was revealed. He checked the three icons again, touching each with his fingertip. Yes, he really had won.

He danced awkwardly round the small room and blew a kiss at his fat-bellied, lucky little Buddha, which sat on his mantelpiece smiling at him. 'Thank you, kind sir.' Then he put the card carefully into his inside pocket.

His luck was turning. He could feel it, taste the joy of it. Oh, yeah!

He didn't need to go and grovel to Henrietta again and he could even pay a little something off his major debt. He shuddered with relief at the thought of that. They'd been threatening to hurt him if he didn't start making payments soon.

He'd make sure he had only just over £100 in his pockets when he went to see them, though. It'd be enough to buy him some time and leave him some money to play with.

The following day he made the payment. The bullies thought it should have been more and one man searched his pockets, even though he assured them it was all he had.

'We'll wait a month, no longer, and there had better be another payment by then, and bigger than this.'

'I'll do my best, my very best, I promise you.'

'And in the meantime you aren't allowed to gamble here again, not until you've paid off all your debts.'

'I wasn't going to,' he lied.

On the way home he stopped to bet on a horse instead,

choosing one whose name included the word Buddha in it, but only risking the tenner that he'd hidden in his sock. Mr Clever Dick hadn't found that, had he?

He waited to see the race on the television in the betting shop and to his delight, his horse won at ten to one.

He didn't push his luck by betting again but collected his winnings, a small but nice amount, then drove home.

It all went to show that he really was starting a lucky streak. He could recognise the signs.

To hell with Henrietta. The old hag didn't deserve a relative who fussed over her and took her flowers.

He'd play it very carefully from now on, though, hiding the money he wasn't using and only placing bets on sure things. He chuckled as he folded up the spare notes and hid them. Buddha would look after these for him in his fat belly, had done it many a time before.

# Chapter Twenty-Two

Simone helped Russ with the final details of setting up his office, feeling satisfied with how it had gone. It had taken most of another morning to sort out the rest of his documents, because all the files and notes from the past year had been in a jumble, having been stuffed into various boxes with neither rhyme nor reason as they arrived.

When the last invoice had been placed in its designated folder, he looked at her with that gorgeous rueful smile that made something inside her grow warm.

'Sorry about that mess, Simone. You've been enormously helpful. After the accident I was thinking more about getting better than about dealing with business paperwork. And I was on strong painkillers for a time.'

'Tell that to the tax man not me. You must owe him quite a lot. You'll need to get yourself a good accountant to sort it all out. I can't help you with that because I don't understand the system here in the UK.'

'I've got an accountant already. He's been pressing me for the paperwork for weeks, so you've done me a really huge favour nudging me to sort it all out and be done with it.'

Silence hung between them. Russ hadn't said anything about the previous night's kiss and perversely she wished he would mention it. Hadn't it meant anything to him?

Pride wouldn't let her be the first to raise the subject and she hadn't been able to decide what she would do if he tried to kiss her again today.

Even worse, what would she do if he made no attempt to kiss her?

Dear heaven, she was such a fool, didn't know what she wanted, was torn every which way.

'I wonder if Henrietta would allow me to go and explore more of her grounds this afternoon?' he asked suddenly. 'Do you think she would?'

'Probably. Phone and ask her. Does it include me this time or is it a preliminary scout round?'

'I need to check it all properly as well as working out what to film and where exactly to go to do it. There's parking on some land to one side of her grounds that used to be a public park, according to the map. I'm looking forward to exploring.'

He beamed at some memory and for a moment she could see exactly what he must have looked like as a boy – which made her foolish heart give another little lurch.

'It'll be better if I go on my own until I've got the area all mapped out in my mind. When we go together, we can take the best path to avoid damage. I'm thinking of featuring the grounds in a couple of episodes if Henrietta agrees.'

'That's wonderful. I'm sure she will. She's very proud of it all. Pity there isn't a family member to inherit. I'm dying to watch you filming it.'

'You'll be sick of the sight of that in the end because I want your face in a lot of the shots.'

She shrugged, still unable to understand him wanting to feature her. Even with the new hairstyle bringing out the best in her, she didn't consider herself good-looking. Unless he thought the viewers would relate better to a middle-aged Mrs Ordinary. Yes, that must be it.

After his second visit to the grounds of Pennerton House, Russ went to report his findings to its owner before he set off for home. He was absolutely thrilled at the flourishing habitat he'd found in the wild section of the grounds.

'I hoped it'd grow like mad if I left it in peace,' Henrietta said. 'Mother Nature can be very clever if you let her get on with things in her own way. They call it wilding, if I remember correctly.'

'I agree. May I come back again tomorrow, or will that be too soon?'

'Of course not. You're welcome any time. Will you be bringing Simone?'

'She'll be joining me in the afternoon. I want her to do some shopping for me first because I'd like to continue filming in your grounds for a while, if you don't mind, and I don't want to wait even a day for anything to be delivered.'

He looked at her earnestly. 'Your grounds will provide enough material for a couple of episodes, just on their own – with your permission of course. And I'd like to use your face in a few scenes.'

She beamed at him. 'Oh, yes! That'll be so exciting. We'll look forward to seeing you both and giving you tea after you've finished your work here tomorrow, then.'

'I'll look forward to that and I know Simone will.'

'She's a very nice young woman,' Henrietta said.

'Yes, she is.'

He smiled as he left the house. To Henrietta he and Simone were both young. To themselves they were what? Middle-aged? No. He smiled as he remembered a friend who always said middle-aged was ten years older than their actual age – and old age kept moving even further ahead as the years passed.

At this rate people would never admit to growing old. Well, Henrietta was a wonderful role model for that. She hadn't grown old where it mattered most, in her head, had she?

He chuckled. He wanted to be just like her when he 'grew up'. If he ever did. An increasing number of oldies didn't totter around looking 'elderly' – horrible word! They dived into every activity they could and refused to pay any attention to their years unless it was forced upon them. Why, Simone's parents were caravanning round Australia. Good for them.

Elizabeth kept watch on Henrietta surreptitiously. The older woman had been rather quiet for the rest of the afternoon, sometimes staring into the distance, at other times scribbling in her little notebook, as she did when making plans.

It was good that Russ had called in to report his latest findings. That had cheered her up.

Henrietta went to bed early without confiding in her companion about what was keeping her so thoughtful.

Feeling worried about her, Elizabeth crept to the doorway of the old lady's bedroom a couple of times during the night to check that she was all right.

The second time, Henrietta said in a low voice, 'I'm not ill, dear, just having a quiet think. I'm going to change my will, you see, and leave Lance out of it entirely. Not that I'd left him much anyway. He's had most of his inheritance over the years.'

'I'm delighted to hear that. He doesn't deserve another penny after stealing from you! You're sure you're feeling all right?'

'Yes, of course. I'm just sad. Anybody would be to be related to that awful creature. The older he gets, the nastier he seems to become. His character shows in his twisted face, don't you think?'

'Yes, definitely. *Ugly soul, ugly face*, my grandma always said. She used to point out people who had lumpy faces but weren't ugly, which she said was because they had nice souls. And then she'd tell me always to wear a friendly expression because that did far more for a woman than putting claggy stuff on her face. Still makes me smile and think of her when I see women covered in greasy make-up.'

'She was right. And you have a lovely friendly expression, which I very much appreciate. Now, go to bed and stay there this time. I'm perfectly all right, Elizabeth, truly I am.'

The younger woman smiled as she returned to her own bedroom. Henrietta enjoyed revamping her will and used a semi-retired lawyer about ten years younger than herself, whose visits didn't cost nearly as much as they should have done and who spent half his time laughing and chatting. No, dear Henrietta couldn't be feeling too bad if she was about to work on her will again.

Thank goodness!

Elizabeth hoped Henrietta would live to be over a hundred, as one of her ancestors had done. She would miss her greatly when she died because Henrietta had been more like a second mother to her than an employer.

Lance was a dreadful creature but the rest of the Pennerton family were pretty decent folk. The ones living nearby visited regularly or invited Henrietta to visit them.

That distant cousin from Australia also seemed pleasant, as well as pretty. The nature-loving chap seemed to think so too. Nice to have someone living next door to you who was charming and quite a hunk. Elizabeth had enjoyed watching Russ's programmes with Henrietta. She did hope he and Simone would get together permanently. They seemed so well suited.

Elizabeth judged people partly by the company they kept and that way of judging had rarely let her down. It suddenly occurred to her that she couldn't remember ever meeting any friends of Lance. Did he have any? His marriage certainly hadn't lasted long and even his son seemed to avoid him as much as possible.

Why didn't Lance turn to Kit when he needed money?

Maybe he'd already tried and been turned down. Probably had, in fact.

Oh, it was all too much at this hour of the night. She snuggled down and started playing number games in her head, which always helped her relax into sleep. Sometimes it took longer than others, though.

When Russ got back to the leisure village he found that Simone had made him a meal.

He eyed it with longing, breathing in the wonderful smells. 'That's above and beyond the call of duty. I shouldn't take advantage of you.'

'It's only a chicken casserole, easy enough to sling together.'

'Twist my arm.'

She pretended to do that, growing suddenly breathless and pulling away to say hastily, 'Let's eat.'

He ate two huge helpings. 'Am I being greedy? It's delicious and I think I forgot to get any lunch.' He frowned as he tried to remember, then nodded. 'Yes, I did forget.'

He hardly stopped talking until he suddenly began to nod off, then jerk awake. It was the result of fresh air and excitement, she thought, watching him fondly.

After a few minutes he closed his eyes and didn't jerk awake, so she shook him gently. 'I think you need to do your sleeping in bed, Russ.'

'What? Oh, sorry. There's nothing like a day in the fresh air for putting a person to sleep, is there?' He hesitated at the door. 'May I kiss you goodnight?'

She nodded, then got angry at herself for such a feeble

response and reached out for him at the same time as he reached out for her.

The result was a very satisfactory encounter that left her smiling as she watched him saunter across the lawn to his home and turn to wave at her from the doorway.

She needn't have worried. He'd definitely wanted to kiss her again. And this time it had been even better.

It was too late to keep her distance from him. She was, she guessed, about to find out what it was like to have a holiday love affair.

Nice start to it. She couldn't resist following up.

She wouldn't think about the inevitability of it ending when she went back to Australia. That would be months away.

When she woke in the morning, Russ's car had gone but a shopping list had been pushed through her letter box and was signed by a smiley face blowing a trail of Xs across the page.

Not as good as real kisses, but still, a nice touch.

A PS said she should join him that afternoon and Henrietta had invited them to tea. Four o'clock at Pennerton House be OK?

Nodding, she beamed at the piece of paper and was foolish enough to plant a kiss on it.


By this time Russ knew his way well enough through the little wood to creep quietly through the pre-dawn greyness to a good hiding place for watching this miniature world come to life as the sun rose properly. He kept very still, camera at the ready and thoroughly enjoyed studying and filming the creatures who lived in the wild garden as they woke up. He was, he knew, picking up some delightful intimate shots of all sorts of animals, birds and insects for his new series.

As the garden settled down after the dawn chorus and first round of activities subsided a little, he found himself a comfortable spot in the shade and lay down, pulling the brim of his hat down to cover his eyes. He could feel himself falling easily asleep as he had so many times before. There was nothing like a quick nap for reviving you after a period of intense concentration and he knew he'd wake up naturally in about fifteen minutes.

As he started to wake up he heard the sound of a twig snapping and half opened his eyes under the brim of his hat, jerking fully alert as he saw a figure creeping slowly towards him with a big stick raised as if to thump him. Lance!

He lay still, trying not to betray that he was awake as he hastily looked for a way to escape. But he'd chosen a cosy spot between a huge tree trunk on one side and a fallen log on the other, and that prevented him from simply rolling aside. All he could do was grab his backpack as he started to get to his feet, hoping to deflect any blows with it.

But before he put that plan into operation, two burly men surged out of the greenery and grabbed his would-be assailant. They were holding Lance, who was struggling feebly.

He had no idea why that nasty little fellow would be attacking him when they'd barely met. Who were the two men? They weren't with Lance. In fact, one of them was holding him with one arm behind his back to prevent him from getting away, and doing it without too much difficulty.

The other man came across to Russ and offered his hand to help him up. He braced himself to fight in case this was a sneaky way of attacking him.

But no. The man pulled him to his feet, let go and stepped back, jerking his head in Lance's direction. 'What does that sod have against you?'

'I have no idea. I hardly know him – unless he's using me to get to the owner of the big house, who is a distant relative of his and who's helping me with this project. Maybe he thinks I'm after something from her. Who knows?'

The man turned to stare at Lance and added, 'Or perhaps he's simply run mad.'

'That sounds more like it. There's no reason whatsoever for him to attack me.'

He scowled across at Lance who had stopped struggling now and was demanding to be let go in a faint, wobbly voice.

Russ said loudly, 'If he tried to attack me again, I'd make him sorry.'

'You'll have to join the queue waiting to sort him out. There are a few people angry at that worm and my boss is at the head of the line.'

The man turned and walked back across the clearing, feigning a sudden punch at Lance. He didn't touch him but Lance collapsed like a punctured balloon and would have fallen if his captor hadn't kept a firm hold on one arm until he was steady then said, 'Listen carefully to what he says, you.'

The man who'd helped Russ stayed in front of Lance, jabbing a finger towards him to emphasise his words, but not actually touching him, let alone trying to hurt him.

'My employer has decided that £100 wasn't nearly enough for a first payment, given how much you owe him. He wants you to pay some more off within the week, Mr Lancelot Bloody Mundy. We've been keeping an eye on you for him. What the hell are you doing here? There isn't a magic money tree in these woods, you know.'

When there was no response to this, his companion said, 'When exactly can our boss expect another payment?'

But Lance didn't answer, couldn't because his face had suddenly frozen into a twisted gargoyle and he was sagging like a rag doll.

Russ called urgently, 'There's something wrong with him. Let him go.'

The man did as he asked and Lance crumpled, not attempting to break his fall and not moving after he hit the ground.

The one who'd been holding him looked down in puzzlement. 'Is he faking it?'

His companion bent over the still figure. 'No!'

'What's wrong?'

'He's just dropped dead on us, that's what.'

'Oh, hell! He can't have done. You didn't touch him.'

The crouching man laid two fingertips on Lance's neck where a pulse should be. 'He's definitely not breathing and he has no pulse.'

Russ moved across to join them. 'Are you sure of that?'

'See for yourself.'

He couldn't feel a pulse either. 'We need to start resuscitation efforts.'

'I don't know how,' one said.

'Me neither. Do you?'

When Russ nodded, they stepped back, gesturing to him to take over.

He put Lance's body into the correct position and tried to get his heart started. But there was something about the limpness of the body and the total lack of any sort of response that made him give up after a short time.

'I don't think he can be revived. He must have had a massive heart attack. Haven't you called for an ambulance yet?'

They shook their heads. 'We thought you were dealing with him.'

'I can't rouse him.'

The two strangers both looked down in puzzlement and one said slowly, 'We didn't do anything except hold him. Wasn't even hard to do that. He couldn't have fought his way out of a paper bag, that little wimp couldn't.'

Before Russ could decide what to do next, Gavin stepped out from behind some bushes and joined them, spreading his hands wide in a common gesture of non-aggression.

'I've been watching what was going on. Are you sure he's dead?'

'Very sure. I can't get the slightest sign of life out of him.'

The two men glanced at each other and turned as if to leave.

Russ yelled, 'Stop!'

They hesitated, looking over their shoulders at him.

'It'll be easier if we all deal with this honestly than if you try to get away. I don't know what you intended to do with Lance, but I doubt it was to kill him and I could see that you didn't hit him. I'm not going to lie to the police, though. I shall tell them you were here. I can describe you two and mention gambling debts and they'll come looking for you.'

'Give us a break. We didn't do anything. There's no need for us to be involved.'

'You *are* involved. I know you didn't do anything and I just said I'll be able to testify to that. I also know that he's not been looking well for a while, according to his family.'

One of the men sighed and shrugged, then came back. He gestured to Russ. 'I'd rather *you* called the police and ambulance, if you don't mind. The police are not my favourite people.'

Russ pulled out his phone and dialled 999, explaining the situation. 'They're on their way.'

Gavin stared down at Lance. 'I watched you carefully as you tried to resuscitate him but there was never the slightest sign of a response, was there? At least the poor sod went quickly.'

Then he looked at the strangers. 'One of you go to the main road by the same route you came into our grounds and show the police and paramedics the way when they get here. Tell them it's a nature reserve and they're to stick to the path and not to trample on anything.'

'Who are you to tell us what to do?'

'I'm the official security guard on this estate, that's who.' He flashed an ID card at them. 'And I'm your best friend if you want to stay on the right side of the law about this incident.'

Russ saw the moment when they gave in completely. Wise of them. They hadn't done anything wrong, after all. Trying to collect debts wasn't against the law. But he wondered what Henrietta was going to say to all this. Would she be relieved to be rid of a nuisance? Or sad that a younger relative had died so suddenly? Both perhaps.

On that thought he rang the house and explained to Elizabeth what had happened, asking her to tell Henrietta and reminding her that Simone was supposed to join them all later. They should probably let her know not to come now. He'd bring her up to date on what had happened later.

Then he waited with the other guys, fretting to lose such good filming weather until he saw a shiny black beetle busy foraging among some leaf litter and started to film that.

Around them the day grew brighter and warmer now the sun was fully up – a perfect day. It seemed particularly sad that a man should have died so abruptly when all around them nature was providing an ongoing chorus of abundant, joyful life.

## Chapter Twenty-Three

When Russ eventually got back to the big house, the two women were waiting for him.

'We phoned Simone to tell her not to come and why,' Elizabeth said.

Henrietta looked at him. 'Tell us exactly how it happened, please. Every detail.'

So Russ went over it all again, ending, 'I did try to revive Lance, I promise you, but he never showed the slightest sign of responding.'

She patted his hand. 'I'm sure you did your best. Lance has been looking ill for a while. I've wondered about him. It may sound fanciful to a young man like you but you'll learn as you get older and see it a few times – some people get a faded, almost translucent look around the eyes when they're approaching death, a natural progression towards death, I mean. I've seen it many a time in the very old. Lance has had that look for some time even though he wasn't all that old. It was one of the several reasons I didn't prosecute him the last time he stole one of my silver pieces.'

She sighed and stared down for a while, then looked across at Russ. 'I'm being very remiss as a hostess. Would you like something to eat or drink?'

'Not really, thank you. I'd like to go and explain it properly to Simone, if you don't mind. And be honest, I'm sure you'd rather not be entertaining guests at present.'

'You're right. I have to call Lance's son and tell him. Sadly, I don't think he'll be desperately upset.' She paused then added as if thinking aloud, 'It always seems worse when a death doesn't upset the closest relatives.'

'It must have been hard for Kit having a father like that.'

'It certainly was. There's never been much love lost between the two of them. Well, Lance was more absent than present as far as his son was concerned, even before he and his wife split up, and he barely kept in touch afterwards, either. Gambling was always his first love.'

After another sigh, she added almost as if speaking to herself, 'I did wonder if Lance really was Kit's father. There isn't the slightest resemblance between them, you know. Which would mean that Kit wasn't really related to me. Not that it matters either way. I like him – and his wife. Young couples who are happy together give us all hope for the future, don't you think?'

'Yes, I do.'

She fell silent and Russ waited until she looked across at him again to take his leave, holding her hand in both of his for a moment, then patting it and moving away.

As he was going he saw her pick up the phone, take a deep breath and prepare to do her duty.

Kit answered his phone straight away.

He listened to Henrietta and gasped, 'No! I can't believe it!' loudly when she told him the news. His workmates looked across at him with concerned expressions.

'Who should I contact?'

'The local police gave me a number.' She read it out to him.

He thanked her and ended the call, then phoned his wife. 'It seems my father dropped dead this morning.'

'What?'

'I have to go and identify the body, do the paperwork.'

Mags was startled at the news. 'Do you want me to come to the police station with you, love?'

He shook his head automatically, remembered she couldn't see him and said, 'No. I'll do this. But if you could come home again and be waiting for me, I'd be grateful for your support.'

'I'll do that, darling.'

Kit was home later than he'd expected, having had to go through the various tedious formalities prescribed by officialdom.

The officers spoke to him in hushed voices and acted as if he was deeply upset, only he wasn't. When he made the mistake of telling them that, they looked at him as if he were a monster. Sometimes you couldn't win.

Once he got home, Mags came running to meet him at the door. He gave her a big hug, rocking to and fro for a few moments, breathing in her perfume, thankful for her mere existence. When he pulled away he asked for a drink. 'I need to brace myself before I call Mum.'

'Oh my, yes. She won't be upset either but she'll go on and on about it.'

'She'll expect me to arrange a fancy funeral with all the trimmings, but I'm not doing that.' He looked at her sideways and said, 'After they've established the cause of death, I'll get the funeral company to take care of the body without any fuss or ceremony whatsoever. I'm not going to be a hypocrite about how I feel, not even now. Anyway, he always refused point-blank to talk about his wishes concerning a funeral, said it'd be a long time before that was needed.' He grimaced. 'Once she realises she'll have to arrange and pay for the funeral if she wants it done in style, Mum will stop complaining. She wouldn't want to waste her money on him either.'

'No one's going to miss him, are they?'

'No. No one that I can think of, anyway.'

'That's sad.'

'It's his own fault. He was a horrible man.'

She gave his cheek a quick kiss. 'We'll be the ones who have to clear out his flat, then, I suppose.'

'I'm not even thinking of that yet.' He went over to get a bottle of chardonnay out of the fridge, ignoring her disapproving look. 'I'm not going to get drunk, love, just take the edge off things. And let's order a takeaway tonight. It's my turn to cook, but I can't be bothered and I bet you can't either.'

'Good idea. Indian?'

'Yes. A nice hot curry to take away the bad taste in my mouth.'

After she'd ordered it, Kit said suddenly, 'I'm going to ask Fern to clear out the flat. I can't face doing it, just can't. She'll let the rest of the family know what's happened, too. She's good at stuff like that.'

He picked up the phone, saying grimly, 'And if she won't do it, I'll pay a junk dealer to go and clear it out. I am *not* going near his place.'

With a firm, satisfied nod at a difficult decision taken and admitted aloud, he called Fern and by the time that conversation ended, the food had been delivered.

When Russ got back to the leisure village, Simone came to her door and beckoned to him. 'You poor thing! What a terrible day! Come into my house. I can feed you if you're hungry.'

'I'm not hungry, but I'd really welcome some company. It upset me to see someone die right at my feet.'

'It's so horribly final, isn't it?'

'Mmm. Oh, sorry. I didn't mean to stir up bad memories for you.'

'It's all right. My husband passed away four years ago and I'm used to it now. And he didn't drop dead at my feet.'

Russ followed her inside and she put her arms round him because it felt to be the right thing to do. He held onto her for a few moments in silence, as if she'd guessed correctly and he welcomed the warmth and comfort of her embrace.

She pulled her head back to look at him but didn't move away. 'Was it very bad?'

'It was brutally sudden. Shocked us all, even the two thugs who were quite literally chasing him for payment of a gambling debt. Why he was trying to attack me I haven't a clue. But I hardly knew Lance, so I don't have a burden of personal sadness to carry, just general regret about anyone's death in such circumstances.'

'How did Henrietta take it?'

'Quietly. She must have experienced a lot of deaths in her long life, in her job as well as in her family and friends. I think she was more accepting of Lance's passing than anyone, had guessed he was growing weaker. Even she didn't like him. Did anyone?'

'I doubt it. How sad to be so alone emotionally. Now, would you like a drink?'

'Yes, please.' He plonked a kiss on her forehead. 'I'm glad I'm not alone emotionally at the moment and I hope that will continue.'

She didn't know what to say, managed a tentative smile and poured him a glass of wine. She had one herself as well, sipping it and watching him stare down into his glass for a while before taking a gulp.

When he'd finished, she asked quietly, 'Do you want to go up to the hotel for a meal or shall I put something simple together for us, like an omelette?'

He stood thinking. 'Will you think me heartless if I say that I'd like to be among people tonight not shut away quietly? But I still want to be with you, that most of all.'

'You're not the heartless type so I doubt I'd ever think it of you. We can stroll across there together after you've freshened up a bit. I'll give them a ring and book a table.'

He looked down at himself in faint surprise. 'Goodness, I am badly crumpled, aren't I? Comes of lying and crouching in the undergrowth photographing creatures, then kneeling down trying to resuscitate Lance. I won't be long.'

At the hotel he was quiet until she got him talking about what he had seen at dawn, and what he'd like to do tomorrow.

She almost invited him to spend the night with her, but something made her hold back. She might be starting to care about him, but she was trying not to care too deeply.

He looked at her as if he was thinking the same thing, but in the end they each went into their own house.

She'd expected to have a wakeful night, but although she did rouse a couple of times, she slept fairly well. She had grown used to the day-night schedule here now, and had always been a sound sleeper.

As she snuggled down, she wished she'd asked Russ to stay with her.

What a pity his life was as closely tied to England as hers was to Australia. Fate was sometimes very unkind. And to make matters worse, he hadn't even had a good experience in Australia, wasn't eager to go back there.

# Chapter Twenty-Four

When Simone picked up the phone early the following morning, it was Fern calling.

'Kit told me about his father's death and he's asked me if I'd go and clear out Lance's flat. He doesn't think there will be much to get rid of, because it's a furnished place. Could I ask you – would you mind coming to help me go through the contents? I don't like the idea of doing it on my own and I know my daughter won't come. She's paranoid about picking up infections since she's had the baby, and Lance has never been famous for his sparkling cleanliness.'

Simone didn't hesitate. 'Of course I'll help you. Um, I'm just being nosey, but why can't Kit do it?'

'He says he isn't going near the place whether I clear it out or not. As far as he's concerned we can throw all his father's possessions into a skip and he'll pay to have it all taken away. Only, he knows I help out at a couple of charities, so he wondered whether some of the stuff might be sellable by them. I hate to waste anything.'

'So poor old you got lumbered with doing this.'

'I seem to be the one who does all the awkward jobs in this family. I took over that role from Henrietta gradually and it was a while before I fully realised what I was letting myself in for.'

'There's always some mother figure in a family, isn't there, the one who organises gatherings and keeps people in touch – and clears up dead men's flats?'

She chuckled. 'Yes. Mama Idiot is *moi*. Kit knows I can be trusted to do a thorough job of it. The other thing I'm going for is to check whether there are any family documents among his father's stuff. Henrietta has been the custodian of the family collection of such memorabilia, and she has some really wonderful old photos and mementoes, dating right back to the 1860s and the early days of photography. She's already informed me she'll be passing the originals on to me when she dies but Elizabeth has made digital copies for everyone else to make sure we don't lose such treasures. You can get a set from her if you're interested.'

'I'd love that. It's kind of you to do it.'

Fern chuckled. 'Henrietta didn't *ask* me to take over the collection after she died, she simply told me I was the one.'

Simone could tell from the tone of the other woman's voice that she was secretly pleased about taking on this role but didn't comment on that, saying merely, 'I'm a bit the same way myself about not wasting things, Fern. Comes of being short of money when I was first married.'

'Yes. We were broke too. It teaches you a lot, doesn't it?'

'Yes. What about the funeral? Will you have to organise that as well?'

'No, thank goodness. Lance left no instructions and Kit isn't going to hold a public ceremony because everyone in the family disliked Lance, who changed steadily for the worse as he grew older. Kit doubts anyone but me would attend. He has to wait until after the autopsy to get the body back anyway, because his father hadn't been seeing a doctor regularly. When he does get permission to take away the body, a funeral company will deal with it.'

After a few seconds' pause, she went on, 'Actually, there's another reason I asked you to come with me. I don't want to go to his flat on my own because Lance was such a creep and I'm sure the place will give me the shivers.'

'Have you never been there?'

'I doubt anyone but Kit has.'

Simone grimaced at her reflection in the mirror as she listened. She too felt Lance had been creepy. But she couldn't refuse this plea from Fern, who had been so kind and welcoming to her. 'I'll come with you, happy to help, but I'll have to let Russ know that I won't be around for a few hours, because I'm working for him now. I don't think he'll be planning to do any photographing today. He's more upset by what happened than he admits and he'll probably welcome some quiet time on his own.'

She could hear the amusement in her own voice as she added, 'I should think he'll calm himself down by keeping company with some animal or other down by the lake.

Hold on a minute. I'll just nip next door and tell him.'

She took the phone with her and Fern couldn't help overhearing the brief conversation with Russ who was indeed intending to relax today.

'Did you hear that?' Simone asked.

'Yes. Thanks a lot. I'm very relieved not to be going on my own. I'll pick you up in about half an hour. You're on my way so we don't need to waste petrol on two cars.'

When Fern's car drew up outside Simone was ready, dressed for practicality and protection in an old pair of well-worn jeans and a faded top. She looked down at herself and wondered what people did when they had dirty jobs to do and had only jeans with big holes in them. That was such a weird fashion.

At the flat, Fern hesitated for a moment then unlocked the door. Neither of them made a move to go inside until she pushed it open and said, 'We're being silly. Let's just get it done.'

But as they walked into the flat, they both gasped in shock and stopped dead because someone had been there before them and the place had been ransacked.

'Oh, hell! What next?' Fern dragged back the curtains and they walked slowly round the living room with its tiny kitchen at one end and a separate single bedroom. 'Don't touch anything.'

Everywhere was in chaos, with clothes, books, scattered slices of bread and pages of newspapers tossed around any old how.

'What do you suppose they were looking for? They even emptied out the bread, for heaven's sake.'

'Who knows? But I bet they didn't find anything of value,' Fern said.

'What should we do?'

'Call the police. I don't want anyone getting away with breaking and entering.'

'Why do you think they did it? I mean, this block of flats is clearly at the lower end of the market. What could they expect to find here that was worth their trouble?'

'Anything of value would be welcome, I suppose. Lance owed a lot of money, all the family are well aware of that,' Fern said. 'And two men were apparently chasing him for a debt when he dropped dead, literally chasing him. I'll phone Kit and let him know about this after I've called the police.'

The police didn't seem at all interested but said grudgingly that an officer would be there within a couple of hours and not to touch anything in the meantime.

Kit didn't think it worth joining them. 'What's the point? I don't know what he owned.'

'Well, I still want to see if I can find any family photos,' Fern said after she'd ended the call to him. She reached up to put her shoulder bag out of the way on the high, old-fashioned mantelpiece and knocked off a garish Buddha statue, which smashed to pieces on the hearth.

'Damn!'

Then she looked at it and exchanged glances with Simone. 'Is that what I think it is?'

They both bent over the mess and Fern reached out to

scrape the top fragments out of the way then held up a roll of banknotes tightly wrapped in a plastic bag.

'This must be where he hid his cash,' Fern said. 'Well, well. At least the burglar didn't find it.'

She glanced at Simone. 'If you agree, I'm not going to say anything to the police about this. I can just give the money to Kit. Who knows how long it'd be before he got it if they took it away as evidence?'

Simone shrugged. 'Seems reasonable. He must be the heir, after all. There's no one else. I'm assuming there's no will.'

Fern rolled her eyes scornfully. 'Oh, we can safely assume that.'

After hunting high and low, they found a folder taped underneath the lowest drawer in the kitchen.

'How on earth did you know to look there?' Simone marvelled.

Fern grinned. 'A lifetime of addiction to whodunnit books and films. Miss Marple has shared everything she knows with me, for a start. We'll look through these documents after the police have gone. For now I'll put them in my car. We won't sweep up the broken bits of Buddha, though, just stir them about a bit so the hiding place doesn't show. I don't think the police will look twice at them.'

Two constables turned up half an hour later and gave the place a cursory looking over.

'There doesn't seem to be anything of value,' one said apologetically. 'We can put this on record but do you really want us to freeze his, um, assets?' Clearly the officer didn't think it worth bothering.

'No. You're right. He hasn't got any real assets, was always trying to cadge money off his relatives. Most of this stuff just needs throwing away. Or giving to charity. I can do that, if it's OK with you?'

'Very OK. The police are overloaded with serious cases, as you may have read in the papers. And there's no harm been done to any person in this crime either, is there? So that gives it an even lower priority. I'll have to check with my sergeant but if he approves, you can clear everything out.'

The officer went outside and made a call, then she came back to tell them it would be fine to clear the flat.

Since it had been rented furnished and Lance didn't seem to have had many possessions, there wasn't much to deal with and it only took the two women a couple of hours. They threw most of his stuff into the big rubbish skip behind the flats, including a linen basket full of dirty clothes. They were left with only two plastic bags of sellable bits and pieces for the charity shops. He hadn't even had much crockery.

Fern called Kit to ask if he wanted to run a final check on the flat and he again denied any interest whatsoever in visiting it.

'We've found a couple of things you might like to keep. Are you at home? Good. We'll bring them round straight away.'

'I can't imagine there's anything worth keeping.'

'Trust me, you'll be glad we came.'

'Oh, very well. I'll put the kettle on. Mags and I have both spent the day at home planning what we'll take with us to Australia. My boss is delighted I've accepted the posting and wants me to leave as quickly as I can because someone's fallen seriously ill in the middle of a project. It's a subject I know quite a bit about, so I know I can deal with the interviews for gathering the necessary information. We're both grateful to Simone for talking to us about Australia.'

On the way home, the two women stopped for a late lunch in a small café Fern knew, then they went on to see Kit.

He stared at the money in shock. 'My father had over four thousand pounds stashed away? *My father!* He must only just have won it, then. He couldn't have kept that much money in his pocket for more than a few days, if that.'

'I suppose so. Anyway, it belongs to you now. Enjoy. Will you have to give your mother a share?'

'No. Her second husband is loaded. She'd tell me to blow the money on a fancy meal. I shan't waste it like that, though. It can go into our long-term mortgage fund, instead.' He chuckled. 'That'd have really upset him.'

'I don't think you should tell anyone about it, then, not even your family. Whoever ransacked your father's flat was looking for something and that could be it.'

'Gosh, yes. I never thought of that.'

'What about the family papers and photos? Will you keep them?'

'I'll go through them in a day or two and see if there are any I want to keep, which won't include any photos of *him*, that's for sure.'

Something bad must definitely have happened between him and Lance to have caused such hatred, Fern thought, but didn't comment. 'Henrietta might like to have the originals, or at least copies of them for the family archives, so don't throw any of them away. Even those of your father.'

'OK. I'll see she gets the originals once I've copied the ones I want digitally.'

Fern stood up. 'Right, then. We'll leave you to it.'

He came to the door with them. 'Thank you. I'm very grateful indeed for your help.' He gave her a sudden hug.

'That's what family are for, to help one another.'

Kit's voice was bitter. '*He* never felt like family.'

She could only pat him on the shoulder and say, 'I know.' The poor lad must have felt the lack of a father, as any child would. His mother's second husband had already raised children of his own when they married. Give Brad his due, he'd not been unkind to Kit, but he hadn't attempted to form a warm, loving bond with him, either.

Kit must have been very lonely before he met Mags and now he was utterly devoted to her. What a lovely young couple they were! They'd see one another through this, she was sure, and the change of country would probably do them a world of good.

# Chapter Twenty-Five

Simone went home to find Russ's car missing and a note from him shoved through her door in an envelope containing his door key. As she was opening it, her phone chimed and she saw that he was calling.

'Sorry. Have to make this quick. I'm on my way to London.'

'Goodness, that was sudden.'

'Well, I mentioned to my agent that I'd put together a pilot episode, just a rough one, shot in the grounds of Pennerton House and she talked to the production people and they want to see it – and me. So I'm taking it to them personally, well, my agent and I are doing that together. They think it might make an extra mini-series, as well as the original series, you see. It'd give me a nice chunk of extra money. So I won't be home tonight.'

'Oh. Well, it's good news about the meeting, isn't it?'

'Yes. But not good news about missing you.'

She couldn't keep the words back. 'I'll miss you, too.'

'If you want to get on with some paperwork I've left my spare key.'

'OK.'

Silence, then he asked, 'How did you and Fern get on today? I didn't like to interrupt your unpleasant job by phoning you there.'

'I'd better tell you about the details in person. We found a couple of things that were useful but mostly all Lance owned was a load of rubbish. And Fern was right. That flat did feel creepy.'

'Oh, heck, we're nearly at the production offices already. I'll have to go. I'll call you tonight.'

She felt disappointed at having to say goodbye, which was stupid. She was used to being on her own, wasn't she? She'd had four years of practice at that. She looked at the clock and did a quick calculation. Still time to ring the girls in Australia and have a quick chat. Neither of them went to bed early.

Why didn't that make her feel more cheerful?

Because she was being stupid about Russ, that was why.

She was starting to realise how much she would miss him when she had to go home to Australia and her family.

Clo picked up the phone. 'Hi, Ma.'

'How are you, darling?'

'Oh, you know. Pregnancy isn't much fun. I get tired pretty quickly these days, then there's all the housework to do after I get home.'

'I hope Bob is helping you more than he did last time.'

'He didn't need to then because *you* were here to help me.'

She sounded tearful but Simone wasn't buying into any guilt about coming to England. Clo's situation wasn't her responsibility, even though she'd help them from time to time, naturally. She tried to speak cheerfully. 'So Bob will have to step up to the mark more this time, won't he?'

'He's busy at work and bringing stuff home as well. It's an important project and he expects it to help him get a promotion. Can't you come back earlier, Ma?'

'No dear, sorry. I have my own life to lead, you know, and I've met a rather nice guy over here.'

'*What?* Who is he? I hope he's not after your money.'

'Why should you think that? Do you think I'm stupid? I learnt my lesson about that from rat man, believe me.'

'No, no. Of course I don't think you're stupid. Who is this guy, then?'

'It's the man I'm working for, the film-maker, so actually he's better off financially than I am.'

'Oh. I see. How old is he?'

'About my age.'

'I bet he's divorced.' Clo's voice sounded sharp.

This was a very weird conversation. 'What's that got to do with anything?'

'You and Dad were so happy together. You'd be taking a big risk getting together with a divorced man who's failed at marriage once. And anyway, I need you far more than he does at the moment.'

'I thought I made it plain before I left that it's not my job to look after you, even during a pregnancy, Clo. It's Bob's responsibility. He is the father, after all.'

'Thanks for nothing.' The phone cut off abruptly at the other end.

Simone was so shocked by this that she sat staring at the tiny screen for ages. Clearly her daughter really did expect her to give up her life to support them. She'd hoped they would be starting to grow used to managing without her. It seemed she was wrong.

She phoned Deb but got an engaged signal. What was the betting Clo had immediately called her sister?

Ten minutes later her phone chimed. She picked it up reluctantly after seeing her other daughter's number. 'Hi, Deb.'

'I've just been speaking to Clo.'

'Oh?'

'I have to say I think you're being absolutely selfish, Ma. She really needs you now and you're only swanning around the UK. You could do that another time.'

'I have a life of my own, something you two seem to forget, and if we're being purely practical, it might have escaped your notice but I've swapped houses with the Dittons for about six months. So even if I wanted to return – which I don't – I've nowhere to come back to.'

'Oh, we noticed you'd gone all right. We've both needed your help, only you've not been around to give it.'

Simone gaped at the phone. Had she raised a pair of selfish monsters or what?

'Is it right what Clo says: you've taken up with a guy?'

'Yes.'

'How could you do that to Dad?'

'Your father's been dead for four years. I've not done anything to him. I'm not quite in my dotage yet, so why shouldn't I go out with a nice guy?'

'Because Dad should have been enough for you.' Simone breathed deeply and before she could speak, Deb went on, 'Anyway, Clo hasn't told you but she's not been at all well this time. The doctor's told her to stop work only she won't because there's the mortgage to pay. She looks awful.'

'Is Bob helping her?'

'He's useless in the house, you know he is.'

'I know she's never let him do much. She's ridiculously fussy about doing things just so.'

'She's a *brilliant* housewife. You should—'

'I'm not going to argue nor am I going to let you two run my life for your own convenience. Phone me when you're calmer and can think about my side of things for a change.' She ended the call.

She tried not to cry but she couldn't help it.

Neither of her daughters phoned back to apologise.

When she realised they weren't going to and they'd be in bed asleep by now, she cried some more.

Later, just as she was getting ready for bed herself, the phone rang. She rushed across the room to pick it up, only it wasn't her daughters, of course it wasn't at this time.

'Hi, Simone. Russ here.'

She sniffed back tears. She wasn't going to weep all

over him. This was for her to sort out. 'Hi, Russ.' Damn! She'd let her voice wobble.

'What's wrong?'

'N-nothing.'

His voice softened. 'Tell me, love.'

'I've just quarrelled with both my daughters. They think I should go home and take over their babysitting again, as well as doing some of Clo's housekeeping.'

'*What?*'

'Clo's pregnant and she's not as well as she was with the other two. I think, no, I *know* I've spoilt them, letting them pile babysitting and other jobs on me. And – and they don't approve of me getting myself a fellow.'

His voice was suddenly full of amusement. 'Is that what I am? Your fellow?'

'Yes.' She was feeling better already, just having him to talk to. 'Or we could say I've "picked up a clue" as my grandma used to call it.'

'Oh, that's a much cuter way of describing it. I'd really like to be your "clue". Or your fellow. Or anything else you need me for. I'm very happy to hear you say that. You've been holding back on committing yourself to a relationship.'

'Because I have to go back to Australia eventually. And your life is here.'

'We'll discuss that another time, face-to-face. Let's stick with the good news now. Though you trumped mine by saying I was your clue.'

'Stop going on about that, you idiot. What's your good news.'

'My *other* good news is that the TV people do want me to make a shorter series about the grounds of Pennerton House, a three-part one, with some shots inside the house to set the scene. They're going to sort out the details of the contract with my agent.'

'That's marvellous. You're doing so well, Russ. I'm proud of you.'

'So you and I are going to be very busy once I get back.'

They chatted for a while and when the call ended she went to bed smiling.

But during the night she woke up a couple of times and inevitably started worrying about her daughters again. What had made them so selfish? Or was Clo really ill? She never had been before, was usually what people called 'disgustingly healthy'.

Worst of all, did they really expect her to spend the rest of her life serving them and retreating to her quiet cave when not needed?

No, even worse was why should they think their father would have hated her finding another man to love? She and Harvey had both told one another that if anything happened to them, they'd want the other to find someone else. If there was one thing they'd agreed about, it was that love was not exclusive, could always expand to include more people.

During her second wakeful period, it was a long time before she felt sleep winning over worrying, because she couldn't work out whether to be angry with or worried about her daughters. Or both.

Angry probably came top. She had still not forgiven them for that holiday weekend when they'd left her alone each evening in the hotel bedroom babysitting their children while they 'partied on' as they called it. She told herself it wasn't worth hanging on to, but it had seemed so utterly selfish.

# Chapter Twenty-Six

Three days later in the evening Elizabeth began opening the doors of the old stables, where they parked their vehicles now, about to park her car under cover. Suddenly she was grabbed from behind and dragged into the old building.

She didn't see her assailants because they slipped a hood over her head and she couldn't scream for help because there were at least two people. One had put his hand over her mouth and gripped her face so tightly it hurt, while the other held her arms behind her.

She heard one voice say clearly, 'Listen, you! Tell the old lady this is a warning. She's to pay off the money Lance Mundy owes if she wants this house to stay intact. He may be dead but the family still has to clear his debts.'

When the rather hoarse voice named a figure and let go of her mouth, she opened her mouth to scream for help, but the man quickly stuffed a gag in her mouth as well as tying her hands behind her. She heard a faint noise and lay still, not knowing what to expect, but as the slow seconds ticked past and nothing happened, she guessed they'd left. When she tried to crawl out into the open, she found they'd also fastened her bound arms to a post behind her.

They must have been well prepared for this, and experienced, too, damn them.

It wasn't until Gavin saw her car in the stable yard some time later with its headlights still on and the driver's door open that anyone came to investigate.

'What happened?' he asked sharply as he sliced the ropes with his pocketknife.

She managed not to cry in sheer relief, but oh, she wanted to.

When she explained and told him what they had demanded, he let out a growling, angry sound. 'First thing to do is to get you to a doctor.'

'No need for that. They didn't hurt me, apart from maybe a bruise or two. It was uncomfortable lying waiting for someone to find me, that's all, and – and it's a bit upsetting. Let's go and check that Henrietta is all right. She must be worrying about me.'

'It has to have been the same men,' Gavin said after Elizabeth had told her tale for a second time.

'They aren't that stupid,' the old lady said. 'Those two will have solid alibis for the time you were attacked.' She sat drumming her fingers on her chair arm, then said, 'Better phone the police, though I doubt they'll be able to do anything. While we're waiting for them to turn up, you can get my mother's little handgun out of the gun safe, Gavin, and load it. Hang the firearm regulations.'

He frowned at that.

'And find suitable guns for yourself and Elizabeth as well.'

As he opened his mouth to protest, she held up one hand. 'I know it's not legal these days for us to arm ourselves, but I'd rather have my own means of defence when they come back. And they will come back. Well, if they expect to find a feeble old lady sitting waiting for them, they're going to be very surprised.'

He looked at Elizabeth. 'I know Miss Henrietta is well acquainted with guns from her job. How about you?'

'I'm country born and bred. I may be out of practice but I know how to handle them – and more importantly, how not to handle them.'

The police were shocked at the attack and the threats, and suggested the ladies go and stay in a hotel or visit friends until they'd caught the attackers.

Henrietta laughed gently. 'Not a chance.'

'Can you hire a couple of bodyguards, then?' He looked round. 'The trouble is, this is a big house, with no other residences close by and it's going to be hard to defend.'

Her usually gentle voice came out more sharply than normal. 'I'll bring in a couple of my young relatives but we have one or two tricks up our sleeves as well. I'm going to get our CCTV system extended and modified. I should have put it in the stables in the first place.'

'Good idea.'

'And please warn any officers coming here not to go down the side of the house with the wall running near it.'

'Oh? Why not?'

'That area was booby-trapped during the Second World War because my mother feared an invasion. It's been kept more or less operational and Gavin can quite easily get it working again. It's one of the things the National Trust particularly want to preserve.'

'You've kept it operational all that time?' one of the younger officers exclaimed. 'Wow, I'd like to see that.'

'Oh, yes. It can still protect us. Quite a few people had hidden systems during the war in case of an invasion. People were grimly determined to resist if we got invaded. Just as I am when it comes to villains invading my home.'

'Are you sure it's safe? You'll be the ones in trouble if you hurt them.'

'I can give you the name of the person at the National Trust who keeps an eye on such places. Our traps won't kill anyone, I promise you, just hold them till the police come.'

'As long as you ladies keep your distance, Miss Pennerton.'

'We'll not let ourselves get hurt,' she said ambiguously.

As she watched the officers drive away, she smiled grimly at Elizabeth. 'We're going to be ready for them, believe me, and I'll only keep my distance if they stay out of my home. I wonder if that nice young photographer would like to set up some cameras down the side of the house. It would be quite a scoop for him to film us repelling an invasion of criminals, don't you think?'

'You're too old and stiff to repel anyone,' Gavin said bluntly.

'I'm still capable of hitting a target, but I'm not able to run, which is why we'll call in one or two of my younger relatives to help.'

She fixed a steely gaze on him. 'I shall only give in to such villains when they nail down my coffin, Gavin. Until then I'll fight back every time, even if I die doing it.'

He grimaced at Elizabeth, who shrugged at him. They both knew the fierce willpower of the indomitable old lady and admired her greatly.

The next week started very pleasantly, with Russ eager to be involved in Henrietta's plans. He spent time buying and fitting new parts to the CCTV system, with a couple of internal electronic 'surprises' that made his hostess chuckle.

After that he set up a mini studio in the old laundry at Pennerton House. When it was finished, he rang Simone to invite her to have dinner with him at the hotel, then realised he should have checked first with Henrietta so went to find her again.

'Do you want me to stay here tonight?'

'No, thank you. Fern's son and a friend are coming to stay with us for a while. They're sturdy and young enough to think it exciting to keep watch for probable intruders.'

'And you? How do you feel about it? You're actually looking very spry.'

She grinned at him then burst out laughing. 'I'm equally excited, if truth be told. Life gets sadly tame at my age.'

'I don't think life can ever have been tame for those living with or near you, Henrietta Pennerton.'

She put on a fake demure expression. 'I had a good example to follow with my mother and I do my best to keep going.'

'I only hope I do half as well as you at that age.'

Which left her beaming with pleasure.

When he got home, Russ changed quickly out of his messy clothes then went next door to share the details of his conversation with Henrietta.

'She's an extraordinary woman!' Simone said.

'So are you.' He pulled her into his arms, not asking permission to kiss her this time, not needing to because she came willingly.

After a few minutes, he moved slightly, to cradle her against him. 'Isn't it about time you and I took these delightful interactions to their natural conclusion?'

'Yes, I think it is.'

He held her slightly away from him and studied her face. 'Am I mistaken, or are you nervous? After kissing me like that you shouldn't be.'

'I am a bit.'

'May I ask why?'

'I have such limited experience.'

'Ah, Simone, you don't need experience to follow your body's instincts. But you need love to do the thing properly and I've definitely fallen in love with you.' He waited.

So she said it, 'I've fallen in love with you too, even though it's not wise.'

'Now when are you going to stop saying that? We can work round it.'

'I can't see how. Our lives are set on such different roads. You're based here in the UK, where you're an expert on small wild creatures and you're just starting to get known. And mine' – her voice choked to a halt for a moment, then she finished saying it aloud – 'mine lies in Australia. I couldn't bear to leave my daughters and grandchildren permanently, to go and live on the other side of the world. I just – couldn't bear to do it. However they treat me at times.'

He reached out to wipe away a tear from her cheek with his fingertip. 'We will definitely find a way round it, my darling.'

She could only shake her head. She felt so shattered by the difficulties that once again they didn't make love.

But for some strange reason the fact that he was sensitive to her feelings and didn't push for it, made her love him all the more. He wasn't at all like rat man. She couldn't imagine Russ trampling on anyone's feelings or taking advantage of a weakness. He was like her first husband in that, considerate.

She fell asleep in his arms. After a while he woke her with a gentle kiss and told her to go to bed. She nodded. It was probably for the best tonight.

As she locked the door behind him she almost called him back. But no. When they made love for the first time she didn't want it to be half sad, half happy, which was how she felt at the moment.

Why did life get so tangled?

She slept badly again and was woken later than usual by her doorbell ringing. When she went down, Russ was there.

'Wake up, sleepyhead. We have to get to work. You're still going to be part of the new series, you know. Breakfast will be served next door in about ten minutes.'

He gave her a mock salute then turned and went back to his house.

She sighed as she went to get showered. He was such a dear love. How could she bear to leave him?

When she went next door, he had what people here called a 'full English breakfast' waiting for her. They hadn't eaten a proper meal last night and she'd thought she wasn't really hungry this morning but she rediscovered her appetite with fresh fruit salad and yoghurt followed by fried eggs, bacon and tomatoes, all eaten in a leisurely manner. Russ even had an extra piece of toast spread thickly with cherry jam to end his meal.

She smiled across the table at him as they finished. 'Thank you. I needed a proper meal.'

'That's all right. But we'd better get to work now.'

'Where are you filming today?'

'Where are *we* filming? At Pennerton House, of course. The TV people want the new mini-series as soon as possible. How about you wear that blue top with your jeans? That shade of blue comes out better on the screen than the patterned one you're wearing.'

'I'd better do something with my hair, too.'

'No, don't. It looks great all tousled like that.' He waggled his eyebrows at her. 'Come-to-bed hair, that is.' Then he gave a shout of laughter. 'You're blushing.'

She escaped quickly and stared at herself in the big bathroom mirror. Come-to-bed hair, indeed.

She hadn't gone to bed with him last night, had she? And was regretting it greatly this morning.

For the following three days they worked on the series and nature seemed to play into their hands, delivering animals, birds and all manner of creatures in a very helpful parade under sunny skies.

It was idyllic. She would never forget it.

When they went home on the third night the casserole she'd put together hastily that morning was simmering gently in the slow cooker and she was able to invite Russ round to share a meal.

She'd planned it carefully, getting up early to set the scene in the bedroom and put the food together.

When he came in she produced the one bottle of sparkling wine she'd bought for a special occasion. As they toasted one another, she smiled across the raised glasses at him.

'It's about time, don't you think?'

She didn't need to explain what she meant. 'You're sure?'

'Yes. The more I get to know you, the more sure I become.'

So they took the half-full glasses upstairs with them and this time nothing interrupted. This time they shared the age-old expression of two people's love with joyful abandon.

And as they lay together afterwards, she knew it was going to be even harder to leave him after this. But she didn't let herself give in to that sad thought now. She wanted to savour every minute they could spend together.

# Chapter Twenty-Seven

That same evening Gavin watched Russ and Simone drive away then came back in to say baldly, 'I reckon they'll be coming tonight, Miss Henrietta. There have been signs in the woods.'

She didn't bother to ask him who he meant or what the signs were. He'd been prowling the grounds for days, setting little giveaway traps made of natural materials. No one but he would notice if they'd been disturbed by someone passing through. If he said it would be tonight, then it would happen that way.

'We must make sure we're ready for them.'

'Yes. But I still don't like you being involved.'

'Who does like being involved in violence? Only fools! But I'd like it even less if we allowed that sort of person to get away without a shock or two. Hopefully it'll frighten them into thinking twice about doing this to some helpless old lady another time.'

'You're not and never have been helpless, Miss Henrietta.'

'I wish you'd stop calling me that. You and I have been friends for such a long time.'

'It wouldn't be proper.'

'You always say that.'

But he stubbornly shook his head.

'Well, it's my home these pests will be breaking into so I'll damn well help drive them away. I'll not hesitate to shoot them if necessary.'

That brought a wry smile from him. 'I never thought I'd see the day you used one of the family's handguns for real again.'

'Neither did I. Not in England, anyway. Now, go and tell the lads to make ready to repel boarders later on. I'll tell Elizabeth.'

The two men spying on the house were sure now of the nightly routine and watched impatiently as the people inside made their preparations for bed.

'Stupid old woman!' Baz muttered. 'She's picked the wrong one to tangle with this time, though. The boss will get what he's owed one way or the other.'

'She's ninety, probably senile. She'd better do as I tell her tonight though. I'm not having an arrogant old biddy disobeying me.'

'You were told not to hurt her, Trev.'

'There's ways of hurting people without killing them or leaving marks that show. It hurts some people if you damage their ornaments or their pets, the silly fools.'

They waited a few more minutes, watched the lights go out one by one, then Baz took charge again. 'That's it.'

They moved forward slowly and carefully.

Inside the house a soft chime warned the occupants waiting upstairs that someone was crossing the stable yard, then another told them the kitchen door had been opened.

'They'd better not have damaged that lock,' Henrietta muttered. 'It's three hundred years old and easy enough to pick.'

The intruders moved quietly but their progress was noted by two excited young men and three older people who were not quite as excited but just as determined when it came to defending their own.

Since she was on the watch for them, Henrietta heard the faint sounds of their approach as they made their way towards her bedroom. She had made sure they knew where she slept, had deliberately stood at the window for a while before drawing the curtains the last couple of nights.

In the bedroom next door she heard Gavin sigh and guessed he'd be fiddling with that cosh he carried with him when he patrolled the grounds after dark. He'd fought against this part of the defence plan, but she had insisted on playing the lead role and he'd agreed in the end. Well, he knew how keenly she felt the physical limitations of old age. He was starting to slow down as well.

When the men crept up the stairs and entered the

bedroom, she smiled. There was no one there to stop them except an old lady sitting sideways on the edge of her bed. And like them she was wearing night goggles.

'I thought I heard something,' she said conversationally, smiling to see them jump in shock. 'Do come in, gentlemen.'

She flicked a switch that turned on the bedside lights and pulled off the goggles with one hand, taking care to keep the handgun pointed at them with the other.

One of the men spoke to her in a patronising tone, as if she were a complete idiot and she glared at him, hoping now that he would give her an excuse to shoot him. Just a little flesh wound to teach him to respect old ladies would be highly satisfying.

He continued in an almost genial tone, 'No need for that gun, missus. Guns are dangerous things. You've no idea how easily they can go off. We're not here to attack you, only to deliver a message and take back your reply.'

'And that message is?'

'You're to pay Lance Mundy's debts or your house will get damaged. And to make sure you understand how serious we are about this, we're going to leave our marks on one or two of your precious pieces before we go and you'll have to watch us do it. No shouting for help or it'll be the last thing you say or do. Now, give me that gun.'

He started to step forward but she aimed the gun more carefully and he stopped, suddenly seeming to realise that she knew how to handle it.

She smiled as she saw the penny drop. 'If you do damage to my possessions, it may be the last thing you say or do for a while – except for screaming in pain. And in case either of you is still not convinced I know how to use this, I was brought up knowing how to shoot and used guns during my military service.'

'You wouldn't do it, though. We aren't even carrying guns.'

'Oh, I would do it, because you're much stronger than I am. Now, I have a reply for your boss, so listen carefully. Tell him I've already gifted my house to the National Trust because neither I nor anyone in my family has the money to maintain it. I certainly don't have enough money to pay Lance's gambling debts even if I wanted to, which I don't.'

'You could still pay some of his debts. Be worth it to stop my boss annoying you.' He stretched out his hand and spoke even more softly. 'Now, give me that gun, there's a good girl.'

The other man suddenly feinted to one side and the one who'd been speaking hurled something at her. But he was too late to stop her firing rapidly at both him and then his companion.

The shots echoed loudly and the larger man cursed, saying in tones of shock, 'She's hit my arm, the bitch.'

The other man had managed to grab Henrietta. 'She got me in the thigh.' He gave her a shake.

She let herself go limp and clutched her chest, groaning as if in pain. 'Oh, oh! It hurts. Need – heart tablets.'

He let go and stepped back. 'Hellfire! She's having a heart attack on us now. That Lance fellow went and died on the others. I'm not risking that.'

She groaned artistically, just a little, and continued to clutch her chest and groan.

'Leave her be. This'll be enough to frighten them into doing as they've been told.'

Henrietta let her head roll back and tried to look unconscious.

'She's stopped moving. I'm getting out of here quick.'

She lay quietly on the bed, smiling happily and listening to what was going on just outside her door. Then, when she was sure the others were playing their parts, she got up and tiptoed to the door to peep out through the hinges.

Baz and Trev had stopped dead on the landing, because the old gardener and a middle-aged woman were standing near the top of the stairs.

'Damned if these two don't have guns as well!' Baz whispered.

'There's others as well.' He indicated two younger men who were standing further along the landing, grinning broadly.

Elizabeth spoke first. 'We're not having our home damaged, so the only way you'll get out without being shot again is by the fire escape at the end of this landing.'

They hesitated, exchanging quick glances.

'You might be able to get away before the police arrive if you hurry. They're on their way. You really ought to get those wounds seen to. You're dripping blood all over our clean carpets.'

'Do as she says but watch out for an ambush,' Baz murmured.

Keeping a careful watch on the group of defenders, they took the alternate route indicated.

'It's a madhouse,' Trev whispered. 'I'll be glad to get out of it.'

'You're telling me.'

As they moved out onto the fire escape, a transparent figure of a woman seemed to float in the air to one side of it.

Baz clutched his friend. 'The damned place is haunted! It would be!'

'Ghosts can't hurt you.' Trev thought he heard a laugh from inside the house and turned to glance that way, but they weren't being pursued. When he turned back he cursed because his companion was clattering recklessly down the fire escape.

Baz got to the bottom of the fire escape first and didn't wait before starting to run along the side of the house in the moonlight. There was a high wall that turned it into a sort of passage so they didn't have much choice about where to go.

Baz speeded up, running recklessly along the side of the house, then suddenly the ground beneath him gave way and with a yell, he disappeared down a hole.

Trev jumped to one side, yelping as this hurt his thigh wound, but managing to scramble away from the soft edge of the trap. He ran along beside the garden wall, ignoring his companion's shouts for help.

Within a few paces he ran into something and found

himself tangled up in what felt like ropes. He swore loudly and struggled but was unable to free himself as he was already being drawn up into the air inside a big net of ropes.

There was applause from behind him and as he looked up he saw the old lady standing at the top of the fire escape – fit as you like, damn her – laughing and clapping. The others who'd seen them out of the house were gathered around her.

'It worked!' the cracked old voice called down to him. 'It really did. Oh, what fun that was! And did you like our tame ghost? Courtesy of a camera trick.'

Only then did she allow her escorts to take her indoors, still laughing with pleasure.

'The police aren't going to approve of those traps,' Gavin said dourly. 'They don't like you touching criminals these days.'

'The National Trust wanted to prove that the wartime defences still worked,' Henrietta commented. 'You did well putting them completely in order again, Gavin. The Trust will be delighted with it all.'

That did draw a slight smile from him.

Henrietta's two young guards didn't follow her into the house. They went down the fire escape and stood peering into the open hole at the man who'd fallen into the old cellar, which now lacked its original delivery chute. He was scrabbling among the chunks of coal.

'Having a good time, are you?' one yelled down to him. 'You won't get out without help. We've locked the inner door.'

'Get me up, then.'

'Nah. We're leaving that to the police. They'll want to see you *in flagrante delicto*.'

'We're sooo frightened of you, we daren't release you,' the other added in a mocking, sing-song voice.

Fern's son nearly choked with laughter as their captive cursed him at length and scrabbled about even more frantically. 'Did you ever see anything like it?'

'No, never. Real slapstick, but it worked.'

'Didn't I tell you Aunt Henrietta was brilliant? I hope I've got the same family genes.'

Inside the house, Elizabeth called the police and they sent the police car that happened to have been patrolling nearby to act as first responders. She explained to a senior officer about the failed raid on the house and how a ninety-year-old woman had designed the trap to catch the burglars.

'Now that I have to see,' he said. 'I'm coming to supervise the rescue operations myself. I've had the pleasure of meeting Miss Pennerton a couple of times. She's amazing.'

It was only five minutes before the first police car arrived, but these officers had been told to keep watch on the two captives until the inspector got there and not to attempt to rescue them unless they were in life-threatening danger.

Even when they did start to sort things out, it took longer than anyone would have expected to free them because all the police officers were laughing so hard. They were also taking photos for evidence of a man hanging in a big rope net with one leg sticking out at a ridiculous angle and the grimy face of a villain well-known locally for his arrogance glaring up at them from a coal cellar.

Henrietta came back out to the fire escape to watch the men being released then finally agreed to go back to bed. She even admitted that she might take half of one of her pills, just to relax her heart a little.

She was smiling happily as she slid down in bed. 'My mother would be proud of us, Elizabeth.'

'Proudest of you most of all, Henrietta. You worked out the plan.'

'I hope she would be proud. I'll never be as good at such trickery as she was, though.'

When the old lady eventually fell asleep, Elizabeth stayed by the side of the bed and left it to Gavin and the two lads to keep an eye on the police as they took away the two intruders.

She had been terrified this might really give Henrietta a heart attack, but it hadn't. She wasn't risking leaving the old lady on her own, though. Not after such an eventful night. There could still be health repercussions.

One day she would lose Henrietta for good, that was inevitable, but thank heavens it hadn't happened tonight.

As far as she was concerned the country would lose a national treasure when her dear friend passed away. She was still helping Henrietta write her memoirs, an unexpurgated tale, and was amazed at how well someone born well before the middle of the twentieth century had coped with change after change, first overseas working secretly for the government, then here at Pennerton House, managing her inheritance.

Downstairs, after smugly explaining how they'd known the intruders would be coming tonight and why the traps were still there, Gavin was relaxing with a broadly smiling police inspector, who was enjoying a glass of single malt whisky with him.

'Well, if those traps are going to be Grade II listed, we can't complain about them being there, can we?' the inspector said in the end.

Gavin nodded and raised the bottle. 'A little more?'

'Just a splash.'

When it was all over Gavin locked up then went to check on the old lady. Miss Henrietta had survived the night and she'd proved yet again what a good marksman she was by only dealing out slight wounds to her two attackers, as she'd boasted she would.

She was incredible.

Most of the action would have been caught on film by Russ's two new in situ cameras, as well as being photographed later by the police. He chuckled suddenly at the memory of the intruders' expressions when a 'ghost' had appeared near them as they ran down the fire escape.

Wasn't technology marvellous? What would people invent next?

# Chapter Twenty-Eight

Next morning Russ and Simone chuckled as they studied the footage of the capture of the two intruders which had been transmitted live to his computer. Then he said thoughtfully, 'I'd love to do a separate programme featuring Henrietta, talking a bit about her background and what made her want to actively help capture two villains at her age. I think it'd go down really well with viewers.' He turned thoughtful for a while then said suddenly, 'Would you mind if I went over to interview her now on my own? I'd like to strike while the iron is hot. I'd better phone my agent first and explain so that she can think about selling it. This could be a very lucrative little extra episode.'

'It'll be lovely to see a ninety-year-old being feted as a heroine instead of being treated like a halfwit.'

'I'll get Henrietta to talk about ageism as well.'

Simone found the house very quiet without him for the rest of the day and wished she could have gone along. But he'd said a couple of times that you often got better interviews when there was just yourself and the person of interest.

She wondered whether to try to phone her daughters today but decided not to. She felt sad being at odds with them, but they had to learn that she had a life of her own still to live.

Life could be hard at times. You just had to get on with things and make changes to your plans if necessary.

It seemed to her that Clo's life would be better without that huge mortgage which was like a millstone weighing down her and Bob. But you couldn't tell other adults how to live their lives, they had to find out, just as she'd had to find out that she could do better than acting as general dogsbody to her daughters.

Well, she made it a rule not to let herself sit around moping so she went out shopping, stocking up the freezer with things which would provide emergency food for herself, or, more enjoyably, for herself and a guest. And buying a few bottles of wine, too.

The only thing that cheered her up about her family was that she'd heard from her parents. The email had come a couple of days ago but for some strange reason had gone into the spam folder. Computers did things like that to you now and then. She had no clue why.

Her parents were glad she'd met Fern and Henrietta, and they were enjoying themselves hugely. They were going off again the following day with a couple who knew a great camping spot far from any town, with incredible views on the way.

They might or might not have access to the Internet for a couple of days, but were sure everything would continue to go well for her.

When Russ came back he was jubilant. 'Henrietta's brilliant. Comes through really well on camera. That must run in your family.'

'I bet she enjoyed herself.'

'Yes, she did. And Elizabeth isn't bad either. Henrietta says she's a mere youngster, only in her sixties.'

He gave Simone a sudden hug, then kissed her and they both forgot everything and everyone else for a while.

As they went downstairs again for some food, he said suddenly. 'I nearly forgot to tell you. I had a message while I was out. Justine has had her baby and it's a boy. He's in a pretty good state of health, thank goodness, in spite of her neglect of good nutrition, though rather small.'

'Is Pierre going to have to fight for custody?'

'No. She'll waive all rights and stay away in return for regular payments from Pierre.'

'I could never have left my children like that.'

'Neither could I. My wife and I lost our baby, and it was a source of great grief to both of us, even though it was also what split us up.'

'I've heard it often happens in that situation. Did you never want to marry again?'

'Not till I met you.'

'Russ, please.'

'I shan't change my mind about that.'

\* \* \*

Two more weeks passed without any further emergencies at Pennerton House or anywhere else, come to that. Most of the time Simone went with Russ on his trips to film the inhabitants of Henrietta's grounds, and found it all fascinating. She'd learnt to ignore the fact that she was on camera and concentrate on the wildlife. He made it so interesting.

She'd watched him make Henrietta feel comfortable as he filmed, too. Clever man, he was, in many ways.

If it hadn't been for her daughters, she would have been blissfully happy, but days passed and neither Clo nor Deb phoned. It hurt a lot because Mags and Kit did get in touch and seemed to have settled in well in Australia. They'd caught up with her daughters but Clo was a bit under the weather, so hadn't done anything socially.

Simone wished she too could catch up with her daughters but didn't intend to be the first to take a step towards reconciliation, not this time.

What was the matter with them, hanging onto their grudge about her going to England like this? She and Harvey must have done something very wrong in the way they'd brought them up. Could you love people too much, give them too much of yourself?

Perhaps it wasn't all her fault but simply one aspect of the spirit of the age that she and her friends had noticed. Some younger people seemed to feel entitled to the best in every aspect of life, even when they were struggling to afford it. Not all young people, of course, just some of them.

She discussed it with Russ one night and he held her close as she wept about her break with her daughters. But he too thought she was doing the right thing in holding firm to her need for a life of her own, and that made her feel better. He was such a sane person.

She managed to forget her worries much of the time because she was learning to live with him, finding it very different from living with Harvey, very stimulating in many ways because he had a curious mind always wanting to learn, to know more.

One day she confided her family problems to Henrietta as they were sitting chatting and waiting for Russ to join them.

'Am I wrong to wait them out on this, Henrietta?'

'Not at all. They'll be thinking hard about the situation, I'm sure. Give them time.'

'I suppose so.'

Henrietta studied her face and reached across to give her hand a squeeze. 'It's difficult for you, I know, Simone, but sometimes you have to be firm with people, especially other members of your close family. Hold firm. It'll be worth it.'

After a few minutes' silence, Henrietta added quietly and rather sadly, 'Nothing can ever be guaranteed where people are concerned, mind you. You just have to know that you've done your best, even if your life and the lives of those you love take different paths from the ones you'd expected.'

'Yes. You're right.'

'And the other thing is, you can never quite predict what people will do in any crisis.'

'My mother said she'd talk to me about my family here, but she never got back to me. She and my father always shy away from talking about the past.'

'They have just as much right as *you* to choose their way in life, even if it's one you don't approve of. In which case you have to live with it. As for your daughters, what they don't have the right to do is expect you, or anyone else, to be at their beck and call.'

The chat was comforting. Henrietta was so wise. Sometimes you just had to move on.

Then one balmy evening Russ came home bubbling with joy. He refused to tell her why until they were at the hotel ordering a meal, then beamed at her across and added a bottle of champagne to their order.

He raised his glass to clink it against hers. 'Today's shoot was *it*.'

'What do you mean?'

'I've done as much as I can with my filming here, so I've come to the end of this stage. I need to work a bit on my editing, then go to London and refine it with a brilliant editor before I turn in my final version.' He grimaced and added, 'And even then the TV company will change things – and change them again. See if they don't.'

'How do you stand it?'

'Because I want the best final product and usually the changes are improvements. Tiny details can make such a difference. And then there's the commentary to record.' He hesitated then added, 'It'd be a waste of your time to come to London with me, darling. You'd just be on your own in the evenings as well as the days. But I'll be home at the weekend. Will you be all right?'

'Yes, of course I will.'

'That's my wonderful independent lady! I love that you don't cling.'

As she waved him goodbye she remembered those words and sighed. Sometimes she wanted to cling, very much wanted to. But she wouldn't allow herself to do it because one day, one dreadful day, she'd have to leave him and go back to Australia. She never let herself forget that and he hadn't managed to persuade her otherwise.

There wasn't a firm date for ending the house exchange, just 'end of August or September'. But she reckoned the Dittons would still want to come home again round about then, so that would be it, more or less.

Her swappees' granddaughter had been born almost exactly on the due date, and they'd sent a couple of delightful photos of themselves holding her and beaming at the world.

Simone had a new grandchild on the way, too. Surely once she was back in Australia, she could sort things out with her girls?

Russ came home at the weekend but he wasn't completely with her. His head seemed still full of the images and the commentary that was now being fitted to them, which included some of her and Henrietta's remarks. This production company, he said, had its own way of doing things and fussed a lot but he liked the results they got for nature programmes better than any other series he'd seen lately.

For two wonderful days they walked round the lake, talked until late, went back to bed in the afternoon to make exquisite love, and then suddenly it was time for him to leave again.

Simone was thoughtful as she settled back into life on her own.

She would never be as totally partner-focused as she had been with Harvey, but maybe something halfway between his way of life and Russ's would suit her better these days, because she was sure some of the ways she'd changed were permanent.

If she ever got over Russ and met someone else, that was.

Make the most of the next few weeks, my girl, she told herself grimly every time she felt a bit down. Even a short time with Russ was such a joy.

# Chapter Twenty-Nine

The world fell apart for Simone sooner than she'd expected – in the middle of that same week to be precise. She was woken at two o'clock in the morning by the phone ringing and when she picked it up, it took her a few seconds to realise that it was her younger daughter who was sobbing at the other end of the line.

'Ma?'

'Deb? Is that you?'

'Don't hang up on me.'

'I wouldn't do that, especially not when you're upset.'

'I'd deserve it if you did refuse to take my call, and so would Clo. We've not treated you very nicely lately and I'm sorry for that.'

For longer than that, but who was counting? 'Well, no one is perfect.' Simone felt happiness surge through her. This meant she and her daughters were going to come together again, which was wonderful, just absolutely wonderful. 'Tell me what the matter is, darling.'

'Ma, it's not good news.'

Deb's voice was so tight and unhappy, Simone's pleasure faded instantly. 'What's wrong? Just tell me straight out.'

'Clo's been rushed into hospital. The baby started coming early and there were complications. Things didn't go well and in the end they had to do a Caesarean.' She let out another tearful choke.

'Did the baby – die?' Oh, please no, please not that!

'No, no. But the poor thing was only just over seven months old and quite small, and – and she's in one of those incubator things. She wasn't due for another few weeks.'

'But Clo's all right?'

'They think she will be. She wants to see you, Ma.'

'And I want to see her.'

'Can you fly back straight away? She needs you so badly.'

'To look after Tommy and Vicki?' In the circumstances she couldn't refuse to take care of her grandchildren, but if it was the main reason for this call, Simone was going to be feel bitterly let down.

'No. Well, not exactly. Bob's parents are doing that, and they're happy to share the job with you when – I mean *if* you return. Clo needs to see you to set things right. She's fretting about it. You will come back and – and reassure her that you haven't given up on her, won't you? Or on me.'

Simone didn't hesitate. 'Of course I will. I'll get online

and see if I can find a flight on that cancellations website. I'll contact you when I have one booked.'

'Thanks, Ma. She'll be so relieved. We all will. You're the pivot of the family, and not just because of the help you've given us, either. You're just – that sort of person.'

After she'd put the phone down, Simone had to blow her nose and wipe her eyes before she could get out of bed. What Deb had said at the end was the nicest compliment she'd ever had. Ever! She got dressed in the first clothes that came to hand, then hurried downstairs. After switching on her computer she made herself a mug of coffee, working out in her head the best order in which to do things.

First she got online and found the site that gave last-minute cancellations.

It took her a few minutes to navigate her way round it and then, to her utter relief, she found a direct flight to Perth being offered. It wasn't a business class seat this time, but she'd manage. She checked the other details quickly, glanced at her watch, then clicked on the icon to reserve the place on that flight, getting out her credit card and paying for it without hesitation.

She now had just under six hours to get to Heathrow Airport. She could do it.

She phoned the local taxi firm, woke up a grumpy chap on 'emergency calls only' and booked a taxi to get her to Heathrow.

'It'll cost £50 extra at this time of night.'

'I don't care. I have a family emergency in Australia.'

'All right, lady. I'll get there as quickly as I can. See you in about twenty minutes.'

After that she rushed round the house pulling all her things out of drawers. Flying what people jokingly called 'cattle class' meant she'd have to pay extra for excess luggage, as well as not being able to lie down on the plane, but that didn't matter.

To hell with packing carefully, she threw everything into her two bags any old how.

She had the suitcases standing outside her front door in fifteen minutes flat, after which she did the hardest thing of all. She phoned Russ in London, waking him up as well.

'Simone? Is something wrong?'

She explained quickly.

'I'm sorry about that. So you're going back to Australia to see her?'

'Yes, of course I am. She needs me. The plane leaves in just under six hours. Look, when you come back to Wiltshire will you clear out the fresh food and any other bits and pieces I've left behind? All the bottles of wine in the rack are mine, so take them and – and think of me when you drink them. I'll shove the Dittons' front door key through your letterbox.'

'Yes, I'll do that. And we'll keep in touch by phone and email until you can come back.'

She took a deep breath. 'I shan't be coming back, Russ.'

There was silence for a moment or two, then, 'What exactly do you mean by that?'

'It'll probably be weeks before I can leave Clo and the baby. Your life is here and mine is there, so it'll be better to make this a clean break. We always knew it was coming.'

'But I thought we—'

Her voice broke as she interrupted. 'Russ, please don't make it harder for me than it is. I love you but we can't make a life together. We knew that from the start.'

'*You* decided that. I never agreed about it. I still don't.'

She couldn't help it, began to sob. 'Please Russ, let's just – remember how wonderful it's been. This emergency only emphasises for me that I have to live near my family. I can't bear to make a life permanently away from them – I just can't.' She was sobbing so harshly now she didn't realise for a few seconds that the doorbell had rung and car headlights were shining through the kitchen windows.

'The taxi's here. Take care, Russ.'

She didn't wait for him to answer but cut the connection and went to open the door, still mopping her eyes. 'S-sorry. I'm a bit upset.'

He gave her a reassuring old man's pat on the shoulder. 'I'll get you to the airport in time, love. This all your luggage?'

'Yes.'

Her phone rang and it was Russ. She didn't answer, just locked up the house and put the key through his letterbox. Then she sat in the back of the taxi and shed a few silent tears. She wanted to howl loudly in anguish and only just managed to hold her grief in.

She couldn't go through another goodbye with Russ after this one. It'd kill her.

The journey seemed interminable and Simone hadn't thought to get a book to read as she walked through the airport. She didn't have any reading material on her phone, didn't like reading electronically anyway.

She tried to watch a film but although she didn't much fancy any of the ones being offered, she settled in the end for a thriller that had good reviews.

After watching it for half an hour she couldn't remember who had done what, because her mind had kept wandering, so she changed to an old musical instead. Since she knew it well, it didn't matter if she missed parts of it. Which she did.

She wasn't the only passenger to heave a loud sigh of relief when they got to Perth.

After she'd gone through customs, she found Deb waiting for her outside, pacing up and down behind the rows of seats.

When she realised that her usually elegant daughter was wearing scruffy old jeans and a top that seemed to have been pulled out of a charity package, Simone's heart gave a lurch of sheer terror.

Her daughter flung her arms round her and they clung to one another for a few seconds, rocking slightly.

'How's Clo?'

'They say she's recovering nicely. If that's "nicely", I hope I never look so awful. They had to do a full hysterectomy, you see, and she was still a bit dopey when I saw her yesterday evening.'

'And the baby?'

'Holding her own. They seem cautiously pleased with her progress. But she's tiny.'

'Thank goodness. Oh, thank goodness!'

Deb stopped to stare at her. 'You look terrible, Ma.'

'So do you.' She looked down at herself in mild surprise. 'Didn't seem to matter what I wore.'

'It was the same for me. I flung on the first thing that came to hand. What about your new guy? I half expected to see him with you.'

Simone hesitated, hating to put it into words, then said it. 'I finished with him.'

'When? You never said.'

Simone drew a deep breath. 'I phoned him to tell him before I set off for the airport. It wouldn't have worked, you see. His whole career is based over there and I couldn't live away from you all. Not permanently anyway.'

Another stare. 'You look sad.'

'Yes, well, I can't help feeling sad. Russ is a wonderful guy but sometimes circumstances don't—' She had to pause to pull herself together enough to continue. 'Our lives are too different. It can't work.'

'Couldn't he photograph the animals here? Or doesn't he want to live in Australia?'

'He's made a speciality of the creatures that live alongside humans in the UK. He brings the whole interaction to life, makes people care about them, see what's been right under their noses. He's making a real contribution to helping save wildlife. He's brilliant. I couldn't stop him doing that. It wouldn't be right.'

'Oh.'

'Besides, even if he came to do some filming in Australia, it'd only be temporary and he'd go away again. I love you all too much to live in England permanently.' She blew her nose hard, trying to hide the tears.

Deb plonked a sudden kiss on her mother's cheek. 'You're still a family first sort of person, aren't you?'

'I suppose so. Let's – talk about something else.' She gave her nose a final blow, then asked brightly, 'How are the kids? I bet they've grown.'

'Parker and Marcie are fine. They're staying with Logan's parents for a day or two. I – wasn't sure about the – the situation with Clo. I wanted to be easily available if things got, you know, really bad. It was a real screaming siren emergency.' She shuddered.

Simone gave her another quick hug. 'Can we go straight to the hospital? I know it's early morning here, but it's night inside my head, thanks to the time differences between the two countries. I didn't manage any sleep on the plane, and I'm tired, but I won't be able to rest before I've seen Clo. Oh, and where am I going to sleep? Did anyone think of that?'

'Of course we did. I rang the Dittons and explained. They're going to move out of your house tomorrow and move in with their daughter until they can change their flight back. Tonight you'll be sleeping at my place, if that's OK?'

'Once I've seen Clo, made sure she's all right, I'll not care if I have to sleep in the garden shed.'

'We can do better than that for you.'

At the hospital, Deb explained to a stern-faced woman at reception that Clo's mother had come all the way from England to see her, so they were allowed in even though it was too early for visiting.

'Just for ten minutes, mind!'

Clo was lying in bed staring blindly into space but when she saw her mother, she tried to sit higher up, winced and held her arms out instead, tears running down her face. 'You've come! Oh, you've come, Ma!'

'Of course I have, you darling dope. Did you think I'd stay away when you needed me?'

'I'd deserve it.'

'How's the baby?'

'She's gorgeous – well, she's going to be gorgeous. She's a bit shrivelled-looking at the moment. They'll let you look at her, but you won't be able to cuddle her and you'll have to wear a mask.'

'She's holding her own, though?'

'Yes. Much better this morning, breathing properly. They brought her in to see me a couple of hours ago and I managed to feed her a bit.'

'She's as stubborn as her mother, then.'

Clo shook her head. 'I've been too stubborn, wanted to be perfect at everything, job, motherhood, running a home.' She blinked her eyes. 'I tried not to let on but I used to get so tired, Ma.'

'Of course you did. No one can be perfect at everything.'

'You always seemed to be. Our home was always immaculate.'

'Is that how you remember it?'

'Yes, of course.'

Simone couldn't help smiling. 'I was the world's best expert at making a place look good once you two had left home – and I had your father to help me. He secretly enjoyed housework, used to take a real pride in how well the furniture polished up.'

Clo blinked furiously. 'I remember Dad giving me a lecture once on how to do that properly.'

Simone waited a moment or two then dared to say, 'You'll have to let Bob share the jobs from now on, darling. No one can do everything.'

'I know. He's said that too. He always intends to do more but he can't always spare the time, so things go downhill.'

'Then you'll have to remind him as well as lowering your standards.'

'Mmm. I suppose so.'

She changed the subject to something more cheerful. 'What are you calling the baby, Clo? You never said.'

'It took us ages to agree about that. Georgie.'

'Short for Georgina?'

'No, just Georgie.'

The nurse came to interrupt them. 'Clo needs to rest now.'

Simone gave her daughter a farewell hug, then said

pleadingly to the nurse, 'Can I just have a peep at my new granddaughter before I leave?'

'You can look but not touch. She's breathing really well now. She's a little Aussie battler, that one.'

The baby was tiny and she did look shrivelled, not plump and beautiful as the other two had been. But she opened her eyes suddenly and it looked as if she was watching the brand-new world around her carefully already.

As she and Deb walked out of the hospital, Simone said, 'Now I can sleep. Am I going to be in your way, though, if I come to your house? I can always go to a motel.'

'Of course you won't be in the way. You're definitely coming home with me. The kids have been getting their junk out of the box room and we can just fit a single bed in it. They'll be all over you once they get home from school. They'll have gone for the day by the time we get back.'

Deb gave her a sudden convulsive hug and clung on for longer than usual before getting into the car.

'What's that in aid of? You're not usually a hugger.'

'In aid of welcome back. You're the only Ma I've got and I've missed you.'

'I've missed you all, too. Did you think I hadn't?'

'I wasn't thinking clearly at first. I am now, I hope.'

Before she went to bed in the tiny box room that evening, Simone checked her phone. Russ had called her ten times, leaving a few loving messages at first, then repeating the same short one: he wasn't giving up on them staying together.

'Get used to that, Simone. We're going to work something out and I'm definitely going to marry you.'

She cried again, shedding tears for her lost dreams. It wasn't going to happen but it was wonderful to be wanted so much. She smiled through the tears: he hadn't asked her, he'd *told* her he was marrying her. Oh, if only!

The following morning she stuffed her clothes into her bags anyhow, then checked her emails. There was one from Henrietta and Elizabeth.

Oh dear, she was going to miss them as well. And Fern. But they'd all stay in touch, she was sure. The modern world was full of ways to communicate. And she'd visit England again, definitely.

Another email came from Russ. She hesitated. Should she block him? No, she couldn't bear to do that.

Should she reply?

No, she couldn't bear to do that either. It would bring him too close to chat to him.

Was she doing the right thing?

What else could she do? Young Parker knocked on her bedroom door to say goodbye before going off to school and she went to the window to watch him get into someone's car.

She'd missed her grandchildren. They seemed to have grown a lot during her absence.

She gave a wry smile. She hadn't missed the school concerts, though, or changed her resolution about never going to one again.

Deb called up that the kettle had just boiled and she went to join her. She was looking forward to moving back into her own home.

She was missing Russ like hell already.

She was so torn between her two worlds.

In Wiltshire, Russ was increasingly thoughtful. He'd never expected Simone to be easy to woo, but the more he'd got to know her, the more he'd fallen in love with her. She'd been so sure that their lives were going to be too different for them to have a successful marriage.

He should have – *could have* – tried harder to persuade her that it was possible, but he'd been lost in his new programmes. Hell, that must have given her all the more reason to doubt that they could stay together long term. Stupid, that's what he'd been. He had taken her presence in England for granted, and his ability to persuade her before she went back that they could work things out.

Well, he might have made a mistake there but he wasn't stupid enough to give her up. He was going to marry Simone, whatever it took.

Why did he love her so much? He smiled fondly as he thought of her. She was a strange mixture of naïve and intense, old-fashioned and modern. And she had a beautiful smile. It lit up her whole face.

The trouble was, he couldn't go after her yet because he really needed to be around for the next week or two, mainly in London.

His guess was that Simone would be more concerned with her daughter and the new baby at the moment.

Premature babies didn't grow bigger overnight.

Simone would make a wonderful wife and life companion, he just knew it. She'd proved that once already with Harvey.

Her first husband must have been a hell of a nice guy, judging by the way she spoke about him. Russ envied her that. His own experience with matrimony had not been nearly as good and had ended in quarrels.

He was going to do better this time, he vowed.

When the Dittons came back from Australia, Russ went next door and explained the situation frankly because he wanted their help. 'Have you seen her? How is she?'

'She's well. We were going to get together with her and her family at our daughter's before we left but it never happened. Did you get on well with her?'

'I fell in love with her almost immediately. We were getting together nicely when she had to rush back.'

'Ah. Her daughters never said.'

'Simone doesn't think it can work between us. I have to persuade her it can.'

'That must be why she looked so sad and quiet when we handed over the house,' Linda said. 'Mystery solved.'

'You think she might be missing me? That would be wonderful.'

'You're still here and she's still there, though.'

'I'm going to change that soon. How are her daughter and the baby getting on? Is your daughter still in touch with them?'

'Yes. She mentions them regularly in her emails.

They've become very good friends. Clo and the baby were only just starting to get better when we left, but the baby's making an excellent recovery from being premature.'

'Well, that's one worry out of the way.'

Linda studied him for a moment or two in silence, then smiled and patted his hand. 'You have got it bad, haven't you?'

'Yes. Very bad. Permanently bad, I hope.'

'So, why aren't you going after her?'

'I am. But not yet. I have to clear the decks here before I can leave. No use going there for a few days and then having to rush back to finish this project. If I did that, it might give her another reason to think that we can't make a life together. She's panicking a little anyway at falling so deeply in love again. I don't think she'd expected to.'

'I wish you well, Russ. If there's anything I can do to help . . .'

'I think this is something I'll have to do myself mainly, but if you hear from her or from anyone there about how she is, I'd be grateful if you'd pass on any news to me. She won't answer her phone to me. But don't say I'm planning to go after her. If she or her daughters ask about me, say I've been very busy and you've hardly seen me.'

She nodded. 'Can do. Good luck.'

As he walked back to his own house, he was feeling highly emotional and kept taking deep breaths in a vain attempt to calm himself.

If he could miss Simone this much after only a few short weeks together, no wonder it had taken her four years to pull herself together after over twenty happy years with Harvey.

He had to sort it out somehow. Just had to. There must be a way for them to get together.

# Chapter Thirty

When Clo was allowed to come home again, a few days later, Bob phoned Simone, who had settled back into her own home, to tell her.

'Can you pick them up from hospital?' he asked. 'Only I've got an important meeting at work and—'

She was startled by the request. 'Don't you want to bring your daughter home for the first time yourself?'

'Of course I do, but it's just a tad awkward today. My boss is panicking about something.'

'Well, I'm afraid I can't help you. I have something else arranged.'

There was dead silence at the other end, then he put on his cajoling voice, 'Can't you change it, Ma?'

'No, Bob, I can't. And I'm quite sure Clo will want *you* to be with her.' When he said nothing, she held in her anger, saying only, 'I have to go now.'

She ended the call then stared at herself in the

mirror. Had she really done that? Said a firm no to her persuasive son-in-law? Yes, she had.

'Good for you!' she told the woman in the mirror. She wondered where to go to prove she had something arranged, then frowned. She didn't need to prove it, she could do as she pleased. She'd planned to clear out the kitchen cupboards today.

The Dittons had left everything clean and well-stocked but they'd rearranged many of the cupboards and it was driving her mad going automatically to get something out and not finding it where she expected.

She walked slowly round the house which had once been her pride and joy. It wasn't a refuge now, didn't wrap itself round her as it had once seemed to do. In fact she was thinking of moving. This place had too many memories and they cascaded down on her at the most inconvenient times.

The phone rang and she checked who it was before picking it up. Deb, phoning from work.

'Hi, Ma. Bob just rang to try to get me to pick up Clo from hospital. He said you couldn't do it.'

'That's right.'

'I told him I couldn't do it either. If he's too lazy to take precautions when he's making love, and doesn't have time to end his fertility, he can wear the consequences, as far as I'm concerned.'

Simone didn't know what to say to that. What a turnaround.

'You still there, Ma?'

'Yes. I was a bit surprised at you saying that.'

Deb laughed. 'I've always been able to say no to Bob. He's Clo's choice of man not mine. And I have taken it on board that *you* need to get a life of your own. I still feel guilty when I think of how we took you for granted. You should join a club or take classes or do something different for yourself.'

'Join a club? Ugh, no thank you!'

'Whatever. Anyway, I just wanted to congratulate you and tell you that Bob is going to have to pick them up himself from the hospital. He should do more to look after his other two kids as well, if you want my opinion.'

'What does your husband say to all this? You've changed too, you know.'

'Being Logan, he's been watching and thinking. I shan't need to make my point too heavily with him. He was never as bad as Bob and I'm not as much a domestic fanatic as Clo. Oops. Got another call on the line. See you!'

That conversation pleased Simone greatly. But she still felt a bit down about her own situation. She'd grown out of the habit of being on her own so much, thanks to Russ and Fern and Henrietta. And now that she'd caught up with the four older grandchildren, Deb was right: she really had to sort her own life out and *do* something worthwhile.

But she wasn't the sort to join clubs, never had been.

What was she the sort for?

It wasn't until she was in bed that she admitted to herself how much she was missing Russ. Even more than she'd expected to and that was saying something.

Was he still missing her? There had been phone calls from him every day. She hadn't answered them, hadn't dared.

Henrietta and Elizabeth hadn't seen him, nor had Fern.

Her parents had been in touch but weren't coming back for months, it sounded like. And why should they? At their age, they wanted to make the most of every single day. She wished them well, emailed when she could because they rarely seemed to switch on their phones.

She couldn't help wondering – just a tiny wonder or two, not a decision – whether she'd been right to break up with Russ so completely.

Maybe she should have come back to Australia and kept in touch, letting their relationship cool gradually.

But what if it hadn't cooled? What would they have done then?

She'd better concentrate on selling the house. That would be her next step. It would take her mind off Russ getting it ready, keep her nice and busy.

Surely a change of surroundings and all the work involved would help?

Only where was she going to move to? She'd been looking at houses and flats and nothing had caught her fancy.

In England, Russ fell into bed late each night, crashing into the sleep of utter exhaustion. Sometimes he didn't get to bed until the early hours. He still tried to phone and she still didn't answer. He didn't want to do this by email. It just wasn't intimate enough.

He was jubilant about pulling the final programmes together. It was his best work ever. In fact he was, as a friend of his would have said, 'thrilled skinny' about what he'd captured on film.

He was surprised at how well Simone had shown up in the filming, not just her appearance but how she talked once he'd coaxed her into relaxing and simply being herself.

She had an on-camera warmth that viewers would relate to, he was sure. And a way of choosing exactly the right word to describe some situations. She wasn't glamorous, but who wanted that when there were so many cute little creatures to watch? The fact that she had a wholesome look to her went really well with Mother Nature's fantastic contributions to his series.

His agent was getting excited about some deal she was cooking up about Henrietta's capture of the burglars, together with the three episodes now nicely polished about the smaller inhabitants of the grounds of Pennerton House.

Being Sally, she was refusing to give him any details until it was all done and dusted, but that hadn't stopped her dropping a hint or two.

He'd started off hoping to get everything finished in two weeks, but it was going to be nearer three, dammit.

He was wondering whether to stop phoning Simone, though that would take all his willpower. He was determined to surprise her in person and make utterly sure that she couldn't avoid speaking to him. He hoped that not hearing from him would make her worry about whether he was all right.

Would she phone him to find out? He doubted it.

But it wouldn't be long now before he could leave. And when he got there, whatever it took, he'd persuade her to stay with him. He knew she loved him and he wasn't leaving her again until she'd agreed to take the next step and marry him.

The Dittons had been helpful. They'd given him some information from their daughter about what she was doing. She sounded to be coping much better with her family these days. From the sounds of it, things had changed and she wasn't allowing them to take advantage. Good for her.

Oh hell, he was missing her dreadfully. It was as if a part of himself was suddenly not there. How had this happened so quickly?

With a sigh of longing he reluctantly continued his efforts to leave things in good order here so that he didn't have to rush back once he got to Australia.

## Chapter Thirty-One

A month after Clo left hospital, Simone decided to throw a final party in her house before it was opened for inspection. It was more than time to let her family know what she was going to do.

She told Deb first.

'Actually, it's a farewell party for the house. I'll be putting it up for sale immediately afterwards.'

Her daughter looked at her in dismay. 'That's why you've been redecorating some parts.'

'Yes.'

'Oh, no! It's such a cosy little house. I love coming here.'

'I've loved living here. But I need to move on.'

'Are you going back to live in England?'

'Why should you think that?'

'I thought you might have made it up with *him*.'

'I haven't been in contact with Russ since I left England.'

'Hasn't he even phoned you?'

'He did at first. Every day. Till this week. He's stopped phoning. Well, it's no wonder. I didn't answer any of his calls.'

Deb looked at her in concern. 'You're still in love with him, aren't you, Ma?'

Simone shrugged, not risking trying to speak about her feelings.

'Why don't *you* try contacting him, talking things over at a time that suits you?'

'Because the same problems will be there between us. His life is in England and I couldn't bear to live so far away from you all – just couldn't. Especially with Georgie added to the grandchildren. What a gorgeous little creature she is!'

And she found herself on the receiving end of one of Deb's rare hugs.

'OK, Ma. I'll let you distract me from asking about Russ.'

Simone forced a smile. 'I told you first about selling the house. How do you think Clo will take it?'

'She'll miss the house too. Has she said anything about this guy of yours?'

'No. She says it's my own business.'

'She won't talk about it to me, either, Ma. I don't know what goes on in her head sometimes.'

'Well, I don't have a guy now, do I, so that's all academic? Nothing to discuss. Now, about details of the party. I think it'll have to be a daytime affair, given that there are four small children and a baby involved.'

'You're probably right. What can I bring?'

'I shall enjoy sorting out the food myself, thanks.' It

would give her something to fill the time. She had trouble settling to anything lately.

'You didn't mean what you said the other night about driving round Australia like Pop and Gran?'

'No. I was just a bit down. You need someone to drive with.'

She'd have enjoyed doing it with Russ.

She had to stop thinking about him. After all, he'd stopped phoning her, hadn't he? Somehow, she hadn't expected that.

Russ answered the door to find Linda Ditton smiling at him. 'Come in.'

'I won't, if you don't mind. We're just going out to our cousins' golden wedding party. You said to let you know if there was anything going on in Australia and some news just came through.'

He was instantly alert. 'Oh? What?'

'Simone is putting her house up for sale and she's giving a farewell party next Sunday for her family and friends.'

'Where is she moving to?'

'No one knows. She keeps saying she hasn't decided yet. She says she's wondering whether to drive round Australia for a while, like her parents are doing, but maybe not for as long.'

'That does it. I'm going to gatecrash the party and persuade her, talk to her. Well, I am if I can get a flight. I've made preliminary enquiries because I'm just about ready to leave but it's impossible to book a seat in that timeframe in the normal way. I've also kept looking at that website where she found last-minute offers so easily but nothing's come up going to Western Australia.'

'Keep trying. Our daughter says Deb thinks Simone is missing you.'

'Really? I do hope so. I'd have kept trying anyway, but now I desperately need to be there for her party. I can't let her leave Perth without seeing me. I have to persuade her that we can work something out. Have to!'

'I doubt she'll have much trouble selling it. It's a really nice little house, a bit old-fashioned but with a welcoming feel to it. We enjoyed living there. It'll probably be bought quite quickly by some young couple looking for a fixer-upper that isn't too expensive.'

Bob sounded the car horn and she took a step away from the door. 'Got to go now. Good luck, Russ.'

Which left him feeling depressed. What the hell was he going to do if he couldn't book a flight?

Then his watch beeped and reminded him that he was taking tea with Henrietta, to hand over a special copy of the capture of the home invaders which was going to be shown on television soon. She had been delighted with the final version.

As he was leaving Pennerton House, Henrietta said, 'Let us know how you get on.'

'I will.'

'Don't look so dubious. She'll agree to marry you.'

'Sometimes I wonder.'

'Well, don't. She loves you too much to say no, especially when you go all that way to ask her properly. Do you have a ring for her?'

'Not yet. There hasn't been time.'

She went across to an elegant sideboard and opened a drawer. 'I was going to leave her this, but it might make a rather nice engagement ring, don't you think?'

The ring was beautiful, a single sapphire framed by tiny diamonds. 'It's lovely.'

'Take it to her then.'

When he got home, he went on the last-minute flights website, but yet again there were no suitable special offers going to Perth. He flung himself down in his favourite chair staring into the distance, feeling very down about the whole situation. He'd been so sure it would all work out once he'd finished what he had to do here workwise, and Simone had been so lucky getting cancellations that he'd expected to get one as well.

It was a good while before he noticed that the light was flashing to say someone had phoned and left a message. Should he answer it?

No. He couldn't be bothered.

But curiosity won and a few minutes later he went to check who it was. Sally. His agent wouldn't have left a message unless it was urgent, so he dialled her number.

'About time, Russ Carden. I've been waiting ages for you to call me back. How dare you be out when I have some further good news for you?'

He didn't feel like being teased and even a new contract wouldn't cheer him up if he couldn't get to Simone. 'I've been busy.'

'Well, you're about to un-busy yourself, if I remember

correctly, and for a very good reason. Are you still intending to go to Australia if you can get a flight?'

'You know I am. Only I haven't been able to get one.'

'Can you be ready to leave in two days' time if I find you one?'

'What do you mean?'

'I have a friend who's flying to Perth. I didn't hesitate to beg a place on his private jet for you.'

'Sally, you wonderful woman! Who is it?'

'A very old friend. Hugo is a reclusive billionaire with a niece getting married in Perth. He's happy to take you there, but you'll have to make your own way back from Australia.'

'Sally, if you were here, I'd give you the biggest kiss you've ever had from a client. That's above and beyond the call of duty. Give me the details.'

# Chapter Thirty-Two

Russ hardly looked at Perth as the taxi drove him away from the airport. He was trying to work out what to say to Simone. He'd been trying to do that on and off during the flight. He didn't want to put his foot in it!

When the taxi stopped, he asked the driver to wait and looked at the house. He was feeling even more nervous now as well as exhausted after the long flight.

The house door was open, the entrance barred only by a mesh flyscreen door. He rang the bell and waited.

Footsteps sounded on a tiled floor and Simone appeared at the other end of the hall. Oh, thank goodness! She hadn't left.

He never said what he'd planned because all sense fled from his mind at the mere sight of her.

She stopped dead and mouthed his name, then surprised him by opening the door and flinging herself into his arms.

'Russ, Russ, is it really you?'

She kissed him first because he was still standing there like an idiot.

But he wasn't too stupid to put his arms round her and kiss her back enthusiastically.

'Don't ever run away from me again,' he growled, kissing her again – on the left ear this time, because it was the closest part of her.

She stared at him and he took a deep breath. Surely she wouldn't refuse him after kissing him like that?

But she spoke first. 'I won't run anywhere ever again. Oh, Russ, I've missed you so much.'

So he had to kiss her some more. Which was far better than building a bridge of words.

Their wonderful reunion was interrupted suddenly by someone chuckling nearby and when they broke apart, Russ realised it was the taxi driver.

'Don't mind me,' the man said. 'I've got all day to hang around.'

'Sorry. I'll, um, pay you now.' Russ got out some of the Australian money he'd picked up at the airport and dumped a few notes into the man's hand. Then he grabbed his suitcase and backpack, and followed her inside.

He dumped his luggage in the hall and kissed her again before taking hold of her hand and letting her lead him through to the back of the house.

The kitchen was full of delicious smells, but the best thing about it was her. 'I'd have come sooner but I had to finish the series off so that I could stay once I got here. If you want me to stay, that is?'

'Of course I do. I thought I could cope with living without you, but it didn't get any easier. And when you stopped phoning I didn't know what to do.'

He took her hand then and raised it to her lips. 'But you never answered my calls.'

'I didn't dare.'

'Well, I can tell you what to do. Marry me.'

'Yes, please.'

'Cross your heart and hope to die?'

She made the gesture. 'Yes, darling, of course I will.'

'How soon can we do it in Australia? I don't want you second-thinking this.'

She gave him one of her steady looks. 'I won't change my mind. I seem to have become utterly addicted to you.'

'Then perhaps you could look at this.' He pulled the little box containing the ring out of his pocket. 'Henrietta sent it. She thought it might make a nice engagement ring. It's an old family piece that she was going to leave you.'

She stared at the ring, open-mouthed. 'It's exquisite.'

'Let's try it on.'

It fitted perfectly and he waited as she turned her hand to and fro, admiring it.

'It's perfect,' she said at last.

'Then we're properly engaged.'

When he waltzed her round the ground floor of the house, she followed his lead, laughing and crying at the same time.

So he had to stop and hold her. 'You're the most

precious creature I've ever encountered, my dearest girl. We're going to be very happy.'

As they went back into the kitchen, his attention was caught suddenly by a tray of biscuits newly out of the oven. 'Those look wonderful.'

She laughed. 'Abandoning romance for food? Rather an abrupt change.'

'I didn't eat much on the plane. I was too nervous.'

'You? Nervous?'

'Yes, darling. I was about to face the most important interview of my whole life.' He frowned. 'But you looked sad for a moment there. What's wrong?'

'Leaving my family. And you coming and going for your work.'

'I've thought it all out. We can spend half the year here and half in England. And since you're going to be helping me present the films from now on, we'll be together even when I'm filming, so I won't be the only one coming and going. Will half the year and the occasional special visit be enough?'

'Oh, yes, yes, yes!'

He watched light and joy come back into her face, then they were kissing again, making up for lost time.

It wasn't until later that he thought of the precious DVD he was carrying in his backpack and she remembered her family.

When he turned round, she was on the phone. 'No, I'm not telling you what we're celebrating, Clo. Just come round, bring the kids and we'll get a takeaway meal for tea. I know you're coming here on Sunday but I want you here tonight as well.'

She ended that call, held up one finger to stop him interrupting and phoned Deb, insisting on the same conditions. It was to be a surprise. No, she wasn't giving any clues.

'Can I grab a shower before they come?' he asked.

'I think you'll just have time if you're quick.'

She went out to the little old fridge she used for wine and oddments and put in an extra bottle of champagne as she took one out. Then she got out the glasses and lined them up, plus a non-alcoholic drink for Clo, who was breastfeeding, and for the four grandchildren who were into lemonade and bitters as their latest craze, she'd found.

Then Russ came downstairs again, damp and smelling of shampoo. 'We can live in this house or you can sell it and we'll buy another. Houses aren't important. You are.'

'We'll sell it and start afresh.'

'No quibbles about details?'

'No quibbles about anything, Russ. I've learnt my lesson. I was only half-alive without you.'

A car drew up outside and he plonked a quick kiss on her cheek. 'Don't let them eat me.'

'They won't. Not when they see how happy I am.'

It was Clo and family, and while Bob brought in the paraphernalia needed for young Miss Georgie, Clo stared suspiciously at Russ.

'I have such wonderful news for you,' Simone began. 'This is Russ and he's just proposed to me. See!' She brandished the ring at them, then turned to him. 'Russ, will you open the bottle of champagne? I'm sure Deb and her lot will arrive any time.'

Clo was still looking from Russ to her mother and back again, and as he dealt with the bottle, he began to worry that she'd not accept him.

Then she held out her hand to him and said quietly. 'Ma's come to life again. I'm glad you're here, Russ. I'm looking forward to getting to know you.'

He gave her a hug, got a mock scolding for squashing the baby, and damned if a tear of happiness didn't escape his control because he'd expected Clo to be harder to win over.

She dabbed it away with the baby's bib. 'I like that you care so much.'

It was going to be all right, he thought, relief spearing through him.

Bob shook his hand next, then Deb and her family arrived, and they went through the introductions again.

It was Clo who raised her glass and gave the toast. 'Here's to you and Russ, Ma. I hope you two will be very happy together.'

Glasses clinked, some eyes were bright with tears and the ring was much admired.

Eventually the four children went out to play in the garden, while the baby ignored the noisy adults and took a nap.

'I'm going to miss you,' Deb told her mother.

Russ smiled at Simone, then turned back to her family and said, 'We haven't worked out the details yet but I reckon we can manage about half the year in each country, give or take. I know better than to separate your mother from you for too long.'

That brought loud cheers and a lot more kissy-kissy.

'That's so wonderful.' It was Clo's turn to dab her eyes.

Russ snapped his finger suddenly. 'I forgot something important. Do you have a DVD player, darling?'

'Yes, why?'

'I've got something to show you and your family.'

He put the DVD in the machine and held up one hand. 'May I introduce the newest small-screen star – Ms Simone Ramsay, or whatever she chooses to call herself in her public persona.'

He moved to put his arm round Simone as they all watched it, her daughters open-mouthed as she appeared in more of the shots.

'She comes up well on screen, doesn't she?'

Dead silence, then Clo and Deb grabbed their mother and danced her round the room.

'Ma, you're a star!'

That had set the seal on it all, he thought. They approved.

He and Simone were going to have a grand life together.

After the family had gone, Simone came to sit quietly with him on the couch. 'I can't believe it all: you here, us getting married, me appearing on TV. I just – can't believe it's all real.'

'Oh, it is. But the best part of it is you and me. I asked you before and you didn't answer me. How quickly can we get married here?'

'I don't know. But we'll find out tomorrow. I'm not waiting a minute longer than I have to.'

A yawn escaped him then. 'Sorry. It's jet lag not boredom.'

'I know how it feels. Let's go to bed and hang any clearing up that's left.'

'I promised Henrietta I'd phone and let them know how things went.'

'Do it tomorrow,' she said firmly. 'Tonight is our time.'

'Yes. Time I got you to bed, my love.' He waggled his eyebrows at her suggestively and she chuckled.

'That's not the way to turn me on, you idiot. I'll just have a quick shower then show you how.'

By the time she joined him in bed, however, he was sound asleep. But that was all right. If they were lucky, they'd have many years to love each other in.

She sighed blissfully and snuggled up to him, starting to fall asleep almost as quickly as he had. They were home together now and that felt so right.

ANNA JACOBS is the author of over ninety novels and is addicted to storytelling. She grew up in Lancashire, emigrated to Australia in the 1970s and writes stories set in both countries. She loves to return to England regularly to visit her family and soak up the history. She has two grown-up daughters and a grandson, and lives with her husband in a spacious home near the Swan Valley, the earliest wine-growing area in Western Australia. Her house is crammed with thousands of books.

annajacobs.com